THE BLISS OF THE GRAVE

CAROLYN HOLLAND

Editor: Tia Ross, WordWiser Ink (www.wordwiserink.com)
Proofreader: Brandy Patton, WordWiser Ink
Cover Design: Navi Robins, North Shore Publishing House Inc.
(www.nsgraphicstudio.com)
Cover Art: The Art of Salaam Muhammad LLC

All rights reserved.
ISBN: 978-1-7324693-1-0

Visit my website at: www.carolynhollandbooks.com

DEDICATION

I dedicate this book to the Ancient One, the beloved ancestor who takes better care of me than I take care of myself.

ACKNOWLEDGEMENT

There is a Yoruba Proverb which states, "A river that forgets its source will surely dry up." (Author unknown)

GLOSSARY OF TERMS

Anakin	Nephilim working class
Brothers of the Dark Veil	First born of the prefects of the Watcher Angel Shemyaza (Ajuma, Antioch, Boaz, Gilead, Nicodemus, Rephidim, Shiloh, Simeon and Zion, the Nephilim king)
The Dark Veil	A supernatural shield erected by the Brothers of the Dark Veil on all seven continents which allows Nephilim to live among humans without detection
The Fallen	Fallen angels turned demons that serve under Zuet
Gateway	A portal of entry between the heavens, hells, and earth
Ghosting	A mode of Nephilim transportation that involves traveling through space and time as particles of gold dust
Gibborim	Nephilim fighting class
Host	A human whose body is inhabited by one of the Fallen
Houses of the Nephilim	Twelve major Houses of Nephilim royalty: Anane, Arazyal, Armers, Asael, Batraal, Ertael, Samsaveel, Saraknyl, Turel, Yomyael, Zavabe, and Shemyaza, the highest House of the king
King Solomon's Grimoire	A demonically inspired textbook of magic with instructions on how to cast spells, create magical objects and evoke or invoke angels, spirits, and demons
Maroon	Community of escaped slaves in the Atchafalaya Swamp
Mind Meld	Telepathic communication

Mind Swipe	A forceful mental invasion to erase human memories
Nephilim	Half angel/half human descendants of the Watcher angels that landed on Mt. Hermon during the days when the Prophet Enoch walked among men
Rephaim	Member of Nephilim royalty
Vessel	A human who gives birth to a child fathered by one of the Fallen
Zion Shemyaza	King of the Nephilim; oldest and most powerful Nephilim in existence
Zuet	Fallen angel turned demon that rules over all seven levels of hell; arch nemesis to the Nephilim people; known as The Satan

PROLOGUE

"You think I don't know what we talking 'bout?" Flossie snapped. "Don't you worry 'bout me, angel girl," she said in a gentler voice. "Surely, after all I have been through, the Gods will expand my resting place and grant me the bliss of the grave and none of the torment."

CHAPTER 1

Zanzibar

MEHWISH WOKE WITH a frown on her face. Her father's words of the previous night still clung to her memory like a twisted limb on an old tree. He dropped a bombshell on her during supper, managing to slip the unwelcomed information in as nice as you please, right between the second course of *pilau* and the third course of *biryani.*

Her stepmother Salme, whom Mehwish despised, was pregnant. Mehwish nearly choked on her food when she heard the disturbing news. She ran from the supper table, barely able to hold back a flood of tears. That night she cried herself to sleep.

Mehwish was no fool. She was well aware that her father had physical needs. It was obvious those needs were met when she looked into the faces of several of the slaves scattered about on his ten *shambas* (plantations). Offspring created with slaves were of no consequence to Mehwish. They were little more than leaves blowing in the wind, easily forgotten.

Her father hadn't warned her of his intention to wed. By the time Mehwish was apprised of his association with the woman that would become her stepmother, it was already a *fait accompli.* The knowledge that her father had remarried had been a bitter pill for Mehwish to swallow. However, the fact that his new wife was already breeding, after being wed less than six months, did not sit well with the pampered little princess at all.

Mehwish envisioned that in four years' time Salme would push out an equal number of brats. With each new birth, Mehwish's connection with her father would grow more tenuous until it diminished and eventually died.

The mere thought was extremely disturbing. She was now wide awake with a dirty taste in her mouth, a spirit filled with meanness, and the inexplicable ire of one far older than her thirteen years.

She covered her eyes with her forearm, more to block out the memories of the night before than to shield against the rays of sunlight burning through the sheer curtains covering her bedroom windows.

Though the hour was late, Mehwish remained in her bed, listening to the routine sounds the slaves and house servants made as they went about their daily tasks in Serengeti. These mundane sounds coming through her open bedroom window blended with the potent scent of cinnamon, nutmeg, vanilla, cloves, and pepper. They only moderately soothed the rough edges of her temper while lending the sense of security that accompanies that which is familiar. She'd slept late. It was time for her to get up and face whatever the day might bring. She swung her legs over the side of her custom-made canopy bed. The bed was so high her feet could not reach the floor.

Binta, the African slave woman who had served as Mehwish's wet nurse, nanny, and surrogate mother since the day she was born, sat in a corner humming a familiar Kiswahili tune as she busily hand-stitched an elaborate appliqué on the collar of one of Mehwish's silk night-rails. Mehwish's mother died in childbirth. Binta was the only mother she had ever known. Binta looked up from her sewing with a smile on her face.

"Well, good morning, sleepy head. 'Bout time you got up. Did you sleep well? Would you like to break your fast?"

When she noticed Mehwish was still too grumpy to engage in any banter, she returned to her sewing. That fact was born out when Mehwish merely grunted in Binta's general direction and ignored her, choosing instead to quietly pace her opulent bedroom in her bare feet.

Binta watched Mehwish under hooded eyes as she moved from one item to the next, first touching a gold hair brush, then a crystal ornament on her dresser bureau. Last, she toyed with an exquisite pair of black diamond ear bobs her father recently gifted her after a trip to South Africa.

She couldn't help but worry about Mehwish. Sometimes her young charge did and said things that were disturbing. The master and mistress had been wed for several months, and still Mehwish had not warmed to her father's new wife. Binta wondered if she ever would. She was even more fearful that Mehwish's impetuous nature would create discord between the master and mistress. Binta quietly watched Mehwish pace until she couldn't take it anymore.

"If you keep on pacing like that, you're liable to wear a hole in the floor, little missy," Binta said in that sugary sweet tone of voice that reminded Mehwish of a beautiful song. "Got something on your mind you want to share with ol' Binta?"

Binta was nowhere near old. She was in the middle years of her life and still very beautiful, with eyes that twinkled with laughter and a perpetual smile upon her lips. She spent more time caring for Mehwish than her own son Hacim.

Mehwish was an only child, and her father Issaiyah fairly doted upon her. She was stubbornly resistant to change. Mehwish liked things the way they used to be when her world consisted of her, her father, and those who lived to serve them. She had no desire to share her father's affections with a half-brother or sister, and she didn't want to share his love with his beautiful new wife, Salme, whom Binta knew for a fact Mehwish was insanely jealous of.

Binta had cleaned Mehwish's little nasty bottom as a babe. She knew her well enough to know when she had something on her mind. She suspected it wasn't anything Mehwish cared to share with her. Binta decided not to push the issue. Some things are best kept to oneself.

Issaiyah bin Said al-Murgebi was wealthy. The foundation of his wealth was derived from the slave trade. He'd cleverly parlayed his blood money into seven spice *shambas* in the tropical paradise known as Zanzibar, or the Spice Islands. His holdings were not only vast, but he was the master of over 10,000 slaves.

Said al-Murgebi was blacker than most of the slaves he owned. It was common knowledge that Mehwish's paternal grandmother had been a pure-blooded black African from the village of Mbwa Maji, a small village south of

Dar es Salaam. The slaves whispered among themselves about it, but no one dared speak of the master's ancestry within his hearing—not if they valued their lives.

He was a cruel man, as was his father before him. The Africans whose villages the master pillaged referred to him as the demonic black beast who sold his own people for profit. Mehwish didn't seem to care. She once told Binta, "My father is black and he might even be a beast, but at least he is a rich one." Binta feared Mehwish had inherited some of her father's tendencies.

Mehwish paused in front of a large mirror to admire her face. For the first time that day, Mehwish deigned to acknowledge Binta's presence.

"Binta, am I pretty?"

Binta couldn't rightly say Mehwish was pretty. There was something in her eyes that kept her from prettiness, but Binta didn't have a mean bone in her body. She could never, ever hurt the innocent child by telling her the truth.

"Well, little missy, with all that lustrous, dark hair and that creamy olive complexion of yours, you have the promise of one day becoming a truly stunning woman," she said diplomatically.

Mehwish scrutinised Binta for a moment while she decided whether she'd been complimented or insulted. She quickly concluded that Binta would never be foolish enough to insult her.

For the first time that day, Mehwish smiled, thinking *Binta is right. I do have beautiful skin.* Mehwish made it a point to never venture out in the sun without both a bonnet and a parasol to preserve her skin colour. She turned her head from the left to the right, capturing every angle of her profile. *One day, when I have breasts and hips like my stepmother, every man who looks at me will fall at my feet.*

"You know what, Binta?" she said, continuing to critique her reflection in the mirror. "I praise Allah every day that I inherited the white skin and aquiline features of my mother and grandfather while benefiting from the wealth of my father."

Binta made no comment. After all, what in the world could she say to that?

CHAPTER 2

OUT OF ALL her father's shambas, Mehwish loved Serengeti the most. It was heaven on earth with an even coastline and a private beach, dotted with coconut trees right outside her bedchamber. Unlike his other holdings, which were located in rural areas, this shamba was located not far from Stone Town, the oldest part of Zanzibar, where the narrow roads were lined with churches, mosques, Hindu halls, and beautiful buildings made of coral stone, lime, and clay.

Mehwish never tired of going into the city. There was so much to see and do in Stone Town, so she was never bored. Serengeti was her father's kingdom, and she was his little queen.

Heaven on earth or not, at the moment Mehwish was so bored she could scream. Expelling a calculated loud sigh to express her boredom and to get Binta's attention, the petulant little girl eventually flounced on the chaise lounge across from Binta with her arms across her chest and her bottom lip poked out. She frowned when Binta continued sewing.

Her lips twisted imperceptively as a thought came to mind. It had been weeks since she'd been to Stone Town.

"Madhe Binta. I would have you take me into town. I have a desire to see the sights and to partake of the delicacies the roadside vendors have for sale."

We can visit the slave market in the Anglican Cathedral. If I am lucky, there may even be a public whipping or execution while we are there!

Binta glanced at her. "I guess the young mistress has forgotten the lunch date with her esteemed father and Mistress Salme. If you do not hurry, you will be late."

Mehwish had, in fact, totally forgotten that she was to lunch with her father and her stepmother. *Agh!* She could not stomach her stepmother's insipid personality under the best of circumstances. She could only assume the dullard would be nigh on intolerable now that she was pregnant.

She let out another lengthy, put-upon sigh. She would have to postpone her trip into Stone Town. In the meantime, she would content herself by playing with a recent gift from her father. A fluffy white kitten with one blue eye and one green eye was sleeping peacefully in a corner of her bedchamber.

She'd named the kitten Confusion because Allah couldn't decide whether its eyes would be blue or green. The kitten slept in a tiny lace-trimmed bed designed by Binta, an exact replica of the elaborate bed Mehwish slept in.

Ignoring Binta's suggestion that she prepare herself for the luncheon, Mehwish reached for the sleeping kitten. Startled, the kitten nipped Mehwish on her hand. She examined her hand carefully. Thankfully, there was no blood. The skin had not been broken.

Mehwish's facial expression didn't change as she grabbed the frightened kitten by the scruff of its neck, marched over to the other side of her bed chamber, and cruelly tossed it out of her open bedroom window. It fell three floors to its death, bursting apart on the flagstones below. Mehwish leaned out of the window to dispassionately watch the whole thing from beginning to end.

Binta didn't have an opportunity to react to Mehwish's cruelty before there was a knock at the bedroom door. She hurried to answer the door, still distraught by what she'd seen. It was the master himself, come to check on his daughter's tardiness for the luncheon.

Mehwish's dark eyes welled up with tears the minute she lay eyes upon her father. He looked toward Binta as if she'd done something wrong as Mehwish ran over to wrap her arms around his waist and bury her face in his abdomen.

"There, there, my love. I hope you are not still upset about the new addition to our family. Everything will be fine. You'll see."

He had hoped a good night's sleep would smooth things over between him and his daughter. He so wanted her and Salme to get on well together. Mehwish nodded, indicating that the discussion of the previous night was not the cause of her current distress.

"Well then, tell Papa what is wrong, little one."

He had a look of puzzlement on his face when Mehwish grabbed hold of his big black hand to lead him to the open window. With quivering lips, she pointed in the direction of the courtyard beneath her bedroom window.

"What the fuck!"

Her father's bellow of outrage when he saw what had become of the kitten named Confusion could be heard throughout the great house.

"Tebeda ena mut!" (*Get fucked and die*) he screamed to no one in particular and everyone at the same time. His sharp retort spilled outside to the courtyard and beyond. The slaves paused in their chores and trembled in fear. The cruel lion who had seemed content with his new state of marriage for the past few months had returned. Anything was liable to happen.

"Tell me who is responsible for this outrage, my darling. I will see that they are punished to fit the crime."

Mehwish's nose was beet red. Tears ran down her face as she dramatically pointed to a young man who, unaware he was the subject of the master's narrow-eyed scrutiny, was busy pruning a bush in the courtyard below. Mehwish blamed the hapless slave for the evil deed, giving Said al-Murgebi a body to vent his anger on.

Binta stood back while Said al-Murgebi sought to console his daughter, shaking her head in disappointment. She'd seen Mehwish do evil things in the past. She'd also seen her throw that kitten out of the window, but she dared not contradict the spoiled child's claim. She pitied the person who would be wrongfully accused of the deed. Said al-Murgebi's punishment was sure to be brutal and swift.

Mehwish and the master brushed past Binta to go out to the courtyard. Binta waited until Mehwish and her father left the room to look out at the pair below the window. Mistress Salme was standing near the front door with her hand shielding her eyes from the sun and a frown on her face.

It wasn't until the master looked up to fix Binta with his cold cruel stare that she realised the unfortunate youth Mehwish had pointed to was her own seventeen-year-old son, Hacim.

"*NOOOOOOOOO!*" Binta screamed, before the floor dropped out beneath her. She grabbed the hem of her skirts and ran to the courtyard as quickly as she could. This had to be a mistake. Missy Mehwish wouldn't break her heart by hurting her only child. She just knew she wouldn't.

But Mehwish intended to do just that. It didn't matter that Hacim was a good boy and that he had never been inside the mansion. And it didn't matter that he had never seen the inside of Mehwish's bedchambers, from where the kitten had been tossed. Those salient facts were of no consequence to Said al-Murgebi when he saw how upset his precious daughter was from the loss of the kitten.

Binta knew Said al-Murgebi to be merciless in his dealings with the slaves. They were of no value to him. Their lives meant nothing, and his daughter had been raised to feel the same. Binta foolishly assumed that since she'd taken care of Mehwish since the day she pushed her way out of her mother's womb that she, and her son by association, would be placed in a different category from the other slaves on Serengeti. Her worst nightmare now played out before her eyes, and there was absolutely nothing she could do about it.

"Oh God, no! Please, young mistress," Binta begged. "Tell the master you made a mistake. Don't let them hurt my son. Please!"

Binta looked crazed with her turban eschew and snot running out of her nose. Both her and Hacim's screams were heard throughout the shamba as her son was summarily dragged to the frequently used whipping post and flogged until the flesh fell off his back like the skin of an overripe banana. The beating went on well after Hacim's spirit had fled the courtyard.

Nothing could stop Binta's lamentation; not even a vicious blow to the mouth could silence her cries.

Young Mehwish looked on barefooted and clad in her night-rail, dispassionately eating an apple while the innocent youth's dead body was pulled down from the post.

Suddenly Mehwish realised she was famished. Other than the apple, she'd yet to break her fast. Mehwish and her father didn't spare Binta a backward glance when they went inside to have lunch.

CHAPTER 3

MEHWISH SCRUTINISED EVERY move Binta made for weeks after Hacim's death, looking for a negative sign in word or deed, but she could find none. Binta continued to serve as before, yet there was no more humming while she went about her chores, no more singing in the morning when she coaxed a reluctant Mehwish out of bed, no more light behind her pretty eyes. She saw only sadness and something else Mehwish couldn't quite put her finger on, but didn't care to try.

Mehwish didn't understand why Binta was so sad. She was not much older than Salme and young enough to have another child—until Mehwish came of age and married, of course. Binta would always have her.

Mehwish decided right then and there she would give Binta a few more days to get over her foolishness before she would demand she be happy again. In the meantime, Mehwish had other matters of importance to attend to.

It had been three months since the kitten incident. Mehwish's father and the men who served under him were in the Congo, sacking African villages for slaves.

Mehwish promised her father she'd make an effort to be nicer to Salme during his absence. She had made a habit of checking in on her stepmother at least twice a day. Salme hadn't been feeling very well of late. She attributed her malaise to her pregnancy, but Mehwish knew better.

While Binta quietly busied herself straightening up her bedchamber, Mehwish secreted a small packet under the sleeve of her day gown. She'd purchased the contents of the packet two weeks ago from a sorceress while in Stone Town.

"Yes, young Mistress," was Binta's only response when Mehwish informed her she was going to her stepmother's suite to visit for a while.

The packet contained a combination of dried pineapple, parsley, evening primrose, Angelica/Dong Quai, Black Cohosh, Blue Cohosh, and Pennyroyal. The sorceress instructed her to place five to fifteen drops in a cup of tea sweetened with honey every four hours to bring about an abortion. She admonished Mehwish not to exceed this dosage.

Mehwish could not allow Salme's pregnancy to go to term. She was afraid Salme would bear her father a son and that he would displace her in their father's affections and become the heir to his wealth. There could be no child to compete with her, be it male or female.

The concoction was working wonderfully. Already Salme had taken to her bed complaining of stomach cramps and nausea. *It shouldn't be long*, she thought, *before the dead baby comes out of her body.*

Every four hours Mehwish had a tea service brought into her stepmother's chambers. She liberally dosed the tea with three times the amount of the herbs recommended by the sorceress. Salme was too weak to resist as Mehwish sat with her, making sure she drank every single drop of the tea.

Mehwish fairly skipped to her stepmother's chambers. She needed Salme to miscarry *before* her father returned. He was ever solicitous of Salme. Since she was not feeling well, he would want to stay by her side and would surely want to join them in their little tea sessions. Her hands would be tied if Salme didn't evacuate that baby soon.

Mehwish encountered frenetic activity when she came upon her stepmother's bedchamber. A frown marred her smooth brow. *What in the world is going on?* She attempted to follow a harried housemaid whose arms were laden with a pile of sheets inside the bedchamber.

"My pardon, Mistress Mehwish," she said, "but the doctor is with Mistress Salme right now, and we cannot allow you inside."

Mehwish's little flat chest puffed up with indignation.

"What do you mean you will not *allow* me inside? Let me pass, you filthy dog! There is no room in this residence that I cannot enter. Now, get out of my way!"

Before the frightened maid could say anything, yet another maid exited the bedchamber with a pile of bloody sheets in her arms. Mehwish took that opportunity to slide inside the partially open door. She skidded to a halt at the foot of the bed as the doctor stepped away from Salme. There was blood everywhere. Mehwish had gotten more than she'd wished. Salme and her baby were dead.

The baby was a boy. Issaiyah named the baby Neverseen because he hadn't lived long enough to see the light of day. Less than twenty minutes after they placed Salme and Neverseen in the grave, Mehwish was happily skipping past the kitchen on her way to the main house. The cook house was always kept separate from the main house for safety reasons and so that cooking smells would not permeate the living area.

Mehwish was feeling well-pleased with how she'd handled the Salme situation. It was unseasonably hot. And the kitchen window was open. She was humming a happy tune when she happened to catch a snatch of a conversation between the cook and one of the kitchen workers.

The slaves were a superstitious, ignorant lot at best, but Mehwish was nonetheless intrigued when one of the slaves made mention of a curse being placed on her family by an old black witch named Zahara. She paused to hear more.

Mehwish giggled to herself when one of the slaves voiced her opinion that the witch's curse had been the cause of Salme and Neverseen's untimely death. She was about to proceed to her intended destination when a voice she clearly recognised as that of the cook's said, "The Masta's mother will not stop cursing him and his issue until every last one of them is dead. Her curse did away with the first wife and now it has taken the second."

The masta's mother?

Mehwish backtracked and barged in on the two frightened slaves. It took less than ten minutes to get all the information she needed. She already knew her father's mother had been a black African. That was obvious by looking at him. But what she hadn't been aware of until that day was that not only was her black grandmother still alive, but she lived less than a twenty-minute ride by horseback from Serengeti. And she was a witch.

How fascinating.

After eliciting the last salient fact from the slaves, Mehwish formulated a plan to meet this witch named Zahara. Her father frequently travelled to check on the profitability of his other shambas or to capture more slaves. Now that Salme and Neverseen were dead, the grief-stricken man sought solace in his work. Salme and his babe's bodies were barely cold in the ground before he set off from Serengeti, leaving Mehwish in Binta's care which virtually amounted to leaving her to her own devices.

Mehwish didn't care that he'd left so quickly. Her father rarely smiled anymore, and wasn't any fun to be around. He'd named her Mehwish, which means "beautiful moon," but she didn't see appreciation for her beauty when she looked in his eyes anymore. All she saw was sadness. She could only hope his attitude would change for the better upon his return. She also hoped that next time her father would know better than to bring another woman into their home. Obviously, things didn't work out well for him when he did.

CHAPTER 4

MEHWISH WAITED UNTIL her father set off on one of his ships before bullying one of the maids into taking her to the nearby village where the woman purported to be her grandmother still resided. Less than a week after she'd gotten rid of Salme and her half-brother—because she refused to think of him as anything else—she was standing in front of her grandmother Zahara the witch.

"Are you *really* my grandmother?"

Two sets of identical obsidian black eyes stared into the other. They were two peas in a pod, one young and one old, one white and one black, both filled to overflowing with the devil's demons.

"Yes. I am your Madhe. I am Zahara. Has no one ever spoken of me?"

At first Mehwish didn't answer, choosing instead to scrutinise every inch of the little wizened woman's face and form, only to return to her fathomless eyes that looked like they had seen the creation of the world. She was falling under the woman's mesmerising spell. Tight-lipped with anger, she forced herself to turn away.

How dare the old crone think herself worthy of mention!

"No," she said arrogantly. "Even though it is apparently common knowledge that you are my father's mother, no one has spoken of you, at least not in my presence. Had I not overheard a conversation between two members of my father's staff on the day of my stepmother Salme's funeral, I would not have known of your existence."

And my life would have continued just fine.

Zahara was not surprised that she wasn't discussed at the Serengeti dinner table. She was the family's dark secret—literally. She had been a member of African royalty, and not even a woman full grown when Mehwish's grandfather stormed into her life like the plague. Rajab bin Mohammed bin Said el Murgebi, whom Zahara called *Mbwa-mwitu* (wild dog), dragged her out of her father's hut, beat her into submission, and raped her in front of all the people who had once held any regard for her.

She used to weep at the knowledge that her poor father's last sight on this side of creation was that of Rajab rutting on top of her. She didn't cry anymore. Hate took up residence where sorrow once resided. The *Mbwa-mwitu* saw to that.

May his soul rot in hell!

When he was done with Zahara, he threw her battered body across the front of his horse and took her back to Serengeti where he continued to rape her until she was pregnant with his child. As a result of the rape, Zahara bore a son, Mehwish's father. She had been beautiful then, comely of face and form, and made to be cherished and loved by a man chosen by her father. The *Mbwa-mwitu* took her future away from her. He took her smile, her joy, and the babies she could have had with a man who loved her.

Unlike each of his three wives who were either barren or could only produce female children, Zahara bore him a strong, healthy son. Rajab named his rape child Issaiyah bin Said al-Murgebi. Although Issaiyah slid out of Zahara's body as black as the ace of spades, Rajab raised the boy as his only son and heir. Her son was now an infamous slaver like his sire.

Rajab would have killed her right after the baby was born had she not been protected by strong witchcraft. Instead, he ripped the babe from her breast before he was even weaned and threw her away like she was little more than garbage. She managed to make her way back to what was left of her village, only to have her people turn their backs on her. Zahara was destined to live out the remainder of her days as an outcast. She had been defiled by the evil Arab and considered to be worse than a leper, unapproachable, and unmarriable.

Zahara snapped back to the present. The day she had been waiting for was here. The daughter of her rape son was standing before her with the same look of evil entitlement as her grandfather. The remembered hurt drove Zahara to strike out at Mehwish.

"Ah. Poor innocent Salme," Zahara said facetiously. "That was a bit of nasty work on your part, now wasn't it, Granddaughter?"

Mehwish sucked in her breath in surprise. "What do you know about Salme's death, old woman?"

Zahara's eyes danced with amusement. "There is not much that I don't know about you. Not only do I know that you killed Salme and her baby, I know you are guilty of many other crimes—some big, some small. Would you like me to take you back to the day you caused your servant Binta's son to be killed for a crime he did not commit?"

Mehwish's dark eyes narrowed in suspicion. Although there was no one around to hear their conversation, she looked around before responding. "Yes," she hissed. "That is exactly what I want," she said in a challenging voice. "Take me back if you can."

She intuitively knew there was no need to lie to this woman. They were kindred spirits. Mehwish felt a darkness in the woman's spirit that mirrored her own. She stepped closer to Zahara in a menacing manner.

"Again, old woman, I asked you a question. What do you know about Salme's death?"

Zahara didn't even flinch. Her laugh was deep and sinister, like scum on the bottom of a nearly dry pond.

"I believe I can show you better than I can tell you, Granddaughter. Come. Follow me."

She led Mehwish to a dark cluttered corner in the back of her hut. Shelves laden with dusty glass jars contained many nasty-looking meaty things. Dried carcasses of furry animals hung from hooks in the wall. None of these items were familiar to Mehwish. She made a mental note to ask the old woman about them at a later date.

Zahara bade Mehwish sit on the hard-packed floor before she pulled out a glass globe and placed it between them. She reverently grasped the globe between her wrinkled, twisted hands, speaking words in a language Mehwish could not understand.

Mehwish covered her mouth with her hands when she clearly saw herself in the globe pouring the deadly herbs inside Salme's teacup. She looked up from the globe in amazement at Zahara's awesome power. Mehwish was more than a little thankful that she had managed to find her way to Zahara. Because of the means and manner in which she found Zahara, Mehwish knew with certainty that she was right where she needed to be.

That first night Mehwish travelled to her grandmother's village would not only herald the beginning of many clandestine visits she would have with the village witch over the next several years, but it would also serve as the beginning of Mehwish's apprenticeship into the art of black majick and witchcraft.

CHAPTER 5

MEHWISH WAS SEVENTEEN years old when she finally met her father's white partner. In Zanzibar, it didn't matter who her father's mother was. He was ruthless, powerful, rich, and the son of Rajab bin Mohammed bin Said el Murgebi. But in the colonies, where an African is considered inferior, Said el Murgebi was forced to use a surrogate to conduct business in the lucrative slave market. He'd taken on a partner, a white American named Martin Henry Singleton. The arrangement was simple. Her father would procure the slaves and Singleton would act as the front man, captaining her father's fleet of ships to transport the slaves for sale in the colonies.

Martin came to Serengeti to square up with her father after disposing of a large shipment of slaves. Mehwish fell madly in love with him in the crazy, irrationally intense manner that only someone of her inexperience and youth could.

Martin was pleasantly surprised at the changes that were wrought in his partner's young daughter. The last time he'd seen Mehwish, she'd been little more than a child. She now bore absolutely no resemblance to the flat-chested, slim-hipped youth whose black knowing eyes were far too large for her face. Her body and her eyes held promise of mysterious sensuality. Being the ladies' man that Martin was, he couldn't help but take notice.

Martin Henry Singleton was breathtakingly handsome, tall and well built, with an aristocratic manner and an impeccable sense of style. He was a mortal god, with chiselled features, hair bleached white-blond from standing on the decks of ships, and mesmerising eyes that were so startling a shade of blue that Mehwish could swear she saw the heavens within their clear blue depths.

Those same clear blue eyes were now looking down on Mehwish, his pants pooled around his ankles, while she serviced him on her knees. Her eyes never left Martin's as she swirled her tongue around his heat, wetting the tip of his cock as she played his organ like a sweetly tuned flute.

"That's right, my darling. Lick me," he urged.

Mehwish did more than lick. She worshipped his stalk. She grabbed him and dragged her tongue from base to tip, leaving a trail of spittle glistening on his skin. Martin moaned like a starving man presented with a royal feast. The only difference was that Mehwish was doing the eating.

She gobbled him up, feeding as much of him into her mouth as it would hold. His tip hit the back of her throat at the same time her mouth connected with the coarse musky blond bush of hair at the base of his cock. She breathed through her nose, inhaling the sweaty musty scent on his skin, and then she swallowed.

At the moment of his release, Martin screamed, "I love you."

Mehwish believed him. After all, why wouldn't she? *I am young, beautiful, and rich. How could he help but love me?*

Mehwish was accustomed to getting everything she wanted and she wanted Martin Singleton—desperately. The very next day she paid an unexpected visit to her grandmother, entreating her to help her. She already had Martin's desire. Now she wanted to gain his love. She fully intended to become his wife.

"Have you given this man your maidenhead yet?"

There was no embarrassment between the two of them. Mehwish was well aware that Zahara knew the liberties she had already allowed Martin.

"No, old woman, I have not allowed him to penetrate my body, but we have engaged in activities I would not desire my father to know about."

Seemingly satisfied with Mehwish's response, Zahara stood on weak legs to retrieve some items from the back of her hut. She returned with two candles.

"This is what you must do, Granddaughter," she advised, handing a pink and purple candle to Mehwish. "This pink candle will induce love. The purple one will induce desire. Scratch Martin's name on the pink candle. You must then burn this candle on the even hours around the clock for seven days.

"Scratch Martin's name on the purple candle. You must burn this candle on the odd hours round the clock for seven days. When is your next flux?" she asked in a no-nonsense tone.

Mehwish answered Zahara's question and listened carefully to the additional instructions she imparted.

Mehwish burned the candles as Zahara instructed. She waited two weeks until she knew her father would be away from the shamba to invite Martin to a very special dinner. She mixed a bit of her first day menstrual blood in a spicy hot Arab soup dish consisting of lentils and spinach and tiny balls of dough. Mehwish sat patiently watching Martin as he ate every mouthful of the ensorcelled food. That afternoon Mehwish surrendered everything to Martin—her maidenhead, her heart, and her trust.

Serengeti was isolated. The Zanzibari nights were hot and sultry—a perfect backdrop for passion. Martin was a man of lusty needs. He indulged Mehwish in her young infatuation, taking advantage of his partner's trust and abusing his hospitality by sneaking behind Issaiyah's back to sleep with his young, impetuous daughter. They made love often, sometimes in Mehwish's bed. Once, they had even sated their desire for one another in Issaiyah's bed.

Now that Mehwish had a taste of what it felt like to have a man inside of her, she was obsessed with Martin. She fully intended to force Martin to accept her inside of his heart. Her greatest desire was to shout her love for Martin to the rooftops. She wanted him to go to her father to ask for her hand. She wanted to share the wonderful feelings she had for him with the world. Martin bade her to wait.

"Sweetheart, we have to keep our relationship a secret. Your father will never consent to our being together. He will see my behaviour as a betrayal of his trust, and that is the very last thing that I want. Run away with me, my love," he declared ardently. "Once we are married and our relationship is a *fait accompli,* your father will have no choice but to accept our being together."

Mehwish happily agreed to run away with Martin. She would do *anything* to be with him.

Not much got past Binta. Her figure blended in with the shadows as she stood at Mehwish's bedroom window, observing Mehwish's late-night departure. For months she'd witnessed Mehwish running after Singleton like a low-class bitch in heat.

Binta knew the date and the time when the little hussy finally lay down with the white man. She'd seen the evidence of Mehwish's lost maidenhead with her own eyes. After all, Binta did her laundry. She could have blown the whistle on her then, but her spirit told her to be silent—to wait.

Binta laughed to herself—not the sweet tinkling laugh of years ago, but a malicious mean-spirited laugh seasoned by years of pent-up rage and unfulfilled vengeance.

Now the evil strumpet fashions herself in love, huh? Well, well, well. This should be more than a little bit interesting.

A set of luggage and two trunks were missing and enough clothing to fill them. It didn't take a genius to figure out Mehwish's intentions. The chit planned to run away with Singleton, and she didn't plan to tell her father about it either.

Serves the devil spawn good and right. Binta knew Mehwish was the only something her wicked sire ever loved. *Why wouldn't he? She's just like him.* She also knew it would break him when he finds her gone. Binta was glad. *Let him suffer as I have.*

The bastard would lose his precious daughter and his trusted partner at the same time. There's no way Singleton could face Issaiyah after a betrayal of this magnitude. Binta prayed every night that she would see him suffer like she'd been forced to suffer when he'd ordered her son beaten to death. She would keep silent until Mehwish and Singleton were long gone, and then she would watch the story unfold.

CHAPTER 6

IT WAS POURING rain on the night Mehwish left Serengeti behind her. She felt eyes on her and looked back toward the main house. She thought she saw the curtains move at her bedroom window, but when she looked again no one was there. She pulled her hood up over her head for protection against the sudden downpour. The rain came down around her like rocks hitting the ground. She had a task to perform. She didn't intend to let a little bit of rain stop her.

Mehwish had made up her mind. She was willing to walk away from everything—her father, the few friends she had, and her current way of life. Martin had far more to offer her. She would take hold of it with both hands and never look back. It was time to move on.

Martin was a member of the southern aristocracy. He was wealthy and madly in love with her. He'd asked her to run away with him. As his future wife, she had no doubt he would see to it that she was pampered according to her station and that her every wish would be met.

He'd already painted a vivid picture of the life they would have together. Martin's family owned a huge plantation in Charleston, South Carolina, with thousands of slaves to wait upon her. They owned a stable packed with the best horseflesh in the world. Mehwish loved to ride.

There would be teas, fêtes, soirees, and balls. As Martin's wife, she would rub shoulders with only the upper crust, and she would have entrée to the most sought-after social events. No longer would she be stuck in the backwoods of Zanzibar, away from gentle society and the excitement enjoyed by the white aristocracy.

Martin said he would see her dressed like a living doll. The best and the most sought-after *modistes* dressed his mother and his sister. They would dress Mehwish as well. Mehwish paused to spin around in a circle, embracing the stormy night as she thought of all the elegant frocks she would order and the priceless jewels Martin would drape her in.

My life will be absolutely wonderful!

Mehwish would leave Zanzibar without regret. She would finally be able to distance herself from any reminder of her African roots. She was already packed and her bags had been secreted onto Martin's ship a few days ago.

They had to go soon. Her father was expected back in three days' time. They would leave on the morning tide. She had one loose end to tie up before she started her new life as Mrs. Martin Henry Singleton.

Zahara knew this day was coming just as sure as she knew the sun would shine on the morrow, whether she was alive to see it or not. She was an oracle and had divined the nature, if not the exact time, of her transition decades ago. She looked up from her silent meditation to find her granddaughter, Mehwish, standing over her, dripping wet from the rain that was pounding on the beach. She was breathing hard with her dark hair plastered to her skull like a shiny black scarf.

Why had she not noticed it before? Zahara thought. Mehwish had the same sharp, ferret-shaped eyes as the man who had raped her over forty years ago and the same eyes as the child she bore him.

If the eyes are windows to the soul, surely Mehwish's dark, emotionless eyes were gateways to hell. The eyes that stared back at Zahara were calculating and devoid of emotion, suggesting sinister, unwholesome thoughts and the promise of evil deeds. Eyes such as Mehwish's were rare in one so young.

Mehwish stared at the old woman, memorising every wrinkle in her face, every grey hair upon her head. This would be the last time she would look upon Zahara's face in *this* world.

Zahara recalled the stormy night her granddaughter had first barged into her small, lonely hut located on the outskirts of her village and asked unceremoniously, "Are you really my grandmother?" That was six years ago, more than enough time for Zahara to apprentice her wicked and intelligent granddaughter in the art of black majick. There was little else she could teach her. It was now time to unleash her granddaughter's special brand of evil upon the unsuspecting world.

Zahara felt no remorse concerning the dangerous powers she had placed at her granddaughter's disposal. Why should she protect the innocent from her granddaughter when Allah had not thought to protect her? Where had Allah been on that fateful day when Rajab bin Mohammed bin Said el Murgebi swooped down upon her peaceful village like a rabid dog on a herd of innocent lambs? Perhaps Allah was otherwise engaged on that day? Or mayhap He was busy assisting someone more worthy than she.

It didn't matter that Zahara would go to hell for it. Allah had turned a blind eye when the rabid dog forced her to carry his evil seed. She would pay Him back by passing that same evil on to others.

The memories were like dung on Zahara's tongue. They flooded in with Mehwish and the storm surrounding her. These were not the thoughts she wished to entertain in her last minutes of life, but she had been filled with hate and bitterness for so long. What else did she have to carry with her? Tears ran unbidden down her face at the bitter memory. Zahara would take the night of her ruin to her grave.

After I pushed out Rajab's demon seed, he threw me across his huge black horse and rode me, still bleeding, to the entrance of what remained of my village. There he threw me to the ground like so much garbage and rode away. I found no succour amongst my people. The few people left that had not been sold into slavery or killed, reviled and ostracised me.

Mehwish knew Zahara to be the most fearless person she'd ever met. She was perplexed by her tears. The look on Mehwish's face was as if she was fascinated by an unusual bug, but hadn't quite decided what to do with.

Should I cherish it? Or should I stomp it into the ground?

Since Mehwish was standing over her on a night not fit for man or beast, and without her ladies' maid, Zahara assumed that Mehwish had finally made up her mind about the bug situation. The decision would not go in her favour.

So, mote it be.

Zahara would not try to fight the inevitable. Even if she thought to petition her granddaughter for mercy, she knew none would be forthcoming. She was tired, and it was time to go.

Her granddaughter hadn't sought her out this night for another life lesson. This time her granddaughter had come to take the last thing left to Zahara.

Zahara's voice was steady and clear. "Go ahead," she said. "Do what you came here to do."

Mehwish took a few more seconds to commit her grandmother's face to memory. She moved closer to embrace the old woman, gently whispering in her ear.

"I am going away, Zahara, to live in the colonies with the man I love. I fear I will never see you again. So, this will be goodbye, Madhe."

That was the first time Mehwish had ever called Zahara "Madhe," the word used for mother and grandmother. Even as the honoured title registered in Zahara's brain, she felt a sharp pain in her belly. When Mehwish stepped out of the embrace, the hilt of Zahara's ceremonial dagger, missing since Mehwish's last visit, was protruding from Zahara's belly. She gasped as Mehwish twisted the dagger even deeper. Before the light of life left Zahara's eyes, Mehwish pushed her feather-light body to the floor and stepped over her.

Mehwish rummaged through Zahara's meagre belongings to retrieve her *Grimoire*. This ancient book of black majick was special, dating back to antiquity and beyond. She never thought to ask her grandmother how she came by this sacred tome. She would never know. Now that she had it, and her grandmother's enchanted necklace and a few other coveted items, she left the old hut and didn't look back.

Martin slipped Mehwish and her servant, Nila, aboard ship while his men enjoyed one last night of carousing in Stone Town. Both women were cloaked in heavy, hooded robes to hide their identities. The skeleton crew on the ship consisted of the night watchman and a handful of sailors. All turned a blind eye as Martin hurriedly led the women to his cabin. Once he'd safely installed the women on the ship, he left them to return ashore. He still had some business to take care of before they set off on the morrow.

Mehwish frantically rummaged through one of her bags until she found the *Grimoire*. She couldn't believe she finally had it. They would be months out at sea. During that time she would familiarise herself with the passages and ancient spells. She intended to become far more powerful than her grandmother ever was.

CHAPTER 7

THEY WERE A third of the way through the protracted voyage. Mehwish was forced to remain hidden in Martin's stuffy cabin the entire time. She used the time wisely, memorising the spells in the *Grimoire* verbatim during the day and allowing Martin to school her in the many physical ways to please him at night. Soon she had read the *Grimoire* cover to cover—twice.

For the most part, the women's presence remained a secret. The few who knew they were aboard, such as the cabin boy who delivered food and water and the first mate, knew not to speak about it.

Having travelled extensively with her father, Mehwish had gained her sea legs at an early age. Unlike her servant, Nila, who spent most of the voyage suffering from a severe case of *mal de mer*, Mehwish generally found travel by sea to be exceptionally pleasurable. This would be her very first time in North America and she was anxious to see her future home and how the colonial aristocracy lived.

The cramped accommodations, coupled with the need for secrecy which forced Mehwish to remain confined to Martin's cabin, made what would otherwise have been an uneventful and rather pleasant trip, nearly unbearable.

As usual, Martin was performing his captain duties, leaving Mehwish to her own devises all day. If Martin's daily pattern remained true to form, she did not expect to see him again until mealtime, which was still several hours away.

Because of her illness, Nila was placed in a much smaller cabin not far from the one Mehwish shared with Martin. Mehwish was lonely and she was bored. There was a paucity of stimulating reading material with which to amuse herself other than the *Grimoire*, and she was heartily sick and tired of sleeping to pass the time. One could sleep but so much. There was nothing to do and there was nothing to see. The view from the one porthole remained the same—sea, sea, and more clear blue sea. She couldn't wait to place her feet on *terra firma*.

Today was particularly bad. Mehwish paced the length of the cramped cabin in agitation. Her only company while Martin was on deck was the creak of the slave-laden ship as it cut a swath through the churning blue-green sea and the smell of miserable humanity stacked like sardines below deck. She continued to pace, her anger steadily burgeoning. Her dark eyes narrowed as her mind focused upon Nila.

How dare Nila take sick at a time such as this!

Mehwish had absolutely no pity for Nila's plight. Since Nila had taken ill, it had been necessary for Mehwish to bathe *and* dress herself and do her own hair like she was a commoner.

Finally, tired of wearing a hole in the cabin floor, she flounced down upon the bed. *What was the purpose of bringing a servant along on a voyage if said servant spends the entire time puking in a chamber pot and lying abed?*

Speaking of puking, Mehwish was becoming ill herself from the stench rising from the hold where the slave cargo was held. They'd stopped off at a warehouse where the captured slaves were being held. Those same slaves were stinking up the ship and everything on it. Each day the smell worsened. As a number of the dead and dying were thrown overboard, the remaining Africans destined to a life of slavery in the Caribbean Islands and the Americas rotted below deck.

Mehwish held a perfumed hanky to her delicate nose in an unsuccessful attempt to block out the rancid odour offending her olfactory sense. The smell of unwashed bodies pressed together in extreme heat, mingled with the smell of fear, irrevocable loss, and human waste, seeped through the floorboards of the ship, tainting the air surrounding it.

At the very least, Nila should be here to fan me or even hold the handkerchief to my nose, she thought. Her arm began to tyre from holding the hanky herself. When Nila recovered, Mehwish vowed to take a strap to the slave girl so hard she wouldn't be able to sit down for a week!

The one good thing about the voyage was that she and Martin were able to make passionate love every single night. Martin would muffle her response with the palm of his rough hand, lest her screams of passion be heard from stem to stern, causing a mutiny. In that aspect, Mehwish had never been happier. She would be Martin's wife and have babies as blond and beautiful as he was. She must try to remain patient.

She nearly tripped over the hem of her skirt when she heard Martin giving meal instructions to his steward on the other side of the door. She was starved for companionship and intelligent conversation.

Martin stiffened involuntarily as Mehwish flung herself into his arms the second he entered the cabin. It had been a particularly hard day, and he was tired and worn. Mehwish refused to see his current state, seeking as always to meet her own personal needs.

"Oh Martin, the day has been interminable without you. I have been out of my mind with boredom! And, Martin, the awful smell of those beasts below is making me ill. How can you abide the smell? Why, if it was not for the perfumed hankies Nila thought to pack, I would choke on the dreadful odour."

For a fleeting moment Martin's face held an unfamiliar expression which he quickly masked with an indulgent smile. He held back what he wanted to say.

Were it not for those stinking beasts below deck, he thought, *your black father would not have been able to purchase the expensive perfume you so liberally doused your delicate lace hankies in.*

But he kept his thoughts to himself. Mehwish's behaviour was to be expected. After all, she had been spoiled her entire life, but that didn't make her infernal complaining any easier for him to bear. He too would be glad when they made land. He disentangled her clinging arms before stepping away from her as he moved to take off his sweat-dampened shirt.

Mehwish could not help but feel Martin was growing tired of her, that he no longer desired her. She hid her hurt by telling herself Martin was merely exhausted from the hours spent on deck in the blazing hot sun. That was why he didn't greet her in his customary enthusiastic fashion. Surely her imagination was running away with her due to her extended stay in the confining cabin. Things would be much different once they arrived at his plantation and she became situated in the bosom of her new family.

Mehwish was in a frenzy of excitement. They were less than a day's sail from a place called Louisiana, where Martin would unload half his cargo before sailing straight to South Carolina. Nila stood before Mehwish on shaky legs, twenty pounds lighter than when she'd first boarded ship. Mehwish gave possession of the heavy *Grimoire* over to Nila.

"Listen here, girl. I want you to guard this book with your life, you hear? It would not pay for my future husband or my in-laws to know about its existence. Let no one know you have it. No one. When we arrive in South Carolina, I want you to hide it on the plantation grounds as soon as you can, but let no one see where you've hidden it. Do you understand?"

"Yes, Mistress."

Nila's eyes were as large as saucers as she nodded her understanding of Mehwish's instructions. Mistress Mehwish was mean through and through. Nila didn't want to do anything to cross her. Truth be told, she hadn't wanted to accompany Mistress Mehwish on this voyage. She knew better than to deny her, and she knew better than to tell anybody about Mistress' plans either.

Since Nila couldn't read, she didn't understand the importance of the tome she'd been asked to hide. She did know, however, that if she didn't guard the thing with her life as instructed, she wouldn't have a life to worry about.

Nila started to feel sick the minute the book was handed off to her. She had a bad feeling about the upcoming journey, Mr. Singleton, and especially about the heavy book which was even now metaphorically burning a hole in her hand.

CHAPTER 8

THE DAY MARTIN'S ship docked in Baton Rouge, the calm ocean water shifted the anchored ship back and forth like a baby in its cradle. Mehwish and Nila remained hidden below deck while the slave cargo was unloaded for the upcoming auction. Less than twenty-four hours later they made their next port of call in Charleston, South Carolina. Mehwish was packed, dressed, and ready when Martin finally came to fetch her. She and Nila were then spirited away in a waiting carriage. Mehwish couldn't contain her happiness. Her new life with Martin was about to begin.

The well-sprung carriage cut through the mass of humanity at the docks with ease. Soon the landscape changed from the busy waterfront to colourful stucco residences in Charleston proper. There was so much to see. Mehwish's excitement knew no bounds.

"Oh, darling, Charleston is absolutely gorgeous! How long before we reach Singleton?" she asked.

Martin brushed an imaginary speck of dust off his trousers. He looked every bit the prosperous country planter, with his tan linen suit, crème-coloured shirt, and a wide-brimmed straw hat to protect his handsome face from the relentless South Carolina sun.

"I've made arrangements for us to stay the night at a small house I own in the city. We'll set off for Singleton in the morning."

Mehwish was disappointed, but she didn't let it show. Martin was right. She would need to look her best when she met Martin's mother and sister. A good night's sleep on solid ground was just what the doctor ordered.

The carriage finally stopped in front of a delightful pink stucco cottage with grey shutters and a black wrought iron fence. Martin gave instructions to the coachman after they alighted, leaving Nila behind to assist with the bags.

Mehwish ran before Martin, laughing playfully. She dashed inside as soon as he opened the door. She was delighted by the tasteful décor. When she spun around to share her pleasure with Martin, he slapped a foul-smelling handkerchief over her mouth and nose. Her eyes rolled to the back of her head, and everything went black.

"How dare you manhandle me in such a manner!" Mehwish exclaimed, staring at Martin with eyes resembling two seething black chips of coal.

Martin looked down the slope of his narrow nose at her, gloating at her beet red face and the tangled bird's nest that had become of her hair, while Nila wailed as if she, and not her mistress, had been struck.

Mehwish pushed away from the floor into a semi-crouching position, shifting into fight or flight mode during the moments it took her to recover from the blow and fully right herself. For Mehwish the choice was simple. She was far too evil to run. No one was going to strike her and get away with it.

She surveyed her surroundings in search of something, anything to wash that condescending smirk off Martin's face. Her eyes landed upon the hearth—more particularly, the metal poker propped against the wall next to it.

Blinded by the sharp sting of Martin's betrayal and oblivious to her precarious position, Mehwish shoved Nila into Martin and made a mad dash for the poker. She had every intention of beating Martin to death, slicing his throat from ear to ear with the sharp pointed tip, and ripping his heart out of his chest like he'd ripped out hers.

She'd barely grasped hold of the poker before Martin was on her, tackling her to the floor. They grappled, with Martin easily disarming her and seriously injuring her wrist in the process.

"Once I am ransomed," she spat, blowing an errant clump of hair away from her eyes, "there will not be a hole on this earth you will be able to hide in to escape my father's wrath. When my father hears how badly you have treated me, he will whip you like the insolent dog you are!"

Martin merely laughed at Mehwish's impotent indignation.

"Why, you vain, stupid little fool! Ransom you? Who said anything about a ransom? Have you forgotten that no one knows where you are?" His lip curled in a sneer as he continued to deride Mehwish. "Never in a million years would your father suspect me of harming his precious little girl. That is why I insisted we keep our trysts a secret. Only a few know about our sordid affair, and they are loyal to me.

You see, I fully intend to continue my business association with your father. Our association has been extremely lucrative over the years for us both. In fact, upon my return to Zanzibar, I will offer my heartfelt assistance in the search your father has most assuredly mounted on your behalf."

At that moment Mehwish's eyes narrowed and her hands curled into claws as she was consumed with a feeling of hate like she'd never known. She wanted to rip the flesh from Martin's handsome face, to gouge his eyes out with her bare hands and shove them down his throat while she watched him choke to death.

"You didn't really think that I would marry the daughter of a Blackamoor, now did you?" Martin queried, in a deceptively soft tone. He wrinkled his long aristocratic nose as though something foul-smelling had invaded the air. "Why, your father is blacker than most of the darkies who work the fields on my plantation! And I declare your grandmother is as black as the ace of spades. That one is a pure black African savage, through and through. You too have a bit of the savage in you, my sweet."

"Look at you," he spat, looking down on Mehwish with revulsion. "You are like a little animal, panting with excessive emotion like a little bitch in heat. You've proven yourself to be a slut already. You showed me your darkie nature every time you spread your dusky thighs to give me entrance to your body. You were born to the role of a whore. I wonder how many others have shared your affection," he asked in a speculative tone.

Mehwish flinched at the cruelty of his words. Never had anyone spoken to her in such a vile and despicable manner, and no man had touched her but him.

Martin's voice held a note of laughter as he continued. "Surely you didn't think my affection for you was so great that I would taint my pristine lineage with your inferior blood, that I would run the risk of a black throwback cropping up in future generations of my family?"

Mehwish was still in shock from the devastating turn of events. She did not know if a question had been put to her or whether his statement was merely a rambling observation. Before she could make up her mind, she was taken by surprise when Martin did what he had been aching to do since the day he met her. He balled up his fist and struck her a blow so vicious, she blacked out—again.

Mehwish was jarred back to consciousness when a bucket of brackish dirty water was thrown smack dab in her face. When she came to, Martin was standing over her. His face showed absolutely no emotion.

"Now that you have a better grasp of where you stand, you will listen to me and you will not speak until I give you leave to do so. You will address me as Master at all times. If you do not, you will be severely beaten. My wife will be addressed as Mistress."

Martin's voice droned on and on as something in Mehwish's mind disconnected from reality.

As soon as Mehwish arrived at Singleton, Martin's family plantation in Charleston, South Carolina, she was introduced to Martin's wife as her new maid. The humiliation and pain was like a knife in her chest. She prevailed upon the decency of his wife at once. Surely the wife that Mehwish didn't even know Martin had would see she didn't belong there.

But when she voiced her indignation, even threatening retribution from her father, Martin's wife declared her insolent. Martin struck Mehwish across the face again, this time drawing blood. He then sounded the alarm, calling all the plantation slaves forth to witness her further humiliation.

Scalding tears ran down her face as Martin ordered his overseer to pull her to her feet. He then ripped the back of her dress open before tying her to a post and nearly peeling the skin off her back with a rawhide whip. She would bear the scars from the brutal beating for the rest of her life.

Mehwish didn't think her circumstances could get any worse than having the man she thought she was going to marry trick her into a life of slavery. Surely her father would leave no stone unturned to find her and offer a ransom for her safe return. After some negotiation, she would be returned to her opulent style of life in Zanzibar with her pride somewhat bruised but her body intact.

Martin's skinny blonde wife looked down her pinched nose at Mehwish and demanded that Martin get rid of her. "I'll take the other one," she said, pointing at Nila, who was shaking with fear. "But I want *her* off our land immediately!"

Martin dragged Mehwish to his carriage and loaded her inside. He took her to the residence of a fat country buffoon with a foul-smelling cigar hanging from his mouth. The man pawed at her as if she was of less value than a piece of horseflesh. She grit her teeth, knowing better than to show her true feelings.

"I don't know, Singleton. She's mighty banged up."

Mehwish had a black eye, a busted lip, and her jaw was swollen. The man pulled down the top of her dress to expose her lacerated back. He tsk-tsked at what he saw.

"These cuts are gonna bring down the asking price considerably, but I think I can get rid of her for you."

"What kind of gul-dern name is May Witch?" the fat fool asked, glancing down at a chart with a list of slaves for sale. Martin let loose that laugh that used to send goose bumps up and down Mehwish's spine. It only made her hate him more, if that was even possible.

"From here on out, gal, you'll answer to the name Hannah. It's a good old-fashioned Christian name and way too good for the likes of you."

In less than ten minutes, Mehwish was herded into the back of a rickety buck wagon. That day Mehwish, the Zanzibari heiress, died and Hannah, the slave, was born.

CHAPTER 9

New Orleans

THE STEADY CLIP-CLOP of the horses' hooves lulled Monique Dubonnet to sleep as her driver navigated her well-appointed carriage through the dark streets of the city. Monique's head bounced in time with the gentle movement of the carriage which was conveying her back to her place of business.

It was late, well past midnight and the usual miscreants quietly hid behind dark shadows waiting for opportunity to knock. They were near the waterfront, a dangerous section of the city even during daylight hours where cutpurses, pickpockets, murderers, and thieves abounded.

Monique could close her eyes without worry or care. She knew that should there be any unexpected trouble, Marcus, the massively built African who served as her driver, bouncer, and trusted protector, had a cocked and loaded pistol within easy access and a couple of lethal knives at his disposal.

A frown marred Monique's smooth brow even in sleep. She was a successful businesswoman of colour, but she knew better than most that there was a price to pay for success. Unfortunately, the nature of Monique's business sometimes made it necessary for her to figuratively get in bed with the devil.

She'd come from the devil's lair a short while ago. This particular devil came in the form of the Honourable Quincy James Topplet, the chief of police and overall dispenser of justice in the city of New Orleans. Topplet was as crooked as they come. No one operated a business, legal or otherwise, in the city without breaking him off a significant piece of their profits. Topplet demanded more than money from Monique, and she was forced, albeit reluctantly, to give him what he wanted.

Their monthly meetings in his mansion on the other side of town would remain a well-kept secret. Each time Monique was forced to visit him, she came away feeling dirty in body and in spirit. But what did she expect?

When you lie down with dogs, you come up with fleas, right?

All she could do now was temporarily shut her mind down and sleep. Blissful, healing sleep was the best remedy to ease her bruised spirit and calm her restless soul. She would have her maid heat water for her bath upon her return to Maison Plaisir. She couldn't wash Topplet's smell and touch off her body quickly enough.

Monique was rudely jostled awake and nearly unseated by the sudden sharp motion of the carriage as Marcus swerved off the road. Her heart was in her mouth. Once she was able to adequately compose herself, she stuck her head out the carriage window.

"My god, Marcus! Please tell me we didn't hit someone!"

"No, but just barely."

Marcus jumped down from the carriage. With a commanding voice, he instructed Monique to stay inside as he headed toward two figures, a man and what appeared to be a woman, at the edge of the waterfront.

Blood flew as the man straddled an unmoving woman, pummelling her with his angry fists. Without a moment's hesitation, Marcus grabbed the woman's assailant by the scruff of his collar and knocked him away like beached flotsam.

The batterer crawled to his knees with the intention of engaging Marcus, but thought better of it when he noted his size and the elegant carriage he'd alighted from. Thinking a person of importance sat in the conveyance, he quickly adopted a solicitous demeanour.

"Listen, boy. You can tell your master that I ain't lookin' for no trouble. This here whore was trying to steal from me. I caught her red-handed and she ain't getting no more than she rightfully deserves. I bought her fair and square, and it's within my rights to feed her to the fish if I want."

Marcus looked down at the woman who appeared more dead than alive. "What use can she possibly be to you in this condition?"

The woman was emaciated and her clothing filthy. She was probably a dock-side whore and the man her pimp.

"Well, I was thinking I might sell her to one of the owners of the fifty cent joints on Iberville. That ways, at least I'll get back the money I invested in her."

Marcus shook his head in disgust. If the woman wasn't dead already, she'd be dead in a few weeks if she ended up in one of the filthy cribs on Iberville. Those women were forced to service up to thirty or forty men a day, many of them poxed or otherwise diseased.

Marcus excused himself when Monique called him to the carriage. He quickly relayed the substance of his conversation with the dock-side pimp. Monique spoke without hesitation.

"Ask him how much he wants for her, Marcus, and put her in the carriage."

And that is how Monique Dubonnet came to meet Mehwish Shumaila bin Said al-Murgebi, now known as Hannah.

Maison Plaisir, New Orleans

Monique generally allowed her girls to buy their freedom after a short period of service. Hannah didn't want to wait. She wanted to get enough money to get back to her life in Zanzibar immediately. All she needed was one big score in order to leave New Orleans and everything it represented behind her. A great deal of money flowed through Maison Plaisir. She intended to get her hands on it. As Monique's trusted friend and right-hand man, Marcus, held the proverbial keys to the kingdom. Hannah decided to seduce Marcus and convince him to betray his beloved employer. She used black majick.

All of the clandestine visits with her grandmother to master the art of baneful majick had born fruit. Hannah was a powerful witch in her own right, and an expert practitioner of black majick. However, every witch requires the tools of their trade. Hannah sought out the Wizard Moultrie, a traitor to the Nephilim Nation and a self-proclaimed arch mage wizard, to provide her with the ingredients for a spell she intended to cast. That is how she successfully ensorcelled Marcus.

The Wizard's aid came with a price. She was to relay any news of note that transpired in Maison Plasir and promptly report same back to the Wizard, for which he promised to assist her with any future needs and handsomely compensate her. Hannah readily agreed.

An opportunity missed is an opportunity forever lost. That was Hannah's credo. She learned at a very young age to pay close attention to her intuition and to the subtle signals her body sent out. Right now, the tips of her ears were tingling like crazy, and it wasn't because of the wet kisses that lumbering oaf, Marcus, was ardently bestowing upon her person.

A similar tingling had taken hold of Hannah a little over five years ago, when she saw a tall, dark-complexioned man materialise before the door to the room right next to the supply closet she now occupied with her clandestine lover. Not only did the man appear in front of the door, seemingly out of nowhere, but he walked through it and into the room.

Hannah had only caught a glimpse of the profile and the back of the magical disappearing man, but she knew a good piece of man flesh when she saw it. She didn't know what his face looked like, but if his face looked even half as good as the back of his body did, she knew him to be extremely handsome—a little too handsome to be human.

Hannah's employer, Monique Dubonnet, was no fool. She prided herself on knowing about everything that went on in her house. However, Hannah was sneaky by nature and clever by necessity. She took great pains to conceal the fact that she was not only stealing from Monique's patrons, but that she was also fucking Monique's trusted bouncer and syphoning information, *ergo* the stealthy meeting in the crowded supply closet.

Hannah had quickly concluded that Monique had to have known there was some kind of preternatural being in her house all those years ago. From the faint voices Hannah heard coming from the other side of the wall on that fateful night, there was more than one. Someone else was now occupying the mystery room. Hannah wanted to know who it was and why they were there. More specifically, she wanted to know what else Monique Dubonnet was hiding. The fact that they were in a seldom-travelled section of the house, behind a door that was always locked, piqued Hannah's interest.

The Wizard Moultrie paid Hannah handsomely for the previous information. Maybe whatever was going on in the room next door would be of equal value to the wizard. For the right price, Hannah would make sure he received it. If the wizard was not interested in whatever she found out, surely this could be valuable information which Hannah could capitalise on later. There was a reason that room stayed locked, and there was a reason Monique didn't want anyone to know who the occupants of that room were.

Using the cunning of a woodland fox trapped by a hound during a hunt, Hannah sidled up to Marcus, fisting the material of his shirt front in her small hands. Marcus' eyes lit with passion when she aggressively backed the big man up against the wall nearest to the supply room door. She needed to get closer to the wall so that she could listen for movement or conversation in the other room. Hannah needed to accomplish this feat while at the same time keeping Marcus preoccupied and ignorant of what she was about.

Hannah hiked up the front of her skirts, brazenly exposing the nakedness underneath. She unbuckled Marcus' pants in a motion made smooth from a great deal of practise. Hannah was a whore, and like any good whore she knew how to perform her duties convincingly, even if her mind was elsewhere. And right now her mind was on the low rumble of voices coming from inside the other room.

By the time Marcus spilled his seed in Hannah's voracious red-lipped mouth, she'd already heard all she needed to know. This was information she would not share with the wizard. She formulated a plan.

CHAPTER 10

THE BLOW MONIQUE delivered to Hannah's face split her bottom lip, nearly taking her head off. The second blow, delivered in quick succession, would have dropped her to her knees had Marcus and Monique's other bouncer, Norman, not been holding Hannah up. Hannah had been at Maison Plaisir for almost six years. She had never seen this side of Monique Dubonnet.

Who would have thought the issy prissy little missy could pack such a solid punch?

It hadn't been difficult to determine the identity of the mole inside Maison Plaisir. Monique laid the trap, and Hannah took the bait like the lying, thieving, ungrateful rat she was. Monique's only regret was that Marcus had allowed himself to be sucked into the black hole surrounding Hannah.

Monique suspected Hannah of theft when several patrons complained of money, rings, and watches going missing. Monique ran a clean house. She couldn't keep anyone around who jeopardised the good name she'd worked so hard to achieve over the years. Monique promptly launched an investigation of all her girls. All fingers pointed in Hannah's direction as the culprit.

A few days ago, one of the other girls observed Hannah slip away from the parlour. She thought it odd for Hannah to leave during their peak business time. She hastened to disclose her observation to Monique. Although a careful search of Hannah's sleeping area failed to disclose the location of the purloined goods, Monique was not convinced of Hannah's innocence. She set Nathan to shadow Hannah's every move. He'd observed her sneaking down to the lower level of the house earlier that evening with Marcus following close on her heels.

Nathan enlisted the assistance of the chimney sweep and two other employees of Monique's to set Hannah up. The men slipped into the seldom-used room next door to the supply closet. They discussed payment for the exchange of stolen goods within Hannah's hearing. The walls are thin in the older portion of the house. They made sure she could hear every word. Monique donated a few pieces of her personal jewellery toward the cause. No sooner did they depart when Hannah slipped into the unlocked room to steal the jewellery. It was wrapped in oil cloth and hidden in a flower vase on one of the tables—in the place where one of the men said he would hide it.

Monique had Nathan follow Hannah. She led Nathan to a small park down the street from Maison Plaisir. He watched her dig a small hole in the arbour to secret the stolen goods and quickly return to the house. Nathan dug up the hole and, lo and behold, there was the cache of stolen goods.

Caught off guard, Hannah's usual facile tongue was unable to come up with a compelling enough lie to convince Monique or any of her other detractors of her innocence. Monique had caught her fair and square. Hannah didn't know how this would play out. She was prepared for the worst.

She knew she couldn't look to her errant lover, Marcus, for assistance. One glance at his stone-cold expression spoke volumes. He knew he'd been used. He would revel in seeing her punished to soothe his bruised ego and get back in Monique's good graces. This time she had no one to turn to who would be willing to save her neck.

She'd been caught stealing. She could only hope that the information she'd previously disclosed to the wizard, which resulted in a surprise demon attack, would never become common knowledge. Hannah remembered every detail of the night Monique allowed a ban of preternatural beings to conduct an illegal meeting in one of the rooms in her house. It was not until after she informed the Wizard of their presence that she realized who and what they were. Moultrie had almost ruined everything! His demons could have at least waited until the superhuman beings were away from the place where she worked and lived before they attacked! So far, no one connected her with the leak. Thinking back to the close call made her quake in her boots.

And where the hell is Moultrie now, when I need him?

The bastard promised her that if she ever got into a jam, he'd know it and come to her aid. Instead, he had left her hanging out to dry—again. Moultrie had earned a place on the list of people against whom she would seek vengeance. If she managed to live through this, she'd see that he paid—and dearly.

Crack!

Monique delivered yet another vicious blow, this time to Hannah's nose to get her attention. The large diamond ring Monique wore on her middle finger cut into the bridge of Hannah's nose, slicing the skin open. A shock wave of pain exploded inside Hannah's head. The last thing she saw as her vision dimmed to black was Monique shaking out the hand she'd used to knock Hannah's lights out.

"Marcus, can I trust you to get this garbage out of my sight?"

Monique had taken Hannah in, cleaned her up, and offered her a job. She had always thought herself to be a good judge of character, but this time she was way off the mark.

The fleeting look of pain that filled Marcus' eyes was replaced with a look of determination. His loyalty had never been questioned before—that is, not until Hannah came into his life. Now that he was looking at her, he wondered what in the world he had seen in her. Her nose was crooked from a previous break. There was a faint scar on the side of her mouth, and she had the coldest black eyes he'd ever seen on a human, male or female. It felt like she had him in some kind of trance that he'd come out of. He would do whatever it took to redeem himself in Monique's eyes.

"Yes, you can trust me," he said with fervour. "I will *never* give you cause to doubt me again."

Monique's voice was terse. "See that you don't."

In that moment, something passed between them. Marcus was holding his breath. Monique couldn't stand the look of guilt on Marcus' face. She realised more than one man had been led astray by the wiles of a cunning woman.

"I believe you, Marcus. And for the record? I trust you with my life."

Marcus exhaled in relief when he saw the smile that followed Monique's statement. That night Hannah found herself on the auction block yet again.

CHAPTER 11

Magnolia Hill

IT WAS JUST past mid-day and already dark as full night, with that eerie calm that almost always presages a bad storm. Even before the arrival of the rain, the moisture-laden air simply wept, burdening the limbs of the trees and covering the whole of Magnolia Hill like a thick, wet blanket. Something bad was going to happen. Flossie could feel it.

An itinerate sea captain, bearing goods for sale along the Mississippi, had confirmed but two days prior of a hurricane that had already cut a merciless swath through Cuba, leaving it in shambles. Now that it was done ravishing Cuba, the violent storm was picking up steam, racing inland from Belize and westward toward the Plaquemines.

Flossie didn't need a wayward seaman to tell her a bad storm was coming. She could feel it in her aching bones. The natural phenomenon had its hungry eye set upon New Orleans, already causing flooding as deep as ten feet in places before veering off and heading directly toward Edgard, the county seat of St. John the Baptist Parish and Magnolia Hill.

Flossie watched a veil of darkness descend as she stood in the kitchen doorway with the strong, hot winds lifting her skirt. The heat felt good on her bare legs. She inhaled deeply. Nothing smelled quite like approaching rain. The unique scent joined forces with the strong smell of cabbage, dirty rice, and decade-old pork fat coming from inside the kitchen that also served as Flossie and her daughter Perline's sleeping quarters.

Cook had gone on to her reward some three years ago. One day Flossie woke to find the woman who had come to be closer than a mother to her slumped over dead at the wooden kitchen table, her face planted in a bowl of shelled peas. Now, Flossie served as the plantation cook, midwife, and healer.

The demons had been restless of late, but something else was eating at Flossie's spirit. Something she couldn't quite put her finger on. That *something* kept her from sleeping last night. She closed her eyes to allow her small solitary figure to sway in time with music only the wind could make, freeing her spirit so that she could pinpoint whatever it was that was nagging at her. She gave up with a sigh on her lips.

As in all things, soon all would be made clear.

There was a great deal of hustle and bustle taking place in preparation for the approaching storm, hammering and boarding up and such. Flossie felt like she was the last human on earth, small, pitiful, and alone.

"Olodumare, somethin' bad is gon' happen sure as my name is Flossie. I can feel it in my bones," she muttered to herself, stepping back into the kitchen.

No sooner had the thought of impending doom crossed Flossie's mind when the wheels of the plantation buck wagon sped over pits and ruts, creating sparks on gravel as its driver raced hell-bent for leather down River Road.

Flossie narrowed her one good eye to see better. It was Drake, the plantation overseer, returning from the city with newly purchased slaves.

Drake's stringy, dirty blond hair lashed his angular face, blowing in the wind as the fast approaching storm greedily licked at the wheels of the buck wagon. They didn't have a moment to spare. It was imperative they seek shelter at once if he was to ensure his safety and that of his cargo. Nine hours of gale force winds had already hit neighbouring plantations not twenty miles up the road from Magnolia Hill, tearing flimsy slave cabins asunder and pulling century-old trees from their roots. The storm left a path of property destruction and death to humans and livestock alike.

One large drop of rain cut through the humidity, landing on Drake's forehead with an explosive plop as the conveyance careened on two wheels through the plantation entrance. The six slaves chained together in the splintery bed of the wagon held on for dear life as they were painfully jostled to and fro.

The first raindrop opened the door to a surge of wind and a blinding rain and hail mixed deluge. Large balls of hail pelted the rain-soaked earth, playing a prickly tune against abandoned farm equipment and boarded up structures. The storm had finally reached Magnolia Hill.

The rain hit so hard, it caused steam to rise from the hot ground, shrouding the plantation in a foggy mist. Drake and the slaves were soon soaked to the bone.

Drake quickly alighted from the wagon, throwing the reigns to a waiting stable boy who could barely maintain his footing against the vengeful wind. Drake was forced to scream over the wind for his instructions to be heard.

"Feed and water the horses and get them stabled now, boy!" he commanded.

Flossie stood with a lantern in hand amidst the fierce winds and driving rain, compelled by some nameless force to approach the wagon. Perline stood at her side. Drake turned to Flossie and Perline.

"You two gals need to stop gawkin'. Make yourself useful. Help me get these here niggas loose."

Flossie and Perline moved as quickly as their twisted bodies would allow. Perline was fifteen and small for her age. Mother and daughter looked like little black sparrows with loose cotton skirts and matching white kerchiefs covering their thick hair.

Among the six slaves were two women. Flossie and Perline led them to the kitchen. The stable boy took the four men to the barn to wait out the storm.

Perline noted that one of the women had skin whiter than the white women she sometimes saw in fancy carriages when she went to town with her mother.

Flossie's skill in midwifery and healing were legendary. Her daughter was equally renowned as an extraordinary seamstress. The Etiennes frequently hired out the services of both mother and daughter, thus they were often in town.

Once inside the kitchen, little Perline moved toward the white-skinned slave. Her gait was painfully slow and awkward due to her crippled leg. Perline had been a breach baby. Instead of turning her in the proper position for birth, the midwife pulled Perline out by her foot. Perline's deformity was a result of her leg being broken at the hip when she was pulled out of Flossie's body. The foot the midwife used to pull Perline out of the birthing canal was broken and was never properly set. Little Perline was fortunate she was able to walk at all.

The woman's clothing was sopping wet, torn in places, and terribly stained. Fascinated with the black white woman, Perline sought to dry her off with a kitchen towel while Flossie offered a similar service to the other woman who said her name was Jane.

Hannah's dark eyes quickly scanned her surroundings. Sixteen years had come and gone, with more "masters" than she could count, yet she still clung to the hope she would one day return to Zanzibar. She was nothing if not persistent.

The white-skinned slave viciously struck out at Perline. "Take your filthy black hands off me!" she screamed, backing away from Perline as though the little girl had the plague. "I demand to speak to your master at once! I will not sleep in this pigsty, not for one night!"

Perline stepped away from the woman in fear. She made it a point to stay out of white folk's way, and she wasn't used to black folks being unkind to her, even if they looked white.

Flossie picked up the lantern and approached the agitated woman. Their eyes locked. It didn't matter how white her skin was nor how straight her hair. Something about the slave screamed "black" as loudly as an African war chant. For the space of a minute, neither of them had the power to tear her eyes away from the other.

"Get behind me, Satan!" exclaimed Flossie, breaking the silence, hastily making the sign of the evil eye in front of the woman. Not only did Flossie detect the woman's blackness in the manner that only another black person could, but she could smell evil pouring from her in waves.

"You welcome to seek out Masta Etienne yourself, gal. That is if you ready to get yourself killed," Flossie warned. "There ain't *nobody* in this here cabin that is gonna fetch nothin' or nobody for you. You can either settle down and take these dry clothes, or you can suffer in the nasty wet ones you got on. Your choice."

With that, Flossie turned her back and began to walk away from the bedraggled slave, dragging her partially paralysed leg behind her, one of several disfiguring injuries she'd sustained during a brutal rape and beating administered by Claude Etienne and several of his cohorts. She turned just in time as Hannah lunged toward her with fingers curled, fully prepared to mount an attack.

"Why, you ugly black crippled little bitch!" Hannah screeched.

Flossie merely raised her pinkie and forefinger in the direction of the charging woman and began chanting in a language the angry woman could not understand.

Hannah was stopped dead in her tracks, momentarily paralysed; however, she remained uncowed.

"You may have won this little battle, old woman, but I will most assuredly win the war! When my father sends for me, I will see you whipped like the mangy dog you are," she threatened in a soft, but menacing tone.

A brand new kind of evil took up residence on Magnolia Hill the day that wicked yella gal arrived. Make no mistake about it, Flossie knew evil when she saw it. It made the little nappy hairs on the nape of her neck stand on end. Despite the hot summer day, she felt a chill that seeped clear to the bone. It was the kind of chill that travelled from the crown of her head to the soles of her feet. It was as if someone was walking on her grave, or the devil himself was standing over her shoulder, slowly blowing the grave's icy cold breath on the back of her neck.

Flossie looked into the slave's dark soulless eyes, black malicious eyes that gave Flossie a little preview of what death and the darkness of the grave might feel like. Flossie likened Hannah's arrival to that of a wicked witch slicing through the stormy night on her broomstick, bringing with her a bucket of heartache and a basket overflowing with pain.

CHAPTER 12

MAGNOLIA HILL SURVIVED the storm. A rooster crowed in the distance, waking Hannah from twisted dreams of the whistling sound the whip made before it sliced through the air to crack against her skin. She felt the remnants of the nightmarish screams that always followed in her spirit, if not on her tongue. She'd come to call it white folks' entertainment at its finest.

During the wee hours of the morning when tomorrow becomes today, Hannah lay in her soaking wet clothing on the hard dirt floor. Purely out of spite, she opted to remain in her wet clothes rather than accept anything from the ugly old crone woman she'd argued with the night before. She'd only served to bite off her own nose to spite herself because now her damp clothing was sticking to her sweaty skin like mould.

Her mind travelled back to the past sixteen years of her life. At one time Hannah thought Singleton's betrayal would be the worst thing that could ever happen to her. Even in a dream state, her laughter was bitter from her remembered naiveté. When Singleton's wife demanded he get rid of her, he put her on the auction block so fast Hannah's head spun. She ended up the property of a crippled dirt farmer with a gambling habit. The farm was located in a rural town called Coward in Florence County, South Carolina.

Her first day on the farm, her new master beat her like a dog with his wooden cane. Her crime was that of steadfastly refusing to answer to anything but her real name, Mehwish Shumaila bin Said al-Murgebi. She would soon learn that nobody on that godforsaken dirt farm gave a hot damn what she said her name was. Her papers said her name was Hannah. He had one of the three slaves he owned drag her outside to the whipping post and watched while the slave beat the living shit out of her.

She had more than enough time to rationally think through her vulnerable position as she lay on her stomach in the barn, smelling of the horse liniment the stable boy applied to her lacerated back. She was proud, but she was not a fool. By the time her new master got through with her, she was answering to the name Hannah quick enough.

Unused to physical labour of any kind, Hannah found it difficult to perform the duties assigned to her as quickly and efficiently as expected. Again, she tried to convince the dirt farmer that a reward would be offered for her if he would contact her father. She was beaten again.

When it was noted that she, as a Muslim, did not partake of the pork rations provided to each of the slaves, her master watched as a huge brutish slave named Cesar beat her, raped her, and shoved chitterlings down her throat. When her stomach rebelled, and she threw up the foul entrails, Cesar forced her to eat the vomit and beat her continuously until she kept the vomit and the pork down. After that, she ate her daily ration of swine along with the other slaves without complaint. Hannah was thankful when, after two years of brutal abuse, the poor white trash dirt farmer wagered her on a hand of cards and lost.

She became the property of a slick, sharp-dressing card shark with a penchant for swindling and a fondness for hard drink. He won Hannah fair and square. Hannah begged him to keep her even though he beat the daylights out of her whenever he got drunk. Anything was better than where she'd been. But there was no place for a slave, female or otherwise in his life. He was gunned down six months later for cheating at cards. His murderer took Hannah and everything else he owned while her former owner lay dying in the street.

Everything was a blur after that. Hannah changed hands more than she could count. She'd been wagered in at least three more poker games, after which she'd been forced to earn money for her masters in more than one whorehouse, brothel, or dockside crib. Each time Hannah found herself sold to someone else, she would try to tell them who she was. All she had were scars to show for her efforts. From the little she'd been able to see last night, Magnolia Hill exceeded the splendour of her father's largest holding in Zanzibar. If she had to be a white man's slave, at least this time it would be a wealthy one.

The only way I will return to Zanzibar will be in my dreams. I am the white man's slave, and I need to make the best of my situation, she thought.

The sound of voices coming through the open kitchen window filtered through the remnants of her foggy dreams.

The other new slave, Jane, and the arrogant old crone she'd met the night before were sitting at a large wooden table that took up the majority of the cooking area, talking quietly while kneading dough. It looked to Hannah like they had been up for hours. There was no sign of the little black green-eyed girl with the twisted leg. Flossie addressed Hannah without looking in her direction.

"'Bout time you woke up."

Something in the crone's tone of voice and the cadence of her words put Hannah in the mind of her old nursemaid Binta. But that was another life ago. Hannah didn't respond to Flossie's statement. Flossie didn't expect her to.

"Mr. Drake say Masta Claude want you up at the Big House. You best get a move on it if you know what's good for you."

Hannah wasn't much for taking orders from somebody's slave, but she was mighty anxious to speak with the master. So, she tidied up as best she could, grabbed a piece of cornbread sitting on the wooden table, and headed up to the Big House.

Hannah was pressed into service in the Big House where she worked day in and day out without a day off. Hannah bore little to no resemblance to the pampered Zanzibari princess she once was. Her skin, which was once smooth and soft from milk baths and daily massages, was now ashy, rough, and callused. Her nails were cracked and broken, and her back was a tapestry of scars. She looked much older than her actual years.

She was forced to attend the infidel's church on Sundays and listen to their devil preacher spouting religious justification to keep the slaves in bondage before she could steal a moment for herself. The once-pampered daughter of an infamous black Zanzibari slaver now worked harder than the slaves who used to serve her.

She waited tables, washed, ironed, took up and put down area rugs, swept floors, dusted furniture, weaved, quilted, and spun linens. She hauled large steaming pots for the preservation of fruits, lifted heavy barrels with cucumbers soaking in brine, hoed and weeded gardens, and collected chicken eggs.

At night when she wanted nothing more than to close her weary eyes and sleep, Hannah was forced to serve old man Etienne's twisted sexual needs and his son Claude's. One of Claude's rotten sons was even digging up her ass and whipping on her whenever he felt like it. He remembered her from frequent visits he'd made to Maison Plaisir.

She no longer belonged to herself. She would suffer the indignity of lying beneath Claude Etienne, whose body perpetually smelled of wet dog fur and the entire Etienne family if she had to. She would do that and far worse to stay alive. She promised herself that one day all of them would pay for what they'd done to her.

CHAPTER 13

LILLY LOOKED UP from the basket of wet laundry at the sound of the back door slamming. Hannah raced past her in the direction of some nearby bushes. She'd come from a session in Masta Clidamont's bedchambers and was now bent over at the waist throwing up in the bushes. Hannah's face was as white as the sheets Lilly was hanging on the line when she was done.

I can't stand that bitch. I hope she chokes to death on her vomit, Lilly thought uncharitably.

Lilly's sentiments were shared by all of the slaves on Magnolia Hill. Hannah made it a point to demonstrate her superiority whenever the opportunity arose. For that reason, among others, she was unilaterally disliked by house and field slaves alike. She'd given Lilly her ass to kiss on more than one occasion. It was now Lilly's time to return the favour by laughing in Hannah's face when she stumbled past on her way back to the house.

Hannah knew she would have to return to Clidamont's little torture chamber. She dreaded doing so. He was a sick old fuck, and he stank of disease. She'd sooner slit his throat than look at him. Not only did she have to go back into that monster's den, but now she would have to deal with whatever punishment Clidamont decided to mete out for her hasty, unauthorised departure.

"That's right, bitch," Lilly said spitefully. "Go back inside and get some more of what you just got! Hmph, if you weren't so damned mean, I might feel sorry for you." Lilly smirked at Hannah's back and returned to her laundry.

Hannah stood in front of Clidamont's door, knowing full well what was waiting for her on the other side. Her hands were damp with sweat and shaking. When she licked her dry cracked lips, the bitter taste of vomit still lingered on her tongue. She grasped the doorknob and took a deep breath before she turned it.

A huge mahogany bed with an ornate headboard that nearly took up an entire wall was the focal point in the suite. Hannah refused to allow her eyes to light upon that bed. Clidamont sat in a nearby chair with one spindly white leg crossed over his knobby knee, a lit cigar in his hand. He was naked except for a white cotton shirt. It was unbuttoned, exposing the grey hair on his sagging neck and chest and the wrinkles on his flabby belly. Hannah's nose twitched like a rabbit at the smell of cigar smoke, old man, sex, and shit in the room. There was also another smell in the room that Hannah wasn't ready to acknowledge.

Clidamont began to disrobe, starting with his shirt. Hannah's frightened eyes followed the shirt as it fell to the floor. His voice—a voice she'd come to hear in her nightmares—snapped her attention back to him.

"Strip and get on the bed, bitch," he said in an uncompromising tone. His eyes were like flint.

Hannah could no longer ignore the bed or what was on it. She'd relived this scenario on more than one occasion. Men like Clidamont couldn't get hard unless he had something dead to fondle. She swallowed the acid climbing up her throat. After she disrobed, she took tiny steps toward the bed. If Hannah had any faith left at all, this would be an excellent time to pray. She didn't have any though.

Clidamont watched with menace in his grey eyes as Hannah pulled back the bloody covers to crawl in beside the little slave boy lying in the middle of Clidamont's massive wooden bed. The boy was no more than six or seven. He looked like he was asleep. Hannah knew he was dead. She'd watched Clidamont beat and torture him, then shove the barrel of his rifle up that little boy's ass to the hilt.

Claude Etienne's Wedding Day
Magnolia Hill Plantation

It seemed the Etienne men had inherited somewhat of a bad reputation when it came to wives. Even though they were land and slave rich, one too many wives buried under the fertile grounds of Magnolia Hill served to cast a pall on their matrimonial suitability among the New Orleans aristocracy.

Clidamont and Claude had to cast a wide net to snare a new chatelaine for their manse. They hit the jackpot in Georgia in the form of Janine Nelson. She wouldn't be coming to Claude fresh though. Rumour had it she'd pushed a baby out a couple of years ago and wouldn't disclose the name of the father. Some said it was one of the stable boys on her grandfather's plantation who did the deed and that the baby was left on Slave Row right after they strung his daddy up.

Be that as it may, Claude could do a lot worse than Janine Nelson, yessiree. The chit's grandfather, Jace Nelson, had one foot in the grave and more money than he could spend in five lifetimes. His son and daughter-in-law died in a carriage accident, leaving his granddaughter, Janine, as his sole heir. Claude wasted no time before he proposed marriage.

The elaborate wedding was the culmination of months of intense negotiations between Clidamont Etienne and Jace Nelson. What with the rumours about the baby flying fast and furious, Jace knew no one in Georgia would take his granddaughter off his hands. He extracted a promise from Clidamont that Janine would be treated well before he packed her up and shipped her off to Claude with a sinfully huge dowry—payment enough to overlook her tarnished reputation, pinched expression, and scarecrow-thin body. What Janine lacked in looks and family name, she more than adequately made up in money.

Now, if his son Claude could keep his dick out of that slave gal, Hannah, long enough to put a baby in his new bride, both Clidamont and Jace could rest easy knowing their combined dynasties would be adequately protected.

Clidamont was forced to make nice with all of the sycophants, of both the neighbourly and business associate variety, in attendance at his son Claude's nuptials. It took a lot out of a man when he had to pull collective noses out of his elderly ass on a regular basis and still keep a smile on his face. He believed he'd comported himself admirably under the circumstances—the circumstances being that he was deep in his cups and desirous of female companionship.

It wasn't often he could rise to the occasion. Wedding or not, he didn't intend to let this opportunity pass him by. A rousing romp with one of Monique Dubonnet's nubile Nubians was just the thing he needed to take the edge off. Accompanied by his two grandsons Henri and Julien, Clidamont slipped away while his son Claude's wedding reception was in full swing to pay a visit to Maison Plaisir.

CHAPTER 14

Maison Plaisir, New Orleans

DOLLY WAS CURLED up in a ball in the corner of one of Monique Dubonnet's elaborately appointed boudoirs trying to protect her pretty face from the same bloody welts crisscrossing her chest, shoulder, and back—unsightly welts inflicted by the seventy-something-year-old grey-eyed devil. Clidamont beat the little black fille de joie so hard his hand hurt.

Bam! Bam! Bam!

"What's going on in there? Monsieur Etienne, please open the door. I demand that you open the door at once!"

Bam! Bam! Bam!

Clidamont stood over the girl with a riding crop clinched tightly in his fist. He was breathing like a Brahma bull in heat with naught but his crisp white wedding shirt covering his wrinkled old body. He was holding the crop so tightly his fingers were numb and tingly. He ignored the loud pounding.

I will open the bloody door when I am done, he thought indignantly.

He placed the crop on the nightstand so that he could flex his wrist, shake out his whipping hand, and fondle his penis—in that order. He was proud of the tent his manhood made under his long dress shirt. It had been a while since he felt this good.

I am not done with you, gal—not by a long shot.

Clidamont was nasty with a penchant for sadism. The girl's pain and torment inflamed his libido like a gust of wind on a brush fire. Her cries for mercy nearly overshadowed the banging on the door and the demands for entry. It was the fear in her eyes that pushed him over the edge, the fear that she would suffer far more than a beating. That fear fed something dark and sinister in Clidamont's soul.

He closed his steel grey eyes to savour the feeling. The whore's fear was the same as he had seen in the eyes of Frieda so long ago—that elusive look he'd chased unsuccessfully for more than thirty years.

Maybe I'll kill this one too.

Residence of Dr. Bernaud Dubonnet
Rampart Street, New Orleans

Clidamont's elder grandson, Henri, looked both left and right before using his personal key to enter the infrequently used side door in the cozy cottage on Rampart Street where Dr. Bernaud René Dubonnet maintained his office and living quarters. The hour was late and the streets were virtually empty of conveyance or pedestrian traffic, yet he took careful note of his surroundings. One couldn't be too cautious.

Once inside, Henri took the steps quickly, two at a time. He strode confidently down the narrow, carpeted corridor to Bernaud's private office. A strip of lantern light shone beneath the closed door. Henri rapped twice, but did not wait for a response before entering.

Bernaud sat behind a large oak desk covered with neatly stacked piles of paper, busy at work. His black-framed spectacles sat on the tip of his long aquiline nose. His shirt sleeves were rolled up, and his face held a look of intense concentration. He removed his glasses and stood when Henri walked in, offering a welcoming smile.

"Well, well. What a pleasant surprise. I did not expect to see you on the night of your father's wedding, Henri." He moved to the front of the desk to wrap Henri in a warm embrace.

"Nor did I expect to see you, Bernaud," Henri said, responding with a smile. "My grandfather was going positively mad from an excessive amount of absinthe and the crush of too many people filling every nook and corner of the house. He suggested my brother and I slip away with him for an evening of pleasure in your dear sister's popular establishment. While he and Julien are partaking of the varied delights as we speak, I thought I would seize the moment to spend some sorely needed time with you, and so here I stand."

Bernaud's genuine smile fairly lit up the office. "Your appearance could not have been any more timely, kind sir. I am in sore need of a break."

To demonstrate his fatigue, Bernaud pinched the bridge of his nose and rubbed his strained eyes.

Henri would never grow tired of looking at Bernaud, fatigued or not. If ever a man could be described as beautiful in a classic sense, Bernaud would be the one. He was tall and well-built, with dark, penetrating eyes and thick, wavy hair. His skin, like his sister Monique's, was so fair, his black blood was near undetectable. Not only was he blessed with exceptional good looks, but he was also one of the most highly respected members of the *gens de couleur* in the city. He was a renowned physician, having studied in France under the patronage of his white sire.

Had he the talent to do so, Henri would have gladly composed an ode to Bernaud's masculine appeal. Since he was sorely lacking in talent in that mode of expression, all he could do was drink in the magnetic aura of the handsome man standing before him.

"Don't get me wrong, Henri. I am extremely glad that you are here, but aren't you a little bit concerned your grandfather and brother will realise you are not in one of the busy rooms at Maison Plaisir?"

Henri's deep, masculine laugh caused Bernaud's smile to widen. "Ah, it is refreshing to have someone worry after me for a change. Have no fear, dear Bernaud. My reckless sibling and dissolute grandfather are legendary rabble-rousing whoremongers of the first order. I've never known either of them to exit the environs of any house of pleasure before the liquor runs out and the sun comes up. When my profligate grandfather and brother drag their drunken, weary feet down the steps at Maison Plaisir, I will be comfortably seated in the parlour with a nice, hot cup of coffee in hand." He dismissed Bernaud's concerns out of hand with a mischievous sparkle in his eyes.

"Enough about them. I didn't come here to discuss my grandpapa or my brother."

Henri stood so close to Bernaud that they shared one breath.

"Come here, baby. I want to kiss your sweet lips."

CHAPTER 15

Maison Plaisir, New Orleans

MARIA NERVOUSLY CHECKED her image in the full-length mirror. Claude Etienne had taken wife number three. His masochistic father, Clidamont, and his mean-spirited son, Julien, were here to celebrate. She and Dolly drew the short straws and would be forced to service them tonight. Maria could only thank God that she didn't get the old man.

As usual, Julien wore meticulously tailored clothing that fit his body like a second skin. No matter the circumstance, Julien Etienne was always well outfitted. Maria saw no reason why the day of his father's wedding would be an exception.

Julien had a fluidity of movement and grace seldom found in large men. Much of that came from the arrogance that derives from wealth and privilege along with confidence in his appearance. It was with that same fluidity and disregard for convention that Julien casually disrobed before Maria.

Julien Etienne was a big, brawny man with a flat nose that looked like it had been broken more than once, a broad chest, and strong, muscular arms one would expect on a pugilist and not the pampered son of a prosperous planter. He had enormous calves that tapered into ankles as svelte as a young girl's. Evidence of his dissolute lifestyle was apparent in the extra folds of flesh at his midriff and under his chin. Maria surmised that in a few short years, the thin layer of fat covering his brawny muscles would take over, burying the remaining muscles beneath it.

Julien's penetrating gunmetal grey eyes and golden blond hair gave him the appearance of a reckless Viking. His older brother, Henri, was as dark as Julien was light. Some said Julien had inherited his frightening grey eyes from his father's side of the family and his fair Nordic features from his mother.

Maria realised she needed to tread lightly. She'd been with a lot of men during her short life, and if she hadn't learned anything else, she knew to be careful when confronted with a big man who was cursed with a small dick.

Don't look down again, she said to herself. *Don't. Look. Down.*

It took a colossal effort for Maria not to allow her eyes to stray back to the part of Julien Etienne's anatomy that was screaming for her attention, nor could she look too long into those eyes that silently dared her to say or do the wrong thing. So, she plastered a fake smile on her pretty face and focused her gaze on the thick mat of hair on his massive chest. There was a dime-sized mole near his right nipple covered with bristling platinum-blond hair.

Julien stood before Maria naked as the day he was born with fists on his broad hips, his prepubescent-sized penis arrogantly on display. He was still as a praying mantis, waiting for that familiar expression of surprise and pity that crosses most women's faces when they spy him unclothed.

There it goes, he thought.

But he had to give the whore credit. She was good. As quickly as the expression washed over her face, she replaced it with the same ingratiating look he received from the slaves on Magnolia Hill. He didn't know what angered him more, pretense or derision. Few lived to tell about the latter.

And if the whore knows what's good for her, she'd better keep that ingratiating look on her face. It might just save her hide.

Julien was paying Monique Dubonnet enough money for her whore to pretend he was hung like a horse, no matter that his manhood looked more like a thimble.

The whore was pretty enough, with large, dark eyes and creamy mocha skin lightly kissed by the sun. A riot of shoulder-length, coal-black, curly hair framed her exotic face. She wore a white peignoir with lace as delicate as a spider's web. Julien liked her lips. They were full, moist, and red as ripe berries.

He could clearly see the pebbles of her nipples and the dark "V" of hair at the juncture of her thighs. She was petite, maybe five feet two, but she appeared even smaller up against Julien's large frame. She dropped to her knees before him. Julien liked his women in that position.

He closed his eyes, leaned his head back, and focused on the heady sensations that erupted everywhere Maria's skilled hands and mouth touched. He ran his thick fingers through her hair, holding on to her soft, shiny mane like it was a lifeline. She took him in her mouth in a languorous, exaggerated fashion, as if there was so much of him that her small mouth could not contain it all.

There was so much worry stomping around in Julien's head that he had to numb it with alcohol and brash behaviour; otherwise, he would go mad. He got lost in the moment, temporarily relinquishing every worry and every care—even the hatred he felt for his elder brother that festered like an infected sore. It killed him that Henri would someday be the master of Magnolia Hill instead of him.

He also let go of the fear that crept up his spine like fire ants on a hill whenever he thought about his pending nuptials and, more particularly, his wedding night. He was engaged to one of the most beautiful girls in the parish. What would his new bride say or think when she saw what the powerful younger Etienne son had to offer her?

He could relax at Maison Plaisir. For a short time, he could close his eyes and pretend the woman servicing him was the woman he would eventually marry. He need not fear what any one of Monique's pretty whores might think about the size of his manhood. They were but one step up from slaves themselves and less than the dirt beneath his feet.

Damn, her mouth is like a suction cup. It feels so good.

Her skilled ministrations temporarily silenced the voices in his head. He heard a wet "plop" sound when she pulled her mouth away from him. He pulled her to her feet so that he could penetrate her mouth deeply with his tongue, like he could only dream of filling her body. She had the taste of him in her mouth, and he liked it.

As their kiss deepened, there was a knock at the door. Julien pulled himself together before grabbing a robe hanging on the back of the dressing screen.

"Go see who it is," he commanded in a sex-drunken voice.

It was Nathan, one of Monique Dubonnet's servants, with a worried expression on his face.

"Excuse this untimely interruption, Monsieur Etienne, but we require your assistance in a matter relating to your grandfather."

CHAPTER 16

THE DISGRUNTLED RIDERS traversed a dark, well-travelled country road on their way back to Magnolia Hill. Bold as brass, Monique Dubonnet had demanded Julien and Clidamont leave Maison Plaisir and never return. Of course, she was backed up by two huge black bodyguards when she did it.

Clidamont had never felt so insulted and humiliated in his life. He had not paused in his vitriolic ranting since he and Julien mounted up over an hour ago. It seemed the closer the two night riders drew to the plantation, the angrier the old reprobate became.

Now that the effect of the alcohol was starting to wear off, Clidamont was forced to admit that he didn't feel too good. His face and neck were redder than a redneck picking cotton under the blistering hot Louisiana sun. He was nauseous. His head was pounding, and he was starting to feel decidedly dizzy. With every step his blasted horse took, his haemorrhoids itched and burned so badly it felt like a red-hot poker was being shoved up his arse. All he wanted was to get back to Magnolia Hill as soon as possible so that he could bite the hair of the dog that bit him, lie down, and shake off his burgeoning malaise.

Not only did he feel unwell, he was seething with rage and sorely in need of a victim upon which he could release his considerable ire. Since there was no one available at the time other than his grandson Julien whose anger matched, if not exceeded, his own, Clidamont's unfortunate mount was forced to bear the brunt of his anger.

The horse screamed in pain, fighting against the cruelly held bit and rearing on its hind legs, nearly unseating Clidamont as he viciously and repeatedly swung the same riding crop he'd used on Monique Dubonnet's girl, drawing bloody welts on the flesh of the hapless horse. Clidamont's breathing was harsh and ragged when he finally got the animal under control.

A low-grade ringing lingered inside his ear, and his vision was starting to blur in one eye. Although the night was unseasonably cool, sweat pooled under his wide-brimmed planter's hat, dripping in hot rivulets down his neck. The handsomely tailored suit he'd looked so dapper in a few short hours ago while at his son's wedding was now rumpled, stained, and extremely uncomfortable.

I'm going to have to leave that Absinthe alone one of these days, Clidamont muttered, before he shook off his malaise and continued to rant at his audience of one.

"Who in the hell does that half-breed wench think she is anyway, getting her lackeys to toss *me* out? I told her I'd pay extra for whatever damage I did to that worthless slut. Hell, I even offered to buy the bitch! It's a sad day in the south when a man can't take his pleasure without some underlings pounding on his *boudoir* door like there was some kind of damn fire in the house," he sputtered.

"Mark my words, Julien. That bitch is going to pay," he vowed, narrowing his cold grey eyes. "She's going to pay in spades because I'm going to see to it. Why, I might even burn that damn place of hers down to the fucking ground, and with her in it!"

Julien was well-accustomed to his grandfather's fits of rage. There were countless bodies of slaves and a few unfortunate whites buried in unmarked graves at Magnolia Hill as a result of that rage. Instead of trying to calm the old man down, Julien chose to stoke the fires even higher.

"*Grand-père*, make sure you don't toast the bitch before I get a crack at her. She's way too high and mighty for her own good, if you ask me. I suspect I'm just the man to bring her down a notch or two. Her and that doctor brother of hers have forgotten who and what they are. It's high time somebody reminded them. When I'm done with her, she'll be broken up in so many pieces her doctor brother won't be able to put her back together again."

"Do a humpty dumpty on her, heh, grandson?"

Clidamont laughed so hard at his own joke that he started to choke. When his laughter finally subsided, his demeanour became serious again.

"I want to know where in the hell your brother was while I was being disrespected."

The two brothers had never been particularly close. Even so, Julien had to admit that Henri had been inordinately secretive of late.

"I told one of those damn servants to rouse him and tell him we were leaving only to find out he'd never checked in. Something suspicious is going on with that boy, Julien, and I plan to get to the bottom of it. I don't like to be deceived, and I like being lied to even less."

Clidamont let go of the reins to shake his right hand out. *There goes that tingling.*

Try as he might to get the circulation flowing again, the damn hand had gone completely numb. Something was seriously wrong because that same numbness was creeping up his leg like ivy on an old building.

The road had narrowed and Julien was riding his horse at a brisk cantor slightly in front of his grandfather. Clidamont was quite alarmed. He couldn't feel his right leg. When he tried to tell his grandson something was terribly wrong, he found he had no voice to do so. He lost control of his bladder at the same time he toppled out of the saddle and onto the ground.

Julien's frightened voice yelling "Grand-pèré!" was the last thing Clidamont heard before he lost consciousness.

Magnolia Hill Plantation

It had been more years than Hannah cared to count since she was catapulted into a life of slavery. Her father was not coming to rescue her. *Who knows, my father may even be dead.* She had also come to accept the reality that the chances of someone else acting as her saviour were slim to none. Yet, even though Hannah was forced to admit these harsh facts, her spirit was far from tamed.

She learned to use her wiles in the nightmare land of servitude in which she now existed—an existence where slaves were all but invisible until those they served had a need for them. She would keep her eyes and ears open, remain watchful and bide her time—for what, she did not yet know. She would know what "it" was when the time came.

It was that same cloak of invisibility that shielded Hannah from detection when Julien Etienne shouldered several guests out of the way to carry the frail figure of his unconscious grandfather through the main entrance of Magnolia Hill. There was a large wet stain in the front and back of Clidamont's trousers. Apparently, the dignified master of Magnolia Hill had peed and shit on himself. For some odd reason, that tickled Hannah.

In an instant, the wedding celebration turned from festive to solemn, forcing the drunken celebrants into sobriety quicker than a bucket of ice-cold water in the face. The invited guests were going crazy, their joy destroyed. Hannah was so glad she could piss herself.

The same people who had run her ragged all weekend with their senseless demands—"gal, go fetch my reticule," "brush and comb my hair," "help me to lace up this dress," and the like—were scurrying around like mice in a maze. Not one of the drunken fools had the mental wherewithal to be of any real assistance. Their discomfiture made Hannah's heart sing. *Maybe my luck will hold out and the evil old coot will die*, she thought spitefully.

Clidamont looked like he was already dead. One whole side of his face was drooping like melted butter; his mouth, twisted in a grotesque pantomime of a smile. It hung open showing what remained of his rotten teeth. A string of spittle dripped from the side of his mouth and onto his dandified grandson's custom waist coat. Julien was vain when it came to his raiment. Hannah had to bite the inside of her mouth to keep from laughing aloud.

Guess he won't be wearing that suit again, Hannah thought merrily. She stood back in the shadows with a few of the other servants, sucking everything in like a sponge and taking note of everyone's reaction.

"What the hell happened?" Claude demanded, shouldering his way through the crowded vestibule with his tie undone and his shirttail hanging outside his trousers.

It was apparent to all that he had been *getting to know* his new bride when word of his father's condition reached him. Claude couldn't hide his fear when he saw his once indomitable father in such a sorry state. His deep, booming voice cut through the banal expressions of worry on nearly everyone's lips. Clidamont Etienne was an irreverent, evil old man to whites and slaves alike. Any expression of concern could not possibly be genuine.

"I don't know what happened, Father," Julien exclaimed, breathless from his race to get his grandfather to safety. "One minute he was ranting and raving like his usual self, and the next thing I knew he'd fallen off his horse. I tried to rouse him, but couldn't."

Claude quickly took charge. Fortunately, Dr. Langston was amongst the wedding guests. For the first time, Claude noticed Hannah standing nearby.

"Hannah, find Dr. Langston. Tell him to meet me in my father's suite at once. Now, hurry!"

Hannah strolled out of the house like she was out for a leisurely evening walk in the park instead of on a mission to find a doctor to save an elderly man's life. Her sharp hawk eyes missed nothing. She'd seen Dr. Langston sneak off nearly an hour ago, and she had seen with whom he'd snuck out.

Even though Hannah knew exactly where he was, she took her good sweet time locating the doctor, who was up to no good in the arbour behind the Big House with the governor's youngest daughter, who incidentally was less than half his age. The old reprobate was heavily in his cups and the young miss in a compromising state of dishabille when Hannah interrupted their little *tête-à-tête*. When she told the doctor the reason she'd sought him out, he quickly pulled himself together and hastened to the Big House as quickly as his drunken legs could carry him.

Hannah led the red-faced doctor up to Clidamont's room. She was about to leave when she heard Claude ask Julien where his brother Henri was. Before Julien could formulate an answer, Hannah spoke up.

"Masta Claude. I believe I know where you can find Masta Henri."

CHAPTER 17

Residence of Dr. Bernaud Dubonnet
Rampart Street, New Orleans

BERNAUD AND HENRI lay naked, their lean, muscular limbs tangled amongst the passion-scented sheets.

If only I could lie like this forever, Henri thought.

Peace. That's what Henri felt when he was with Bernaud. When he was with Bernaud, he could quiet his troubled mind, be still, and enjoy blessed peace.

No matter the trials or tribulations he faced day to day, and there were many because it wasn't easy being the grandson of Clidamont Etienne or the son of Claude Etienne. God knew it had *always* been difficult and singularly unpleasant being the elder brother of Julien Etienne. At times Henri felt Julien begrudged the very air he breathed, especially in light of the fact Henri was the firstborn and not Julien.

Much was expected of Henri as the Etienne heir-apparent, and no matter how hard he tried, he always fell short of his father's and his *Grand-père's* expectations. One day he would be expected to take over the reins of Magnolia Hill even though that was his brother Julien's dream, not his. If he could but reverse their birthdates, Henri would have gladly done so.

While Julien and that bunch of rabble-rousing, trouble-making sons of neighbouring plantation owners he ran around with were out wenching and drinking, Henri generally had his nose in a book and his head in the clouds. He'd spend hour after hour capturing the beauty of the countryside on canvas or pondering man's purpose and why anyone would consider a man like Bernaud to be inferior because he had a miniscule amount of African blood flowing through his veins. More often than not he would dream of being in another place and having another life anywhere else but Magnolia Hill.

It seemed the hours since he'd first crossed Bernaud's threshold had sped by. Although he was now wide awake, Henri kept his eyes tightly shut. To open his eyes would only serve to break the wonderful spell he was under. With his eyes shut, he became keenly aware of his surroundings. Except for the sound of Bernaud's soft, rhythmic breathing, all was blessedly silent.

Even with his eyes closed, Henri could not stop his worries from forcing their way into his brain and pushing away his peace. A frown marred his handsome face. Soon he would be expected to take a wife and to have children. He knew he would never want any woman the way he wanted the man lying in his arms. He didn't want to think about that right now—not while he was so desperately trying to hold on to the sweet intimacy he and Bernaud shared. His brother, Julien, was engaged to wed in a year's time. Hopefully, all the family's attention would be focused upon his younger brother for a while.

Bernaud barely stirred when Henri pulled him more closely into his embrace, kissing the side of his slightly opened mouth. Henri didn't know when next he would have an opportunity to see him. He only wanted to hold Bernaud in his arms a little bit longer. Soon he would have to get dressed and return to Bernaud's sister's establishment where he would continue the farce he'd been forced to play for most of his life. No one must know his secret.

When Julien set out to retrieve his brother, he didn't travel alone. He never travelled alone when he intended to do harm. Julien was a coward by nature and there was safety in numbers. Not only was the angel of death riding shotgun with Julien and his companions, but the angel of death brought along one of his helpers. The night would be a busy one.

Julien had a posse of four of his closest friends. Each was a rapscallion son of a prosperous River Road plantation owner. All of them were looking for trouble and knew where to find it. They rode into the city, hell-bent for leather with the wind in their faces and their coattails flying behind them. There was work to be done and Julien would see it through before the day was over.

If what that Hannah gal told them was true, his brother Henri had a longstanding friendship with Monique Dubonnet's brother, Bernaud. The wench said she'd seen them talking together on more than one occasion when she worked at Maison Plaisir. Once she'd even seen Henri enter Bernaud's house on Rampart Street. Julien intended to put an end to that friendship and teach Monique Dubonnet a long overdue lesson at the same time.

What better way to destroy my older brother's friendship with Bernaud Dubonnet than to force him to watch while we burn that uppity gal's establishment to the ground? Julien thought.

His laugh was maniacal as he whipped the spirited black destrier he rode into a frenzy, forcing it to run faster. He couldn't wait to get back to town.

They made it to the city in record time, barely taking a moment to hitch their exhausted horses in front of Bernaud Dubonnet's residence before they forced their way past the startled butler and into the quiet, tastefully appointed house.

Henri's eyelids began to flutter at the sound of the grandfather clock in Bernaud's parlour chiming the even hour, yet he fought the temptation to open them. Something was disrupting the quiet serenity in Bernaud's house. The rude smell of stale alcohol, manly musk, and evil assaulted his senses.

Henri opened his eyes mere seconds before the door to Bernaud's bedroom flew open, crashing against the wall with such force that the knob left a hole in the wall. Several small paintings he'd recently given Bernaud crashed to the floor.

Bernaud came awake with a start. Both men were frozen in a nightmare tableau, too stunned to react, as Julien and his cohorts piled into the bedroom like non-paying guests at an upscale hotel.

"Well, I'll be damned," was all Julien could say when he took in the scene before him.

His brother, all six feet, two inches of him, was naked as the day he was born and lying abed with the equally naked octoroon doctor.

"Well, I'll be motherfucking damn," Julien repeated.

Julien didn't know what he had expected to find when he forced his way into Bernaud Dubonnet's residence, but he sure as hell didn't expect anything like this. The mussed hair and kiss-swollen lips of both men put the lie to the possibility that what he was looking at was anything other than what it was.

Now I know why I've always hated Henri. The moment put a sense of rationality to the years of abuse he'd been compelled to heap upon his older sibling.

Bernaud was the first one to react. Aware that he was at a distinct disadvantage in his present state of undress, Bernaud made to get out of the bed to put some clothes on. Henri grabbed hold of his wrist. Bernaud's handsome face instantly grew mottled with rage. His privacy had been invaded by four strange white men, and Henri expected him to suffer their abuse unclothed.

Surely, he asks too much, Bernaud thought. His anger was clouding his judgement.

Technically, only two of the four were strangers since he recognised Henri's brother Julien. He also recognised George Raveneau's mentally defective son, Jacques, who was blind in one eye from the pox his diseased father passed on to him at birth. He was a mean-spirited character if ever there was one. Jacques looked at Bernaud with condemnation while his filmy blind eye remained as useless as a chipped stone in a bowl of porridge. The other two men were known to Bernaud by reputation. Both had been unwelcome visitors at his sister's establishment and subsequently banned.

Nestor French's boy, Tremont, was a small man with ferret features like his sire. He was ugly, with a huge misshapen nose, a face covered with pimples, and a nervous girlish giggle. Tremont shuffled from foot to foot, like a racehorse chomping at the bit. His excited giggle reminded Bernaud of a patient in the madhouse he visited once a month. Tremont, or "Tre" as they called him, was a follower and frequently the butt of cruel jokes instigated by Julien. His family didn't have nearly as much money or land as the Etiennes or the Raveneaus. They kept him around like a pet wildebeest, to be unleashed on hapless victims when they were seeking entertainment, usually at his expense or the expense of others. He would do just about anything, no matter how craven, to fulfil his desire to belong.

The last member of the quartet was Parker Villareale's son, Pierre. The Villareales were considered to be New Orleans royalty, and their son Pierre was one of the most eligible bachelors in Louisiana. His was an old family, dating back to the original settlers. He was handsome. He was rich. He was cruel. He also had the reputation of having lynched more than a few Blacks, slave and free alike.

Bernaud sat up in his bed, somehow managing to maintain his dignity even with the bed sheet clutched to his chest to hide his nudity.

CHAPTER 18

"**W**HAT IS THE meaning of this? What gives you the right to barge into my home uninvited?" he asked angrily.

The look of indignation on Bernaud's face sent Julien over the edge.

"You don't presume to question me. I'll do the questioning, mongrel. By the way, which one of you is the cunt?" Julien demanded.

The situation was quickly going from bad to worst. Bernaud didn't know whether it was paranoia or fact, but it appeared to him that French, Villareale, and Raveneau were silently closing in on him and Henri in an aggressive manner.

Julien walked over to a nearby chair where Henri had strewn his clothing the night before. Never taking his eyes off of Bernaud's face, he threw Henri's pants in his brother's face.

"Here. Make yourself decent," he commanded as Henri stumbled out of the bed, his hands shaking like an old man with palsy as he clumsily pulled his trousers on.

Hate flared in Julien's eyes at the sight of his brother. He couldn't help but notice that, even flaccid, his brother's member was of prodigious dimensions and his body a work of art.

Henri barely had his trousers on when Julien spat in his face. Julien's face was contorted with every ounce of hate he'd felt for his elder brother his entire life.

"*Maricon!*" he shouted viperously.

Henri flinched at the vile insult. "I swear on my mother's grave that this isn't what it looks like, Julien," Henri pleaded, glancing toward Julien's companions. "Give Bernaud a chance to put his clothes on so that the three of us can talk. This is a family matter. There is no need to involve outsiders. If you would just ask your friends to wait in the parlour, we can talk this out."

Other than a look of profound disgust on Julien's face, he appeared to be as unmoved by his brother's request as a statue in the middle of the French quarter. Henri misread his brother's silence as acquiescence and was momentarily encouraged when Julien drew near.

Maybe, just maybe, he thought, *we can work this out without Father or Grand-père getting wind of it.*

Henri squealed like a ten-year-old girl when his brother, who outweighed him by some thirty-odd pounds, backhanded him, knocking him to his knees, quickly dispelling any hope with the ferocity of his attack.

"Shut your mouth and don't open it again until I give you leave to do so, you filthy sodomite!" Julien ordered. He spat in Henri's face again, then turned the brunt of his monstrous anger upon Bernaud.

"What have you done to my brother? Was it black magic? Was it voodoo?"

Julien's words were all the more frightening due to the lack of emotion behind them, but his evil grey eyes told a tale more frightening than words could convey.

At that moment the cloud of anger blocking Bernaud's sense of reasoning lifted enough for him to realise the untenable situation he was in. He was naked (metaphorically and physically), weaponless, and surrounded by four hate-filled white men in a city where there was no justice for someone like him.

Bernaud had encountered this brand of hate before. He'd felt this same kind of hate while dressing the wounds of slaves beaten within an inch of their lives and while stemming the flow of blood of women raped with a savagery far more suited to beasts than men. Bernaud was reminded of this kind of irrational hatred in the wails of despair he encountered each time he was called upon to cut down bodies swinging from trees, when innocent men were lynched for irrational offences, such as not moving out of the path of a white man quick enough or for allegedly gazing too long upon the face of a white woman. The look of hatred in Julien and his companion's eyes nearly blinded Bernaud.

Bernaud tore his eyes away from Julien to look upon Henri's frightened face. Henri's eyes were the same steel grey colour as Julien's, yet the two men could not have been less alike. The irony was not lost on Bernaud that poor, sweet Henri, whose soft grey eyes would well up with tears while reading poetry or the passages in a well-written book, could be born into the infamous Etienne family. What a cruel twist of fate that he should fall in love with this particular white man.

He could smell the fear coming off Henri in waves, taste it on his tongue. He knew he need not look for any help in that direction. In one glance, they shared a silent message. Both knew how this situation would end. Julien Etienne was out for blood, and he would have it. Bernaud knew today was the day he would die, yet he still tried to reason with Julien.

"Monsieur Etienne. Would you please allow me to at least clothe myself?"

Julien's response was short. He hammered his fist into the side of Bernaud's face, causing his head to slam into the thick mahogany headboard. The pain was so intense, Bernaud could barely think straight. From the moment of birth every man starts his journey toward death. Julien's blow propelled Bernaud on the last leg of his personal journey. The first blow had been struck. There was no turning back now.

Julien experienced what felt like a spike of adrenalin coursing through his body. In fact, what he was really feeling was the indescribable rush humans feel when a host of demons invade the portal of their soul. His body and his soul were wide open for the taking. Julien shook his head like a shaggy dog that had come in from the rain as each demon slipped inside his body. When Julien spoke, his voice was not his own. It was deeper, gravelly, and each word echoed as though uttered in a canyon.

"I asked you a question, boy, and I demand an answer."

"If my recollection serves me right, Julien," Pierre interjected with a sinister smile on his attractive face, "I believe you asked him two questions, the second being which one of them was the cunt in their seamy relationship.

I, for one, am more interested in an answer to *that* particular question," he stated in a droll voice.

They all laughed, but none louder than Tre French. The funny-looking little man was near doubled over with laughter, his behaviour far exceeding the level of levity Pierre's cruel comment deserved. Julien would not be detracted.

"Now, I'm going to ask you one more time. What kind of African hoodoo spell have you cast on my brother?"

Henri had never been as frightened of his brother as he was at that moment. He'd lost all sense of reason and dignity. Afraid to stand, he crawled toward his brother, answering Julien's question in Bernaud's stead.

"Nothing, Julien. He's done nothing to me. Please don't hurt him, Julien. I beg of you. Please don't hurt him!"

By now Henri was on all fours, his head slightly bent with a thick glob of spittle and blood dangling from his busted lips. Tre French chose that moment to deliver a cruel kick to Henri's belly with his boot-shod foot. Tre spun around with his head thrown back, giggling at the pain he'd inflicted. Bernaud visibly cringed when he heard Henri's ribs crack. Henri's lips were moving, but no words would come out.

Wake me up. Wake me up, God. Wake me up. Wake me up, God. Wake me up. Wake me up, God. Wake me up. Wake me up, God. This can't be happening. Pleeeeese, God. Wake. Me. Up!

This was no dream. Henri watched as all four men converged upon his lover en masse, and there was nothing he could do to stop them. They dragged Bernaud from the bed, and they beat him, and beat him, and kept on beating him until their fists and clothing were covered with blood and there was nothing left of him that would identify him as a man.

Somewhere amidst the beating, Pierre Villareale paused to unbutton his trousers and drop to his knees in the midst of Bernaud's attackers. They cheered him on as his buttocks rose and fell upon Bernaud. They resumed the beating when Pierre was done.

Henri curled up in a ball and covered his ears to block out the thud of fists connecting with flesh, shattering organs, and breaking bones. Bernaud piteously begged for his life, screaming like a wounded horse after each brutal blow landed, yet still they continued to pummel him. They were without mercy. Their fists rose and fell until flecks of flesh, bone, and blood peppered the walls.

The screams abruptly stopped. The silence was ominous. Only the sound of heavy breathing generated from exertion clawed its way through the silence as Julien and his friends stood over what was left of Bernaud Dubonnet to admire their handiwork.

Suddenly, the screaming commenced again.

Was that me screaming? Henri wondered.

At this point Henri couldn't tell because one of the connections between his brain and reality had snapped. A swift kick to his head rendered Henri as quiet as his lover.

Henri had no idea how long he lay unconscious. It could have been seconds, minutes, or even hours. It could have been a lifetime, and still it would not have been long enough. His thoughts were a swirling maelstrom of darkness as a scene of horror he would carry with him until the end of his days unfolded before him. He caught a glimpse of Bernaud when Julien raised his leg to retrieve a knife he kept in the calf of his knee-high riding boots. Henri remembered saying to himself, *now what in the world does Julien plan to do with that knife?* He would soon have his answer.

Like a maestro's baton, the thick metal blade of Julien's knife briefly caught the light coming in through the bedroom window before its graceful descent. It came away bloody after Julien castrated Bernaud. Bernaud's body twitched for a few seconds and finally went still. All four men shouted in victory as if they had defeated a dangerous foe and not an innocent, unarmed man. Julien held his bloody trophy in his raised fist.

There was that infernal giggling again. French was giggling like a maniac and the others joined in while Henri vomited up every hope, every dream, and every inch of his sanity onto the ornate oriental rug. Henri passed out yet again after Julien shoved Bernaud's manhood inside the opening where his mouth had once been.

CHAPTER 19

New Orleans

MONIQUE'S CLOTHES WERE sopping wet. They reeked with the sour smell of fear. Her heart was pounding so hard she was forced to place her hand to the centre of her breast to still its erratic racing, else it might break through the wall of her chest, killing her instantly. Maybe that form of death would be merciful.

She was on the run, with no money and no place to hide from her pursuers. Far better to die alone in a garbage-strewn New Orleans alley than to be caught in the clutches of that devil Julien Etienne and the demons he rode with.

There was to be a big party that evening. Thankfully, many of her girls and a few of the servants were out running errands, thus escaping the carnage. Those who remained were busy doing menial tasks about the house or resting from the night before when the murderers arrived.

She squeezed her eyes shut and choked back a sob, trying to block out the last image she had of her brother. Bernaud was dead. They'd killed him. She saw his mutilated body swinging from the poplar tree in front of Maison Plaisir with her own eyes. *How he must have suffered.* God only knew how many others would die this day.

It was a massacre at high noon. Julien hung Bernaud's body in front of Maison Plaisir for all to see, then they torched Maison Plaisir from all sides. After that, it was a turkey shoot. They wagered amongst each other, taking bets as to which of them was the best shot. They sat like mediaeval kings upon their big stallions, laughing as they carefully took aim, shooting any and everyone who attempted to escape the fiery death intended for them.

Were it not for Nathan's quick thinking, Monique had no doubt her body would be swinging right next to her brother's. He'd tossed her the pot boy's britches, a cap, and a jacket at least two sizes too big. She pushed her waist-length hair up under the cap and donned the boy's clothing while thick clouds of billowing black smoke filled the lower rooms of the house, cutting off their air supply.

Her dear friend had sacrificed his life, taking a bullet in the back of his head while creating a diversion to allow her escape. She mourned his loss and shuddered to think what would have happened had those animals gotten their hands on her. Death would have been a welcome surcease, but she wasn't out of the woods yet.

She pressed her back against a refuge bin in the rear of an alley between a bakery and a cobbler's shop. There she hid in constant fear of discovery until nightfall. Her only company was her throat-throttling fear, and the overwhelming stench of rotting food, discarded leather, and rodents.

She could hear the clip-clop of horses and the wheels of carriages rolling upon the uneven street pavement. There were sounds of conversation and laughter from people going about their day as if nothing was amiss while her world catapulted upside-down and spiralled out of control.

She dared not leave her hiding place to seek aid. She doubted anyone would be suicidal enough to come to her aid anyway. She had been sheltered too well. For that reason, she'd forgotten who she was—a woman without kith, kin, or country. No free person of colour would risk their lives to help her. She represented everything her darker brothers and sisters despised. She was a Black woman who lived almost as well as the whites.

If I live through this, I vow to never forget my African blood again.

She knew she couldn't remain in the alley. To do so would mean she would run the risk of someone eventually discovering her and betraying her whereabouts to Julien Etienne. A chill went down her spine just thinking his name. She would wait until nightfall and make her way to the waterfront. There she hoped to board a ship—to disappear.

Barataria Bay, Louisiana

When the United States government barred American ships from docking at foreign ports, three half-brothers—Jean and Pierre Lafitte, and Dominique You—devised an ingenious solution to the problem faced by many New Orleans merchants who relied on foreign trade.

They set up a thriving port for the purchase of smuggled goods on Barataria Bay, a sparsely populated island located between the barrier islands of Grande Terre and Grande Isle. The location was perfect for their illegal enterprise since it was located far enough from the U.S. naval base for their ships to smuggle the pirated goods past the noses of the custom officials, yet close enough to New Orleans for the exchange of goods.

Rephidim and Jean Lafitte watched as Lafitte's workers carefully transferred a large shipment of goods onto the Celestial, a ship owned by King Zion, from one of two privateers docked at Barataria Bay. Yet another crew was loading goods from a platform onto seven pirogues for transport through the bayous to New Orleans where the Lafittes kept a warehouse. Rephidim had already inspected his purchases.

Straddling the great divide between the Creator's heavenly host and those fallen angels ruled by the Satan known as demons is the Dark Veil. The Dark Veil is a mystical wall of protection behind which preternatural half-human/half angelic beings known as Nephilim can exist in tandem, yet undetected by the angels who revile them, the demons who hunt them, and humans who fear them.

The Nephilim Nation is under the protection of seven powerful Nephilim generals, one for each of the world continents, and are collectively referred to as Brothers of the Dark Veil. Each member of the elite corps command an army consisting of thousands of soldiers and has the ability to raise or lower the Dark Veil at will. They answer directly to Zion of the House of Shemyaza, the oldest Nephilim in existence and their mighty matchless king. They are Nicodemus of the House of Urakabarameel; Ajuma of the House of Akibeel; Gilead of the House of Tamiel; Simeon of the House of Ramuel; Boaz of the House of Danel; Antioch of the House of Asael; and Rephidim of the House of Turel.

It was Rephidim who arranged the clandestine meeting in Monique Dubonnet's house of pleasure which culminated in a demonic attack so many years ago. Lafitte was in the presence of a member of the Nephilim King's Supreme Court and didn't even know it.

Rephidim was six and one-half feet tall and 225 pounds of hard muscle. He positively dwarfed the infamous smuggler who, by his many exploits, seemed larger than life. More than a few young female camp followers who made their homes on Barataria found an excuse to wander to the docking area to get a closer look at Jean Lafitte's handsome visitor. Rephidim was accustomed to the admiring stares of human females. His otherworldly good looks were a magnet to the opposite sex. He took their flirtatious smiles and sultry looks of longing in stride.

Jean Lafitte looked more the businessman than the vicious pirate his arch nemesis, Governor William Claiborne, claimed him to be. Make no mistake about it; the Lafittes were bloodthirsty killers, and absolutely no one was more deadly than Jean's right-hand man, Dominic You.

Unlike his brother Pierre, who could only be described as rough around the edges, and Dominic, who was a pirate in every sense of the word, Jean was not only gifted with good looks, but he was a natural-born leader with an enterprising spirit and refined tastes.

Jean spent the majority of his time managing the business of outfitting the privateers and smuggling stolen goods into the city. His half-brother Pierre looked after their many interests in the city while his other half-brother Dominique captained one of their three largest ships. The audacious human who started out as a slaver, fell in love with an octoroon, and eventually became known as the Terror of the Gulf of Mexico intrigued Rephidim.

The Lafittes were the go-to men for a lot of the precious jewels confiscated off Spanish ships and the velvets, silks, and lace finery that graced the bodies of the wealthy Nephilim males and females behind and outside the Dark Veil. Rephidim had also purchased several of the more modern European furnishings in the aristos' homes. Over the years they became fast friends.

Jean and Rephidim took in the hustle and bustle of the thriving port. It was the middle of the night, yet the island was alive with working sailors loading and unloading stolen goods from all over the world. The pirated finery was destined to grace many of the homes in New Orleans. Finally, the last crate was loaded onto King Zion's ship. Rephidim prepared to leave.

"Can you at least have one drink with me, my friend?" Pierre asked. "I have an exquisite brandy that I know you will enjoy. In fact, I had my men load a case onto your ship. It is my small way of saying thank you to you and your mysterious patron for your continued business. Your patronage alone has made me a very wealthy man." He laughed.

Jean assumed Rephidim was a free man of colour, acting as an agent to a wealthy white benefactor. Rephidim never bothered to dissuade him in that assumption. The Nephilim aristocracy was accustomed to a certain standard of living, and they had the resources to pay for it. The Lafittes were in a position to meet Nephilim's discerning demands. It was as simple as that. Over the years, the Nephilim communities in and around Louisiana had fattened the Lafitte's coffers significantly.

Rephidim had already tendered half the asking price to Pierre for the goods he would deliver to the king's residence in Baton Rouge. His plan was to return to the city to settle the balance with Pierre before sailing back to *Grato Quies*. It had been a long time since he'd seen the inside of his own home. He longed to do so.

"As much as I would love to enjoy a drink with you, Jean, there are other things I need to take care of before the night is out. One of them is settling up with your esteemed sibling. Regretfully, I will have to bid you adieu until we next meet."

"Reph, promise me you'll be careful tonight," Jean entreated. His face wore a grave expression when the two men clasped hands in farewell. "It's not safe for a Black man of means or otherwise to be about. Earlier today a vigilante group went ape on a prominent Black physician in the city. What they did to the man wasn't pretty. Watch yourself, my friend."

Rephidim nodded in acknowledgement. "I will guide myself accordingly," he said solemnly. "Until we meet again, I bid you *adieu*." Rephidim bowed formally and turned to board one of the waiting pirogues where a sailor waited to row him back to King Zion's ship.

CHAPTER 20

New Orleans

THE HOUR WAS late, but the city was alive and teaming with excitement. Brilliantly lit chandeliers and lanterns illuminated figures through the windows of stately mansions dancing the night away.

Scions of New Orleans society and their privileged male offspring arrogantly rode expensive horseflesh to exclusive clubs or establishments similar to Maison Plaisir. Horse-drawn carriages conveying elegantly dressed women and debonair gentlemen returning from a night at the theatre or a fancy fête or ball, clip-clopped on the cobblestone streets.

One such conveyance rode past Monique who now appeared more like a poor white urchin boy than the sophisticated madam of a once popular bordello. The wheels of the carriage splashed mud and water upon her while the occupants laughed inside.

Less than a block over, the rubble that had once been Maison Plaisir still smouldered, and the smell of charred human flesh left its distinctive perfume in the air. *My brother Bernaud is dead. The sun will rise on tomorrow. The whites will continue to live, love, and laugh as if neither he nor I ever existed.* Monique quickly dashed away the hot tears that rose in her eyes. She no longer had the luxury to cry.

Monique had once lived on the fringe of this elegant white society, but now she hunched her shoulders and lowered her head as she darted from one dark alley to the next in an effort to make herself invisible. With each step

Monique took, she was distancing herself from the only way of life she had ever known. She didn't know how she would live. All she knew was that she was not ready to die. She would need to put as much distance between herself and her beloved New Orleans as possible.

Soon the music and lights coming from the stately mansions was replaced with the desperately loud laughter and raucous music of working-class men and the low-class women who served them at local bars and ale houses. The elegant conveyances she'd seen earlier were now replaced with hard-ridden steeds and harder-faced riders who were either running from trouble or planning to stir some up. Monique jumped like a frightened cat at every sound and shivered in her oversized boots at every movement in the shadows. The closer she got to her ultimate destination, the Port, the stronger the smell of fish and the sea became, and the more isolated and seamy her surroundings. She felt like an innocent babe left out in the woods.

She stood at a distance watching the ships gently bob in the calm waters at the Port. The ships represented freedom at the tip of her fingers. Now that she was here, she didn't know what to do. She had no idea which one she would stow away upon nor how she would accomplish the task.

Most of the sailors were out carousing in the local bars or cat houses. Surely there would be a skeleton crew on each of the ships. She couldn't just stroll aboard like a paying passenger—or could she?

She fingered the bag of gold she had stashed deep inside her trouser pocket. If she couldn't prevail upon the mercy and decency of one of the crew members, she could appeal to good old-fashioned greed.

She wasn't going to accomplish anything by staring at the ships. She had to act now. She closed her eyes, said a quick prayer, and made the sign of the cross before taking off from her hiding place toward the nearest ship.

Halfway to the ship she heard the sound of a single rider bearing down on her. She glanced in that direction. Her bowels turned to liquid. She let out a scream of terror when she recognised that it was none other than Julien Etienne on his big, black horse, gaining on her like the devil himself.

After a good meal and a quick tumble with an accommodating Nephilim acquaintance, Rephidim was blood and sex satiated. He headed back to the Celestial with significantly lighter pockets. He'd already settled the King's account with Pierre Lafitte and was well satisfied with the bargain he'd struck. Pierre assured him he would be in a position to provide several anxiously awaited items in his next shipment. Rephidim promised Pierre he would return to the city within a fortnight when a shipment of exquisite silks from the Orient and laces from Paris would be available for purchase. The wives of the wealthy Nephilim aristos behind the Dark Veil would be especially pleased when the merchandise arrived. *Maybe the unrest will have blown over by the time I return.*

Before Rephidim could go home to get some well-deserved rest, he would have to supervise the unloading of the King's ship upon arrival in Baton Rouge. Only after that was done would he be free to head off to the estate he owned in Mississippi.

Horse and rider moved as one as Rephidim rode at a moderate cantor through the dark, lonely streets of New Orleans. The preternatural being feared no man—white or otherwise.

A frown suddenly marred his striking face. Something was off. It took but a second for him to realise what it was. Other than an isolated coachman here and there awaiting his master's pleasure outside a couple of local gentlemen's clubs or upscale bars, Rephidim had not seen any people of colour, slave or freeman. It was as if the city had been bleached of that special something that made New Orleans both unique and intriguing. Jean warned him to be careful. Apparently, the black humans were doing the same.

Suddenly, the overpowering smell of fresh human blood tinged with anguish and the subtle scent of the delicate lily of the valley slammed into Rephidim's gut like a red-hot anvil. His body reacted immediately. He tightened his hands on the reigns.

Rephidim's fangs punched through his gums at the same time as he saw someone huddled over an unmoving figure in the middle of the street. A knife-wielding man was raising his hand to deliver what Rephidim concluded would be the final death blow to his hapless victim.

Rephidim rarely got involved in human business, and it was rarer still when he intervened in situations surrounding white humans. But something inside of him urged him to spur his horse to greater speed. Even as he sped forward, the man's hand came down to make a slicing motion. The blade came away wet with bright red blood. Rephidim's mouth filled with saliva—he was so hungry.

Rephidim got a good look at the man's hate-filled face when he looked over his shoulder at the sound of Rephidim's horse's pounding hooves. The man dropped the knife on the cobbled stone street with a clatter as if it were acid in his fist. He leapt into the saddle of a nearby horse and rode like a rat escaping a burning ship to disappear in the distance. The only evidence that he had ever been there was in the diminishing sound of his horse's pounding hooves.

Rephidim vaunted off his horse to kneel in the pool of blood surrounding the small figure. The air exited his lungs in an exhale. He looked into a pair of huge dark-brown eyes frozen in a death stare. A beautiful woman dressed like a lad lay in a widening pool of blood. Her throat was a gaping gushing wound, slit from ear to ear.

Rephidim acted without thought, first sealing the grievous wound to her throat with his large hand. Next, he brought his wrist to his mouth to open a vein, then knelt forward to give Monique Dubonnet the dark kiss, linking her to him forever.

CHAPTER 21

Magnolia Hill

THE BLOOM HAD long since worn off the rose, and Claude and Janine Etienne rarely slept together. Most nights found them adjourning to their separate bedchambers which adjoined one another on the second level of the house. Hannah was made to sleep on the hardwood floor outside Janine Etienne's bedchamber door like a faithful family hound in case the mistress had a need for her.

Lately, Hannah's sleep had been fitful. In spite of the herbs she drank daily to prevent pregnancy, she now found herself with child. *Surely there has to be some advantage to birthing the master's bastard*, she thought.

Well, the deed was done, and only time would tell what the future held. Hannah fully intended to milk the situation for all it was worth.

All was quiet save for the sounds of the house settling for the night. Hannah lay curled up in a ball outside Mistress's bedchamber when she heard the familiar creak of Claude Etienne's bedchamber door opening. A dim light from inside the chamber illuminated the far wall, extending a silent invitation for her to enter. Hannah quietly rose from the floor, entered Claude's chambers, and closed the door behind her.

Now that Clidamont was out of commission, Hannah's nocturnal visits to Claude Etienne's bedchambers had become a near nightly ritual, and this night would be no different. There was a degree of excitement in putting horns on the mistress while she slept right next door.

Claude Etienne lacked the virility of the field hands Hannah sometimes dallied with; however, his lack of stamina had its advantages. Hannah was in and out of his bedchamber in less than ten minutes, leaving the master of the manse fast asleep and well satisfied.

She was a novelty, a white slave who was not averse to using her body to better her living conditions or to bring pain to anyone who stood in the way of her wants. Hannah had targeted countless men—and even a few women— for a specific purpose and discarded them as soon as they were no longer considered useful. She saw no reason for changing the manner in which she did things upon her arrival at Magnolia Hill.

Excitement was racing through her veins. There was no way she could return to sleep now. With hours to go before dawn, Hannah's eyes were drawn to a closed door at the end of the hallway. She padded quietly toward the door on bare feet.

Every once in a while, Hannah liked to slip into Clidamont's room and stand over him so she could gloat. In his heyday he had been hell on wheels, making the lives of every slave on Magnolia Hill miserable, including Hannah's. He was a murderous, depraved beast who deserved to suffer the worst punishment imaginable.

Hannah was charged with feeding Clidamont his mid-day meal. At least once a day, she'd pop into his bedchamber to pinch him, poke him, or pull out some of his hair. She'd do anything to cause him pain that wouldn't leave a telltale mark.

Since Clidamont couldn't talk or move, he was at Hannah's mercy, but this was the first time she'd paid him a visit during the night. The look of fear in his rheumy grey eyes when she entered the room more than made up for the orgasm his ineffectual, drunken son Claude could never give her.

The sickening smell of old man rot consumed the large chamber. The smell was exacerbated by the roaring fire that was kept burning in the fireplace around the clock, no matter how hot the temperature. Clidamont lay dwarfed under multiple blankets on a massive wooden hand-carved four-poster bed in the centre of the room, dominating the chamber.

The wooden legs upon which the bed sat were as thick as hundred-year-old trees. The size of the bed swallowed Clidamont's shrivelled form. He looked like the little slave boy whose cold dead body he'd once forced Hannah to hold on to while he pounded the pale pink meat between his legs into her unwilling body.

Hannah stood at Clidamont's bedside. She remained quiet for a spell and glared at the wasted old man to give her presence greater effect. When she did speak, it was in a low whisper so as not to alert anyone to her presence in Clidamont's chambers.

"It sure does my heart glad to see you laid low. I can't tell you how long and hard I prayed to Allah that you would be stricken. And guess what? He answered my prayers in a manner that exceeded my wildest expectations. Tell me, how does it feel to be trapped inside that wicked old body of yours, unable to talk or walk or even scratch yourself when you itch?"

"*Ibn Al-Kalb.* Do you want to know what I just said?" she asked with a wicked smile on her face. "I said you are the son of a dog. That's what I said. Let me add that you and your son and your son's sons are lower than camel dung. I spit on you, and I spit on them. And do you want to know something else? I piss and put pieces of shit in the food they have me feed you each day."

Tears of rage sprang from Clidamont's eyes. Hannah could see he was struggling to speak, to no avail. She leaned closer, so close she could smell the sour odour wafting off the surface of his thin skin.

"I will not be satisfied until every one of you is dead, rotting in your graves, and this house is burnt to the ground. You are going to lead the vanguard, old man. I plan to dispatch your ass tonight." She moved closer to the bed.

Hannah wore a speculative look on her face as she took in Clidamont's current condition.

"I guess the boll weevils done ate the flesh off that boy's body by now," she said tauntingly. She knew she didn't have to tell Clidamont which boy she was talking about. It could have been any one of many he'd killed over the years.

"He's probably nothing but a sack of dry bones, along with the bodies of all the other little boys and girls you tortured and murdered in this here bed, you stinking piece of shit."

She slapped the old man upside his head, bringing fresh tears to his eyes.

"Well, Masta Clidamont…" Hannah emphasised the word "Masta." "I'm gon' share a little secret with you." She moved close enough to whisper in his ear. "You bout to join 'em."

She pulled back his blanket, exposing him to the cool night air. Goosebumps peppered his skin. He wore a nightgown to make it easier to clean him up when he pissed and shit on himself. Hannah lifted the hem of his gown up over his loose, flabby belly, exposing his shrivelled, aged genitals and subjecting him to an unspeakable indignity. She grabbed a handful of thin grey hair behind his scrotum and pulled it out by the root. Clidamont's eyes bulged. A copious stream of tears covered his twisted face.

Hannah quickly tired of playing her wicked game. It was time to end this charade once and for all. She scrounged through his belongings to see if there was anything of value. Her search produced some money, several small pieces of jewellery that would probably go unmissed, and a small wooden box she found hidden in his dressing room. Hannah opened the box. Inside was more money and an old handbill for a convicted murderer named Pierre Antoine Wolf. The likeness on the handbill bore an uncanny resemblance to Clidamont.

Well, well, well, if this ain't some shit, Hannah thought. *Masta Clidamont is an escaped, convicted murderer.* She wondered how much that information would have been worth six months ago. She stuffed the stolen goods in her top and returned to Clidamont's bedside. It was time to get rid of the old bastard.

But how will I accomplish the deed and get away unscathed?

If she was going to do it, she had to do it now. Her eyes surveyed Clidamont's chambers. At first glance, she saw nothing that would serve her purpose, and then her eyes landed upon the neat stack of white gentlemen's hankies near the nightstand that were used to wipe the constant flow of spittle that dribbled from Clidamont's mouth.

She grabbed a handful of the hankies and wadded them into a ball. She shoved the hankies down Clidamont's throat, fully enjoying watching him choke to death. Once the last death rattle sounded its knell, Hannah pulled the hankies out and rearranged Clidamont's bed clothing.

"Bye bye, Masta Wolf."

She left as quietly as she had come.

CHAPTER 22

CLIDAMONT ETIENNE'S BODY lay in his bedchamber under the watchful guard of two house slaves. Janine didn't think to wonder how it might feel to be forced to sit in a room with the dead body of someone you utterly and completely despised. She assumed the chosen slaves were well-suited to the morbid task. After all, their level of intellect and emotion was not much higher than that of the family hound. She would not have been able to do it. She hoped God would forgive her, but she was glad her father-in-law was gone.

Clidamont Etienne had treated her abominably from the very start. He'd been a mean-spirited, cruel, and extremely evil old man, quick to point out her past and current faults. It became patently clear before she married Claude that she would serve as a brood mare with a large dowry. The options left to her had been limited. She married Claude anyway.

She'd been hopeful that Claude would promptly get her with child and that some tender emotions would grow between them. Neither event occurred. In fact, she feared both her womb and her husband's heart might well be barren.

Claude left early that morning to make the necessary arrangements to get his father put in the ground. It was early evening, and he had yet to return. Janine would face another supper alone and, more likely than not, another night alone as well. It didn't matter; Claude had stopped coming to her bed years ago.

Frowning, Lilly quickly glanced over at Hannah as she poured Mistress

Janine yet another glass of wine. Hannah had a smug look on her face. Mistress's dinner plate was untouched, yet she'd already been through two carafes of wine and was about to finish a third.

The sound of the wine being poured into the large crystal tumbler brought terror to Lilly's heart. Hannah filled the glass to the brim. It was obvious that Hannah's intent was to get the Mistress drunk, but that was the last thing Lilly wanted or needed. Mistress was a mean, ugly drunk.

There was not one slave on Magnolia Hill, house or field, who didn't know that Hannah was fucking Masta Claude every which way but loose. Rumour travelled from plantation to plantation that Mistress Janine liked her meat dark and that the Masta knew all about it. It wouldn't surprise Lilly one bit if it was Masta Claude's intent to plant Janine up on the hill next to the other dead Etienne wives right after she pushed out a son.

Flossie told Lilly that Mistress Janine was desperate enough to come to her for herbs to quicken her womb. Lilly didn't know a slave on Magnolia Hill that hated those Etiennes more than Flossie did. Instead of giving the mistress something to get her with child, Flossie gave her an herb that dried up her womb just as her constant drinking had her scarecrow-thin body.

Flossie had later laughed with Lilly about it.

"Hmph. Why in the hell would anybody on Magnolia Hill want to bring another Etienne into the world?"

Lilly wholeheartedly agreed with her. *Why indeed would any slave want that?*

Hannah hid a secret smile with each glass of wine Mistress gulped down. If the bitch remained true to form, she would soon be passed out cold in her plate of food, and Hannah and Lilly would drag the blubbering, pitiful woman upstairs to sleep it off. Hannah would then have some precious free time to herself.

Memories of the contents of the *Grimoire* she'd stolen from her grandmother, Zahara, were coming to her as clearly as the proverbial handwriting on the wall. Zahara's voice came to her at the most unexpected times, exhorting her to write the recitations down. Hannah felt like her mind would explode if she didn't memorialise Zahara's words. Her enterprise was risky business at best, since reading and writing was outlawed for slaves, but the only way to silence Zahara's voice was to put her words down on paper.

One of the trunks Hannah unpacked for Mistress Janine upon her arrival to Magnolia Hill contained ten thick, leather-bound journals with blank pages. At the end of each day Janine would sit at her escritoire, writing in one of the large books.

Hannah stole one of Mistress Janine's journals and for the past eight months had been feverishly transferring the invocations, evocations, and black magick spells into the journal through a hand that could not possibly be her own. Hannah's head was pounding with an inexplicable urgency to get back to her book.

Janine's hand shook as she raised the full glass of wine to her lips. She was drunk yet again and so lonely she felt like crying. Claude had abandoned her—left her to waste away—to wither and dry up while he rutted on her own maid right under her nose.

She knew Hannah was sleeping with her husband. It was not at all unusual for a wealthy planter to use his stock in that manner. That was the custom in the south. Custom or not, that didn't mean Janine wanted Claude's affair with that arrogant slave rubbed in her face.

Hannah's slightly spreading middle hadn't escaped Janine's notice either. She could not countenance having the pregnant woman in her presence, especially since she could not conceive a child of her own. Janine suspected the baby Hannah was carrying was Claude's. She wanted Hannah out of the house and out of her sight before she was forced to endure the indignity of looking at yet another baby with the distinctive Etienne gunmetal-grey eyes.

The wine had taken over. Now she was getting angry—angry enough to hurt someone as much as she was hurting. Something inside of Janine finally broke as she looked up through glassy red-rimmed eyes in time to catch a mixture of pity and disgust on Lilly's face. Lilly tried to lower her eyes. Too late. That look lit a fire under Janine.

Janine stood on wobbly legs, knocking over the glass of wine. A circle of wine spread on the pristine white tablecloth and dripped off the edge of the table and onto her skirt like a widening pool of blood. Spit flew out of Janine's mouth.

"What in the hell are you looking at, gal?" Her voice slurred from too much drink.

When Lilly didn't answer, Janine tossed her plate of food at Lilly, barely missing the slave's startled face and painting the light green walls behind her with grits and gravy. Janine's hands were fisted at her side and her breath coming in heaves.

"Why, you stupid little bitch! Look what you made me do."

Lilly took a step back, afraid Janine would lob another missile at her. Maybe next time she wouldn't miss.

"Clean this mess up before I take the strap to you."

She then turned eyes made mad from pent-up jealousy and inebriation upon Hannah, who was taking in the recent state of affairs with no expression on her face.

"This is one of my favourite gowns. If it is ruined because of your clumsiness, I will tan your ignorant black hide until the skin falls off!"

Janine painted a ludicrous picture to Hannah who followed behind her as she staggered and stumbled twice on her way up the stairway to her bedchambers, her head held high.

Less than an hour later, Hannah returned to her mistress' chambers with the gown draped over her arm, having managed to get every single wine stain out. Janine had drunk an inordinate amount of wine. Hannah hoped she would be passed out on her canopy bed so that she could slip away to write in her journal. When Hannah knocked to gain entry to Janine's chambers, she heard a solemn response instead of the expected silence.

"You may enter."

Not only was Janine not passed out drunk on her bed, but she was at her escritoire, busily writing in one of her journals. Hannah held up the recently laundered gown before her. Janine nodded her approval.

"Hang the gown up and see that it does not get wrinkled, then come back here. I would have a word with you."

Hannah couldn't help but wonder what that fool woman might want to discuss with her. As she turned to exit the closet, she was met with Janine's journal, planted square in the centre of her face, knocking her off her feet. Hannah saw stars.

Janine stood over her like a conquering Viking. "You are not just a dirty little whore, but you're also a thief. Do you think I didn't notice you'd taken one of my precious journals?"

Janine had, in fact, discovered one of the journals was missing that evening. When she reached the last page of the one in which she'd been writing, she went through her trunk for another. Finally, Hannah had given Janine the excuse she'd been waiting for to have her thrown out of the Big House.

Janine beat Hannah about the head and face, first with one of her journals and then one of her silver hairbrushes, calling her all nature of foul names with each savage blow.

Hannah wanted to grab that bug-eyed bitch by the neck and slowly squeeze the life out of her until her watery blue eyes popped out of her head. Instead, she not only took the beating, but dared not raise her eyes from the floor for fear the hatred in them would burn a hole through anything she looked upon.

From that day forward, Hannah was forced to live among the same lowly slaves she'd previously disdained during her elevated status as a house servant. The day Hannah was banished to live in the slave quarters was the same day Clidamont Etienne, née Pierre Antoine Wolf, was buried, and the day she went into labour.

CHAPTER 23

FLOSSIE WAS OLD and tired. She was a human jigsaw puzzle whose pieces had been cast in the wind, some lost forever. To add insult to injury, her joints ached like a bad tooth. The slow throbbing pain emanated from the marrow. Nonetheless, it didn't matter how bad she felt. There was work to be done.

Today would be no different than the day before. Flossie got up early every morning to cook breakfast. No sooner than that was done, she had to prepare for lunch, dinner, and anything else the white folks at the Big House desired. Her day didn't end until she'd cleaned up after dinner and gathered firewood for the next day.

The cabin she inhabited with her daughter Perline was slightly larger than that of the other slaves since it also served as the plantation kitchen.

None of the slave cabins had windows. The side of each cabin had only one opening covered by an ineffectual shutter to let in or keep out light. This opening also let in the elements. It caused the cabins to be unbearably hot and humid in the heart of the summer.

During the rainy season, the wind insinuated its way through numerous openings in each cabin, making a mockery of the flimsy shutters covering what served as windows and the slaves' efforts to pack the cracks in their cabins with mud and rocks. The rain would blow in through the cracks, soaking the dirt floor, and forcing the slaves to live in a miserable muddy mess. Flossie counted herself fortunate to reside with her daughter in the plantation kitchen, but today the cooking fires turned the cabin into a living hell.

Flossie wiped the sweat from her brow with an old rag that doubled as a potholder. It was late afternoon. The sun was at its zenith, slow-cooking everything in its path, even as Flossie slow-cooked the evening meal for the occupants of the Big House.

All the cooking for the whites and slaves was done in heavy metal pots and skillets over an open fireplace. Only half of the smoke from the cooking fire exited the brick chimney. The other half backed up into the cabin, making breathing difficult. The heat from the fireplace was unbearable. That uppity yella wench Hannah could not have chosen a worse day to push out her piccanniny.

Reeking of sweat, onions, and other food smells, Flossie looked toward the stained quilt that served as a privacy partition between Hannah and the remainder of the cabin, alternately cooking and humming an old Negro spiritual as Hannah laboured to bring her child into the world.

"Steal away, steal away, steal away to Jesus."

Her rich alto voice travelled out the open window. The tune was soon picked up by other slaves and became a chorus amongst the labourers. The song meant there would be a ritual that evening and that all who were desirous to participate should slip off into the woods at a prearranged time.

I sure hope that heifer has that baby before nightfall. I got things to do, Flossie thought.

Flossie sat on a rough-hewn stool near the fireplace stirring a large pot of beans, impervious to Hannah's screams. She took her time, checking the contents of each pot before steeping her herbs. She had decided not to gather any pain-killing herbs for Hannah whom she referred to as "heifer," "that gal," or that "yella gal." *Suffering is redemptive*, she thought spitefully. *Maybe the little heifer will keep her nasty legs closed next time!*

Death is the universal equaliser. Eventually it comes knocking at everybody's door. It just so happened that the unwelcomed angel was right up the road, heading at a steady pace toward Flossie's cabin. The most frightening thing about it was that Hannah knew it was coming and she was helpless to do anything about it. At the moment, she felt like she'd been chained to a post in a burning barn with no means of escape.

For the past forty-eight hours, pain was Hannah's constant companion, holding her in its cruel grip as it took ruthless advantage of her body. The pain insidiously gnawed its way through the thin pallet barely separating Hannah's body from the hard dirt-packed floor so that it could viciously attack her insides. Hannah was experiencing the kind of pain that tortures you just short of unconsciousness so you can't miss a minute of its work.

What a cruel twist of fate that an act that could bring such pleasure would result in such pain. The pain was all-encompassing. Thankfully—for the time being, at least—it was intermittent.

Hannah was no novice when it came to pain. The raised weals on her slender back were a testament to that fact. This was a different kind of pain. This was the kind of pain that tiptoed on your nerve endings in pike-soled shoes to see how much you could take before your sanity exited the room.

Hannah braced herself. It wouldn't be long before the pain would tyre of toying with her—no, not long at all before the pain would take a bite out of her flagging self-control and send her spiralling into the realm of unremitting agony. When the next contraction arrived, Hannah let out a scream that was heard the length of the slave quarters and clear up to the Big House.

CHAPTER 24

HANNAH TOOK A deep, shaky breath when the pain finally subsided. Hatred and anger swirled through the kaleidoscope of her mind. She refused to acknowledge her own part in her current circumstances.

Were it not for a fucking man, I would not be in this predicament!

Between bouts of pain, she thought about methods by which she could bring suffering and total destruction to those ruddy-faced infidels who held the power of life and death in this purgatory she was trapped in.

She wished a similar fate upon the mindless black chattel who were forced to serve them. Human beasts of burden is what they were. Why, in her native land, they existed only to serve their betters. She was now forced to serve right alongside them.

But, alas, these were but fanciful thoughts and delusional pain-washed dreams. Instead, she would content herself with use of the evil spells she'd learned under the tutelage of her paternal grandmother. She only hoped she would live long enough to see the fruit of her labour.

Finally, the pain began to ebb a bit. Hannah ventured to move her head slightly. The cabin was empty. She'd heard the old woman dragging that dead leg of hers out of the cabin before muttering something about fetching some herbs for pain.

Most of the slaves were either in the sugar fields or otherwise occupied on the plantation. Other than Flossie, there was no one to attend her. The fact of the matter was that no one cared enough about Hannah to attend her during her delivery.

There was no one to hold her hand or wipe the sweat from her brow. She had made many enemies during her stay on Magnolia Hill. There was no one to sit by her side as she laboured, no one to give her a cool drink of water to soothe her sore parched throat or moisten her dry cracked lips. There was not one single person she could call friend. To have a friend, you had to be a friend. Hannah had no idea what that looked like. As far as she was concerned, they could all go straight to hell in a fucking hand basket. She didn't need them before, and she damn sure didn't need them now.

Hannah knew this delivery was not a normal one. She had witnessed more than a few births in the past year, and none were like this. Something was drastically wrong. A fleeting thought crossed her mind. Maybe this was punishment for some of the things she had been forced to do to survive, but she could not think about that right now.

She just might end up dying. If she did, there would be no one to mourn her passing. Life would go on long after she was dead and buried. Many would consider themselves better off if she did die. Shit, a few would probably dance on her grave!

If anyone else found themselves in a situation similar to Hannah's, they would, more likely than not, be prayerful and penitent, humbly seeking God's mercy and forgiveness. Why not? If you have to die, you may as well get on God's good side, just in case. Hannah was nowhere near humble nor was she penitent. God's name didn't pass her lips or enter her mind unless it was followed by a blistering profanity.

Hannah was enraged because she didn't know which of the men she'd lain with had fathered her child and therefore could not mete out a suitable punishment. She lost count of all the men she had carelessly spread her thighs for.

There was Martin Henry Singleton before I left Zanzibar. Then there were the men who raped me on the dirt farm in South Carolina. I can't forget all the men who fucked me at the filthy crib by the waterfront. Of course, there was Monique Dubonnet's house of pleasure in New Orleans, and, lastly, the good old Etiennes.

There were so many more who'd known her intimately while on Magnolia

Hill. Most of them merely tickled her insides, offering a prelude to the unachievable.

If she knew which he was, she'd slice his pecker off and shove it up his ass! Most of the clandestine trysts had not been satisfying anyway. It would be a shame to go in such a painful manner, after not even having had the pleasure of cumming.

Before Hannah could complete her last thought, another sharp contraction took hold of her, gripping her at her core, twisting and rending her internal organs. Once the pain subsided, it was all she could do to prepare herself for the next one.

The contractions were now coming closer together. Her face was awash with sweat as she gritted her teeth, bracing herself against yet another indescribable wave of pain. The last contraction was more intense than the one before it, nearly jackknifing her body off the bloody pallet. Hannah sought to conserve what little strength she had in preparation for the next physical assault. *Dammit, I am not dead yet. Fuck if I will give these illiterate, ignorant niggers the satisfaction of seeing me die*, she ranted, panting like a thirsty dog left too long in the hot sun.

If death was determined to claim her this day, Hannah was equally determined to not go without a fight. She would stand up to the demon of death in the same fashion she'd faced down each of the myriad obstacles she'd been forced to confront in what had become her wretched life. She would spit in death's eyes, facing it boldly, irreverently, and without fear.

Shit. Gotdammit. Fuck!

Hannah screamed so loud and for so long her throat felt as if it were packed with cotton. She writhed in agony, finding it difficult to breath. The pain was so unbearable, yet her mind would not shut down.

Where the fuck is that ugly little troll? She's had more than enough time to gather the herbs necessary to ease my pain. If I live through this, I swear to God, I will slice her head off and spit in the cavity!

Hannah was beside herself with pain and a little fear. Her life and the life of her unborn child were in the hands of a woman who had never hidden the fact that she hated her. The moment their eyes met, each recognised the power in the other. On that day, an unspoken challenge was made. Hannah was afraid because she knew that, were the tables reversed, she would take this opportunity to permanently dispose of Flossie. She was at the mercy of her worst enemy.

Hannah could hear her heartbeat in her head. It was pounding hard enough to split her skull in two. A relentless, steady rhythm resounded inside her brain like the sinister beat of jungle drums.

There is nothing pretty about childbirth. It's an immodest, messy, and smelly affair. Through sheer dent of will, fueled by hatred and a deep-seated desire for revenge, Hannah was determined to force out the *thing* that stubbornly maintained a stranglehold on her dilated womb. She cared not whether it lived or died; she just wanted it *out*.

Although the pain was more than she could bear, Hannah put chin to her chest and pushed with all her might. She was determined not to die. She pushed until the blood vessels in her eyes burst, expelling gas and excrement as she tried in vain to force the life out of her rapidly weakening body.

"Stop pushing, gal," Flossie commanded. "I can see the baby. It's comin' ass first. Don't push no more!"

Mindless of the bloody mess on the pallet and the blood-soaked dirt floor beneath it, Flossie held Hannah's knees wide apart while she squatted between her open thighs.

Hannah was too weak to fight her. Determined to get the life out of her body after more than two days of long, hard labour, Hannah ignored the instructions of the midwife and kept on pushing. She pushed even though the pain was excruciating.

Hatred was the impetus which afforded her the strength to continue to push while the midwife shoved both hands elbow deep inside of her body. Hatred helped her to keep her grasp on sanity as Flossie turned the breached baby into proper birthing position. Hatred kept her conscious through the unbearable pain.

Hannah's blood pressure soared, slamming against her skull like waters cresting in an angry sea. High-pitched ringing resounded in her ears as her body began to weaken from loss of blood. But hatred and her refusal to die until she'd had an opportunity to make all those who'd wronged her suffer gave her the near superhuman strength to keep pushing, even as the life within her body was literally tearing her inside out.

Before she lost her grasp on consciousness, Hannah heard the faint cry of her baby. The sounds around her became more and more distant until she could barely hear anything at all. Her feelings of hatred may have sustained her through the delivery, but it could not keep her life's blood from copiously gushing from her body.

No intervention could have prevented Hannah's spirit from departing her battered body on that date and time, but that didn't keep Flossie from trying anyway. There was a loud popping sound before Hannah's spirit disconnected from her body. Flossie's were the last words Hannah heard before she gave up the ghost, transitioning from agony to a pain-free existence and a weightless state of being.

"Look lak Massa got hisself another white-lookin' pickaninny, and it look like I done won the war, now don't it, gal!"

CHAPTER 25

HANNAH DISPASSIONATELY surveyed the carnage childbirth had wrought on her body from the height of her lofty perch.

So, this is what being dead feels like, she thought.

Her dead body was a mess. Her mouth was open in a silent scream. Her legs were splayed wide open, and she could clearly see where that damn baby had ripped her open clear down to her shit hole.

Damn. If I wasn't dead already, I'd strangle the little bastard with my bare hands.

She wondered whether Flossie would leave her dead body lying on the floor while she went back to cooking dinner. *Surely Flossie doesn't want the folks in the Big House to have Drake take the strap to her because their food was late,* she thought facetiously.

Before Hannah could further ruminate on what would be done with her broken body, her spirit was sucked through the cabin ceiling and into the heart of a spinning vortex. When the spinning finally stopped, she landed with a bone-jarring crash onto a narrow ledge about five feet in width. The force of the impact split both of her knees wide open. In fact, one of her knees appeared to be fractured with the bony kneecap fully exposed. The pain was mind-boggling, eradicating the pain-free serenity she felt immediately after her death.

Who would have thought one could experience pain beyond the grave?

"Shit!"

Dragging her injured leg, she crawled toward the edge of a ledge that overlooked a steep precipice. Her head began to spin. A seemingly endless abyss greeted her. She was assaulted by a sense of vertigo, as unseen hands threatened to pull her over the ledge, forcing her to spiral into an endless free fall.

Can a person die more than once? she wondered.

Terrified, she scooted as far away from the ledge as possible, flattening her back against the hard rock face. The sound of her heavy breathing and her fear took up every space in her brain, blocking out all rational thought. She had always been afraid of heights and dared not venture near the edge of her precarious perch again.

She dug her fingers into the rock's craggy surface with a white-knuckled grip to keep from pitching forward. It seemed an eternity before she got her breathing under control. When her heart stopped pounding its fear-filled percussion and her pulse returned to normal, she was able to take note of her surroundings and assess her situation.

Obviously, she had crossed over into another realm of existence and was now in that mysterious divide between the world of the living and that of the dead. From the look of things, she had landed smack dab in the middle of hell.

From her vantage point, she could see a swirling dark mist surrounding the tops of a range of massive mountains. The mountains, which were ten times higher than the Himalayas and 100 times longer than the Andes, appeared to be bordered by highlands and separated by valleys and passes.

Huge winged creatures soared around the mountaintops, slicing through the mist-shrouded sky. Their majestic wings sounded like huge leather fans flapping in the wind. There was not one star to brighten the blue-black sky. Hannah was tempted to call out. She wanted to see whether her voice would answer her in this massive desolate place, but common sense prevailed. She instinctively knew it would not be safe for her to remain in her current location nor call attention to herself. She had no desire to become food for the flying creatures who made this string of mountains their home.

Spying a dark crevice about fifty feet to her left, Hannah cautiously positioned herself on all fours, leaving a trail of blood behind her as she slowly and painfully crawled toward the opening, hoping against hope to find shelter until daybreak.

The crevice opened up into a large cave with ample room for Hannah to stand erect and spread her arms wide. Using the slimy cave wall to stabilise herself, she tentatively ventured deeper into the darkness of the cave, breathing in the smell of mould and rot as she travelled. Something that felt like dried leaves and other unfamiliar vegetation served as a cushion for her bare feet. Hannah froze suddenly like a deer in the woods.

What was that sound? she wondered.

She heard the sound of distant voices. Exhilarated that she was not alone in this frightening new world, she hastened her steps in the direction from whence the voices came.

The cave turned out to be surprisingly large with numerous twists, turns, and tunnels. The voices served as her compass. As Hannah drew nearer to the source of the voices, she spied a faint light reflecting off the walls of the cave. *Where there is light, there is warmth and maybe even food.* She hobbled as fast as her injured leg could take her, stumbling toward the blessed light like a moth drawn to a flame.

What Hannah saw when she staggered into the cave clearing rivalled even the most horrific scene from Dante's Inferno. The huge space was brightly lit with wall sconces made of human skulls. Hannah felt gorge rising from the pervasive metallic smell of blood and smoke. She bent over, wanting to vomit, but she could only dry heave throat-burning bile as she choked in a paroxysm of coughing. Frozen in time, Hannah took it all in.

Upon a stone altar lay a thing that had been human at one time. All that remained of it now was a screaming mass of exposed muscle, tendons, and sinew. Someone had taken the time to skin the person alive. There was not one strip of flesh left on its body, yet it still lived, mewling like a tortured animal, begging to be put out of its misery.

A ten by fifteen block of concrete was suspended above the altar, bearing a legend written in what looked suspiciously like dried blood.

"This is the punishment meted out to murderers," Hannah read, gulping at the thought of how she had murdered her grandmother before she left

Zanzibar and how she'd later dispatched Clidamont. Now, she prayed this would not be her fate.

She saw midget men with huge, distorted phalluses and abnormally large heads. Some cavorted with quill-skinned animals and others savaged horribly diseased men and women. Dead bodies lay strewn about like so much garbage. Thick bloodworms burrowed under the skin of the discarded bodies, crawling in and out of every orifice. A nearby cement sign indicated this was the punishment for those who committed incest and child abuse.

A wrinkled-visaged witch performed aberrant sex acts while an orchestra of naked priests wearing naught but clerical collars played chamber music in sync with the wicked witches' salacious grunts and moans. Standing behind the performers were two angels of punishment, flaying skin from their backs with fiery, barb-studded whips.

"This is the punishment for men and woman of God who practise unlawful fornication."

Hannah looked up only to see the unimaginable. Lifeless bodies swung like marionettes from thick, smoke-charred oak beams. People were suspended from the beams by large hooks embedded to the hilt in their eye sockets. This was but one of the many punishments meted out to those who coveted and sought to take that which belonged to others.

Naked women hung horizontally with metal shipping hooks buried between their thighs. Similarly, naked men hung by their necks with their manhoods protruding from their mouths, their sightless eyes bulging from their heads. Several other dead bodies hung by their hair; others, by their breasts.

Each of the dead was suspended from chains of fire, yet the fire never completely consumed them. These unfortunate souls were being punished for adultery and licentiousness.

Elsewhere were screaming people staked to cave walls by their ears. Bloody metal spikes decorated both sides of their faces. The only means of escape would be to rip both ears from their heads, a fitting punishment for those who listened to vicious gossip.

One man sat strapped upon a metal throne. Upon his head was a steel helmet which was secured to the back of the throne, holding his head immobile. His tongue protruded through a mouthpiece fashioned within the helmet. Both of his hands and his tongue were pierced clear through with smoking hot metal rods. The smell of his burning flesh filled the cave. This was the punishment meted out to liars and thieves.

Hannah covered her mouth to keep from screaming. Sinners were suspended by their feet with their heads facing downward and their bodies covered with fat, black, blood-engorged worms. These were people who swore false testimony, causing unjust punishment or death to innocents.

Angels of destruction alternated between lashing other sinners with red-hot chains and breaking their teeth with fiery stones as continual torture from morning until evening. During the night the sinners' teeth would grow back and their flayed flesh would heal only to be beaten into bloody mush again and again. These were the agnostics and the atheists. Apparently, both groups had decided to believe in the existence of God because they called His name again and again, but He no longer heard their cries. It was too late for redemption.

CHAPTER 26

A BEAUTIFUL MAN with the face of an angel and the body of Adonis took note of Hannah standing at the mouth of the stone chamber.

"Come, little lovely," he said, beckoning her with his eyes. "You look thirsty and hungry. I will feed you. I will give you drink and protect you. Come. Don't be afraid."

All this was said without opening his mouth. Hannah heard his voice in her head as clear as day. Hypnotised by this one beam of light in the midst of a chamber of horrors, Hannah hesitantly stepped forward, only to retreat when his tongue, which was black and at least two feet in length, lashed out to whip her with its barbed tip.

Hannah began to shake all over, slowly backing away. Paying no attention to her injuries, she turned and ran in the opposite direction. She didn't care where she ran as long as it was away from the memories of what she'd seen in that cave clearing.

She ran faster at the sound of pounding feet behind her, gaining on her. She didn't know who or what was following her, but she knew she did not want whatever it was to catch up to her. She ran, and ran, and kept running until her chest burned like someone had set off a bonfire inside of her.

She ran until she literally slammed into a stone wall. She had nowhere else to run. Her eyes frantically searched her surroundings, looking for anything that might serve as a weapon, but there was nothing. She was trapped and would probably be forced to endure the fate of one of those poor souls being tortured in the clearing.

"Psssst. Psssst."

Hannah froze. She held her breath, tilting her head to listen with a keen ear. There it was again.

"Psssst. Psssst. Quick. Over here!"

Hannah turned in the direction of the voice. Partially hidden behind a stalagmite was a young man, probably Hannah's age or slightly older. He stepped from his hiding place, beckoning her to follow him. Since Hannah was not trustworthy herself, she found it difficult to place her trust in others. When she hesitated, the young man quickly let her know what she was up against.

"Listen. You can stay here and wait for them to catch you, or you can follow me to safety. In any event, I'm not sticking around to see what they do to you."

The echo of multiple feet drawing ever nearer to their location decided Hannah. Without a backward glance, she followed the young man through a barely discernible fissure in the cave wall. The opening they took led to another tunnel. From there, it veered off into yet another tunnel, seemingly descending deeper into the belly of the cave. The mountain was a mysterious maze filled with a labyrinth of tunnels, paths, and clearings. She was grateful for her newfound companion.

They travelled in companionable silence for what seemed an interminable amount of time. The sounds made by Hannah's pursuers were replaced with the sound of trickling water and that of the scampering feet of critters who called this mountain their home. Deer mice, snakes, and salamanders made way for the two-legged trespassers. Spiders, beetles, and bats folded into the fissures in the cave wall as Hannah and her erstwhile guide passed by.

The floor of the cold, dark cave was wet and muddy and, in many places, uneven. Hannah's feet were cut in places and her ankles throbbed. She was hard-pressed to keep up with her companion.

"Wait!" she cried out, now out of breath.

The young man continued walking as though he hadn't heard her. Hannah rushed to catch up with him, struggling to navigate the slopes and cracks in the rock floor on her road-weary bare feet. She had quite a few questions, and she was determined to get answers to them.

"I *said* wait a minute, damn you!"

Now that she was out of imminent danger, Hannah was determined not to take another step until she knew where the hell she was and where her silent guide was taking her.

The young man stopped and slowly turned. Hannah was nearly poleaxed by his beauty. He was as slender as a young girl. His arms and legs were reed thin but perfectly formed, with exquisitely detailed musculature. It seemed his maker had taken a knife and hand-carved every detail of his body to craft this perfect specimen of a man.

Hannah drank him in. He waited patiently as Hannah's greedy eyes took her fill. She raised her eyes to look upon his face. His complexion was smooth, rich, and dark as a sun-dried cocoa bean. His facial features were as perfect as his body. He had huge, expressive brown eyes with sinfully long lashes, a noble nose, high cheekbones, and succulent bow-shaped lips. His tightly curled hair capped a perfectly shaped head. Hannah entreated him in a gentler voice.

"Please. Might we stop for a moment? I need to know where you are taking me."

At first she thought he would ignore her again. Instead, he surprised her by taking her by the hand and leading her to a nearby rock upon which they sat. He spoke to her in the language of her ancestors. His voice was soft and cultured, music to her ears. It had been so long since she'd heard the language of Zanzibar.

"I am known as Micah," he said, pointing to himself.

Hannah was quick to respond to his introduction. "And I am known as Hannah."

"I know who you are, Hannah," Micah stated with a smile. "I know all about you and I know why you are here, Hannah of Zanzibar who was made a slave."

Sensing her confusion, Micah sought to answer Hannah's unasked questions.

"You have died and gone to hell," he said, pausing a moment to allow the information to sink in.

No kidding, she thought. *Based on what I saw in that fuckin' cave, I'm damn sure not in heaven!* Hannah bit her tongue to refrain from verbalising the smart retort.

"Hell has seven divisions, one atop the other. They are known as *Sheol, Abaddon, Beer Shahat, Tit ha-Yawen, Sha'are Mawet, Sha'are Zalmawet,* and *Gehenna.* Each division is similar to a country on earth, but much larger in size than all earth's countries combined.

"There are seven subdivisions within each of the divisions. The subdivisions are similar to states on earth. Within each of the subdivisions are seven compartments which are similar to earth's cities. In each of the seven compartments are seven thousand caves.

"In every cave, there are seven thousand crevices. In every crevice are seven thousand scorpions. The scorpions are slumbering now. Each of the scorpions has three hundred rings around its body. Inside every one of those rings are seven thousand pouches of deadly venom, more than enough to fill the seven rivers of the underworld to overflowing with their poison.

"These rivers are the *River Styx, Phlegethon, Acheron, Cocytus, Lethe, Erianos,* and *Alpheus.* Each of these rivers flow with seething, live coals and are filled with pitch, sulphur, and other unmentionable things.

"I don't mean to push you, Hannah, but it is imperative we make haste. We are currently on *Gehenna* in one of those 7,000 caves I mentioned. In less than two hours, the archangels of punishment, one of which you saw in the clearing, will exhort the scorpions to exit their crevices so that they may do what they do best. If we do not make haste, we will heartily regret it!"

Having said his piece, Micah gave Hannah a hand up and they proceeded on their journey with Hannah making no further complaint.

Micah led Hannah to a rocky outcrop when they exited the cave. The depression in the mountain wall was about a quarter mile in height from the valley below and deep and wide enough for both to sit comfortably.

Hannah was not at all pleased to find herself on yet another mountain ledge, albeit much wider than the previous ledge. Thankfully, her circumstances were not as precarious as they had been earlier.

Hannah had hoped to put as much distance between herself and this godforsaken mountain as possible, but she was apparently going to have to exercise patience, something she had in small commodity. She didn't get an opportunity to share her thoughts with Micah, however. It seemed no sooner were they situated inside the mountain depression than she heard a loud roar. The mountain began to quake with what sounded like the heavy feet of thousands upon thousands of stampeding elephants, all attempting to break through the rock walls.

The mountain rumbled, virtually bursting at the seams as the paralysing transparent pre-venom of 7,000 scorpions flooded its interior. The pre-venom was followed by enough viscous poisonous fluid to fill an ocean. Dense, cloudy venom spewed out of every cave opening, causing lateral and fissure eruptions the length and breadth of the mountain.

Milky, liquid death ran down the walls of the mountain, killing everything in its path as it flooded the valley below and rapidly filled the rivers to overflowing. Hannah clutched Micah's arm, her sharp nails biting into his flesh as the venom overflow created a waterfall curtain across the opening of the depression in which they hid. Their spirits would be doomed to experience the agonising death again and again, with no surcease from the venomous stings, if one drop of the liquid touched their flesh.

Hannah watched on as though hypnotised while thick globs of venom rained down on everything, coating the side of the mountain and the floor of the valley below with a venomous white paint.

When the venom finally ceased to flow, Hannah and Micah ventured from their place of sanctuary to the valley below. Their descent was long and arduous. Micah led Hannah back through the mountain to reach the valley floor. By the time they reached the valley below, there was not a trace of scorpion venom anywhere.

They passed skeletons in their travels. Micah explained these were the remains of servants who, though themselves free of sin, had decided to follow their masters into hell.

Shit, Hannah thought. *There is absolutely nothing anyone could say or do to induce me to follow them into this hell-hole. Ain't that much loyalty in the world, especially after what I have seen in the cave torture chamber.*

When Hannah and Micah finally exited the cave, they ended up near the base of the mountain. Hannah looked up, hoping to see the ledge she'd originally landed upon, but the mountain was so high and the ledges and precipices so numerous, it was impossible to determine which one was stained with her blood. She became dizzy from the sheer immensity of the mountain range surrounding her.

Hannah examined her arms and legs for the source of the blood and found all her previous wounds miraculously healed! When she turned her attention to Micah to exclaim over her newfound healing, she noted a strange look on his face that he quickly masked.

It was not divine providence that led Hannah to the cave of punishment in *Gehenna*. All dead are assigned a guide. However, the guide will not risk his or her life to preserve the existence of his charge. Micah was assigned to be Hannah's guide.

It was preordained that she be judged for her deeds. Her escape with Micah merely postponed the inevitable. Micah held this treasured secret close to his heart for he knew that the Angels of Destruction were simply toying with her. At any time at all, they could pluck her from her current location and squash her like a bug.

All deceased souls are given a three-day period to circumvent their punishment. To do so, one must make it to the Kingdom of the Dead and petition Incarnadine, the Son of Darkness, for their soul. Micah would lead Hannah to the Dark Castle.

CHAPTER 27

THANKS TO MICAH, Hannah had already survived the caves in the mountains of Gehenna. Micah would see to it that she survived The Valley of the Shadow of Death as well. The last leg of their journey would take them through the Enchanted Forest, which Micah informed Hannah was anything but enchanting. If she succumbed to the perils in the Valley of the Shadow of Death or within the forest, she would be brought before the Angels of Punishment where she too would meet the same fate as those in the cave of tortures.

Hannah did not know how much time had elapsed while she travelled with Micah through the maze of tunnels in the cave nor did she know how long they had waited for the rivers of venom to cease flowing, but she knew more than enough time had passed for the arrival of daybreak. A shroud of darkness continued to cover the entire valley, hovering like a death pall over every twisted, leafless tree and black blade of grass.

"Micah. The darkness of this place dampens my spirits. I crave the feel of the sun upon my face. Tell me, did the day come and go while we travelled through the cave?"

Now that they were safely away from the dangers the cave presented, Micah seemed more relaxed and willing to converse with Hannah.

"No. You did not lose a day in the caves, Hannah. When we exited the mountain, we entered into *Be'er Shahat*. You are now in the Valley of the Shadow of Death, a city within *Be'er Shahat*. Here there is no light, only perpetual darkness."

A wrinkle appeared between Hannah's dark brows as a recollection came to mind. *So, this is that infamous place referred to in the twenty-third psalm of that book the whites and their dark puppets put so much stock in. If only she could give the poor fools evidence of its actual authenticity!*

The first thing Hannah noticed when she and Micah entered The Valley of the Shadow of Death was the bone-chilling, teeth-chattering cold. Her only protection against the cold was the thin night-rail she'd died in. It afforded virtually no protection against the numbing cold. No matter how hard she tried, she couldn't stop shaking. It was hard to discern whether her uncontrollable shivers were a result of the cold, her fear, or a combination of both. After all, she had barely escaped the harrowing experience in the cave and the scorpions.

Micah, clad only in tattered knee britches and sandals, seemed unaffected by the sub-zero temperature. Be'er Shahat was known as the land of hellfire and ice. A thick layer of steaming hot ice coated the surface of everything as far as the eye could see.

Her arrival in The Valley of the Shadow of Death had not been heralded by any blinding bright light nor were there any long-lost family members present to ease her mounting disquiet. Instead, she was greeted by a troubling symphony of anguish and a beautiful semi-androgynous male who fortunately possessed intimate knowledge of this mysterious dark world. She shuddered to think what her fate might have been were it not for Micah's timely intervention.

The next thing Hannah realised was that her feet were no longer touching the ground. With little or no concentration, she was able to travel while suspended in mid-air, floating about two inches above the ground. She looked at Micah in wonder, noting that he too was travelling in the same manner as she. He would later explain to her that, having survived the perils of the cave, she would acquire certain preternatural powers, one by one, and grow more powerful with each new obstacle she survived.

Hannah encountered stygian darkness everywhere she looked. In her spirit mind, she could see and hear clearer than ever before. It was amazing. She could see a bat-like creature feeding upon a rotten carcass of an animal at least five miles away. Hannah could actually hear the crunch as bone and teeth met. She could hear the sopping sound that loose decayed flesh makes when it is pulled away from the bone. Hannah paused to better take in the unfettered sounds of decadence and depravity all around her.

The sinister surroundings began to envelope Hannah, becoming one with her spirit. The air was redolent with the smell of blood, decay, and filth. She took a deep, lung-filling breath. Like an animal in search of prey, she could smell everything. She had been loosed from the shackles of mortality and made invincible. Her dark eyes began to sparkle with bloodlust and her fear began to subside. Her excitement was contagious. Micah's demeanour had changed from that of caution to unbridled excitement as well. In this place of evil in its purest form, Hannah felt as though she had finally come home.

Hannah and Micah exited the Valley of the Shadow of Death for *Tit ha-Yawen,* the Hell of Man's Own Making, better known as Tartarus. Here the Prince of Darkness reigned supreme in the huge Castle of the Dead. Hannah would present herself before this self-proclaimed prince to be judged for her crimes or have her sentence commuted.

They'd successfully made it through the Valley of the Shadow of Death when they stopped to take a well-deserved rest from the bone-numbing cold. Micah led Hannah to an abandoned cabin in a wooded area abutting the valley. Hannah surmised this wasn't the first time Micah sought shelter in the cabin and that she wasn't the first soul he'd led on this journey. Hannah couldn't help but compare it to one of the cabins on Slave Row at Magnolia Hill.

The rickety cabin door squeaked in protest when Hannah followed Micah inside. The cabin boasted only the barest necessities. Inside the damp, musty interior and stacked neatly beside the front door was a pile of wood for the fireplace with a rusty hand hatchet lying nearby.

Beyond that were a small wooden table and two chairs. A dust-covered lantern and flint sat atop the table. A ratty blanket was folded in a corner on the floor. It didn't matter that there was no food or water since Hannah felt no hunger and, surprisingly enough, no thirst. Without a word, Hannah took the blanket up and wrapped it around her cold body.

She was more fatigued than she'd ever been, both in body and in spirit. All she wanted to do is sleep—to lie down and wake up outside this nightmare she found herself in. Before she could rest, Micah needed her to know what lay ahead.

"Our final destination will be *Tit ha-Yawen*. We'll have to cross the River Styxx, make our way through the dark forest, and enter through one of the seven gates of *Sha'are Zalmawet*, which is also known as the Hell of Seven Hells. *Sha'are Zalmawet* is a portal to *Tit ha-Yawen* where The Underworld is located. Our journey has just begun, Hannah." Micah was still talking when Hannah drifted off to sleep.

CHAPTER 28

IT SEEMED HANNAH had just closed her eyes when all too soon they were on their way. They travelled to the mouth of the River Styxx to hitch a ride on ferryman Charon's barge. Hannah had no tribute to give Charon in payment for her transport, and no matter how strongly she entreated he refused to take her to the opposite bank. Micah had coin, but not enough for both of them.

Hannah had come too far to let the matter of coin hinder her. Frustrated and determined to get to the other side, Hannah and Micah lay in wait for the next hapless soul to attempt crossing. They didn't have to wait long before an elderly man with a spring in his step approached the implacable oarsman.

Unlike Hannah, this was a beloved soul. His family had buried him with love and honour after a protracted illness. Hannah didn't know what this poor soul could have possibly done to earn a place in the same part of hell that she had. She didn't care. All she knew was that he probably had money in the pocket of his natty brown burial suit and nickels under the lids of his wrinkled eyes.

The old man didn't know what hit him. Hannah picked up a jagged rock on the bank of the river and bashed his head in. When he went down to his knees, she straddled him and, with the evil oarsman Charon looking on, pushed his head beneath the surface of the raging river, rendering him dead for the second time.

After the dirty deed was done, Hannah rifled through the man's pockets and extracted his coin, a box of flint, and a gold pocket watch with a picture of a white woman inside.

Huh. He probably stole it, she thought uncharitably.

Then she removed the nickels beneath the twice dead man's eyes. She didn't care if she had spirit blood on her hands. She now had sufficient coin with which to pay the ferry fee. At long last, she was on her way to meet the Prince of Darkness.

Tired and footsore after walking for what seemed like hours, they finally reached *Sha'are Zalmawet*, the Hell of Seven Hells. They came upon a dark narrow road leading up to a long stone wall at least fifteen feet in height with seven wrought-iron gates. Hannah looked to Micah in confusion when he stopped at the path in front of the first gate.

"Why are we stopping, Micah?" Hannah didn't like the look on Micah's face, and she cared even less for this place he'd led her to.

"*We* are not stopping, Hannah. I am. It is up to you to determine which of the seven gates you shall enter to reach your ultimate destination," he responded, leaving Hannah flabbergasted.

"Surely you don't intend for me to go in alone, Micah!"

Micah's responding laugh was anything but comforting. In fact, it bordered on mockery.

"Of course I don't expect you to enter alone, you silly girl. I have taken you this far, haven't I? I will accompany you on whichever path you choose, but the choice will be yours and yours alone, Hannah."

Hannah was mollified in the knowledge Micah would accompany her on yet another trial, but only moderately so. She slowly approached the first gate where a painfully thin man stood with huge, hungry eyes, a red slit for a mouth, and a long-beaked nose with a runny pink pimple on its bridge. His clothing was tattered and dirty and hung off his emaciated frame like a wooden coat rack. The man grabbed hold of two of the black iron bars, bringing his face flush with the gate.

"Come closer, Hannah," he entreated in an oily voice. "I have a secret to share with you, one that your companion cannot hear. Please come a little bit closer so that I can tell you my secret."

Hannah got no assistance from Micah, who sat comfortably perched upon the black grass with his legs twisted under him yogi style. She wondered briefly how the ugly man knew her name.

"How do you know me, demon?"

The thin man laughed. He didn't seem at all surprised that she knew what he was, but not who.

"Come closer to the gate, little witch woman, and I will tell you," he replied.

Cunning and careful were the credos for the day. Hannah did not trust this demon one bit.

"I am no witch, skeleton man. You'd do best to tell me what you want me to know from this distance."

"Alas, would that I could, but if I deliver my message from this distance, surely your companion over there will hear my words. Like I said, the message I have is meant for your ears and your ears alone." He gave Micah a glance and then sighed in an exaggerated dramatic fashion. "I fear we have ourselves a bit of a conundrum."

Hannah was curious, as he knew she would be. Against her better judgement, she drew nearer to the skeletal man, thinking maybe he would lead her directly to the castle. When she was within a few inches of the gate, he hawked up a thick, nasty glob of brownish-red spittle from the depths of his stomach and spat full in her face.

"That is for Salme and her unborn babe, you murdering bitch!" he roared.

Hannah recoiled as the foul-smelling spittle slammed into her face like a gunshot. A great deal of it struck her in the left eye before running down her cheek and into her mouth. She swiped her face repeatedly in an effort to wipe the thick slimy substance off, to no avail. It stuck to her hands and her face like black sorghum. Her eye began to itch and burn as if a spike covered with live fire ants had been shoved into the socket.

She spun around like a whirling dervish, wild with pain and screaming for Micah to help her, but no help was forthcoming. She was unable to open her eye. Taking deep measured breaths, she forced herself to calm down.

Breathe, she told herself. *Breathe. I don't know what the fuck is going on with Micah or that monster behind the gate, but I will not perish this close to my destination!*

She remembered a shallow creek they'd passed about a quarter mile back. *Can I make it there half blind? Can I make it alone?* She didn't want to go back through the frightening forest, especially not alone, but she had to clean out her eye which was now itching horribly. The same burrowing itching was beginning on her face and hands.

Hannah brought her hand up to her one good eye to see what was causing the itching. What she saw made her scream again and again. Inside the foul-smelling demon spittle were hundreds—maybe thousands—of baby maggots. Hannah dropped to her knees, spitting and retching to the sound of the thin man's maniacal laughter.

She must have passed out because the next thing she remembered was lying on the hard, cold ground a few feet from the first gate. Micah was now kneeling over her with a concerned look on his face. Somehow, he had miraculously located a source of water closer than the creek she'd spied earlier. He gently wiped her face with a cool wet rag he'd fashioned from a piece of the lower portion of his shirt. Hannah remained still as he ministered to her.

"You will have to let me clean out that eye," he said, tisking as he worked with deft efficiency. Micah was trying to pry Hannah's left eye open when she grabbed hold of his wrist, staying his hand. Her eye was sealed shut like a two-ton crypt door made of stone, and it hurt like the devil.

Not to be deterred, Micah extricated his wrist from Hannah's grasp and forced the swollen lids apart with his thumb and forefinger. Hannah's eye was an angry blood-red and crawling with white miniature maggots. The eye emitted copious tears and started to burn anew when the air hit it.

Hannah thrashed in discomfort while Micah held her head still. He used the wet rag to gently wipe inside the eye and under the swollen lid, sloughing away the maggots who were laying eggs and feeding upon the optic flesh.

Cool water ran down the side of her face and neck, and she felt immediate relief as Micah irrigated the eye. After he'd flushed her eye out for several minutes, Micah tied the wet cloth over Hannah's injured eye, deeming her fit to travel. She resembled a female pirate, with her tattered night clothes and makeshift eye patch. He took her arm and pulled her to her feet.

It didn't matter that Micah thought Hannah could continue on. Try as she might, she could not manage to place one foot in front of the other. Her feet felt like they were weighed down with lead anvils. She was afraid to move.

The thin spitting man was no longer at the first gate, but she heard the clanging of metal against metal coming from the direction of the second gate. Hannah canted her ear in the direction of the sound and tilted her head so that she could see through her one good eye.

The noise was coming from a naked man with skin the colour of Zanzibari sand and shrivelled black genitals that appeared to have been burned in a fire. He was baldheaded with no lashes, brows, or hair anywhere on his body.

The man paced back and forth like a caged animal on the prowl, running a long stick against the iron rungs of the gate. Sparks flew off the metal bars as he snarled, bearing long, sharp, yellow-fanged teeth. After what happened behind the first gate, Hannah knew to keep her distance from this demon. Evil radiated off this being like the heat from a funeral pyre. Unlike the demon behind the first gate, this one didn't hide his enmity.

He looks like he wants to tear me from limb to limb and sup on my brains, she thought. There was *nothing* that could make Hannah walk through this particular gate and she told Micah so.

"If I draw any closer to this evil being, I will suffer far worse than a maggot-filled eye, Micah. I will not enter this gate. Please accompany me to the next."

Micah reminded Hannah of her purpose.

"As you wish, Hannah, but remember we had but three days to make it to the castle and already we have used two. You must choose your path. You cannot remain on this side of the wall much longer. You must choose one of the seven gates or suffer the consequences."

Hannah didn't bother to ask exactly what would happen if they remained on this side of the stone wall. She already knew something horrible would happen. From what she could see, however, something equally horrible awaited her on the other side of the wall.

Hannah approached the third gate with Micah by her side and trepidation in her heart. She was surprised to find the third gate partially open and no one behind it. A natural sense of self-preservation screamed out to her.

Do not enter this gate.

But even as her psyche trumpeted a warning, she knew this was the gate she would ultimately walk through. One of Hannah's eyes was covered, but she could see well enough with the other. There was danger behind that gate. Micah didn't hesitate to state the obvious.

"Look, Hannah. This gate is already open." He demonstrated the safety behind the gate by pushing it further open and stepping through. "There are no menacing demons to threaten your well-being behind this gate," he assured, extending his hand to her. "Come with me. Let us face your destiny together."

Hannah could see no threat on the other side of the gate, but she felt imminent danger as keenly as a forest animal before a storm. "I cannot, Micah. I am sorry, but I cannot.

With that, the hair stood up on the back of her neck. She heard a terrible howling further down the path. The sound didn't come from the wind. It was coming from one of the other gates.

Although the gate hung partially open, it was anything but welcoming. It protested with a sinister rusty squeal when Micah pushed it the rest of the way open to allow Hannah entrance.

Before she lost her courage or had time to think better of it, Hannah took Micah's extended hand and stepped through the portal of the third gate. As soon as her foot touched the other side, the gate automatically closed and the lock clicked shut.

There was no turning back now.

CHAPTER 29

MICAH LED HANNAH through the perils of hell for two and a half days without her voicing one single complaint. During that time Hannah felt neither thirst, hunger, nor excessive fatigue. The wounds she received outside the cave had miraculously healed, and though it was bitterly cold she was no worse for wear. Not once during her odyssey had she felt the urge to perform any natural bodily functions.

But when Hannah stepped through the entrance of the third gate, every single human frailty came back with a vengeance. Thirst hit her in the face like a bag of rusty nails. Her tongue and mouth became bone dry, her throat lined with sandpaper. She would have done just about anything for a cup of cool water.

I thirst like a camel too long on the desert, yet I have to pee so badly I feel my bladder will burst.

The unremitting thirst and need to eliminate did nothing to overshadow her hunger. She was so hungry she'd have taken a bite out of Micah if she didn't need him to escort her through this hellish new existence. It was while she was looking for a bush or tree behind which to relieve herself that she finally adjusted her uninjured eye to the darkness and was able to take note of her surroundings.

Mile upon mile of dark barren wasteland separated by a long twisted walkway and hideous trees encompassed this place of perpetual night. The trees that flanked both sides of the walkway were blackened as if burnt by the devil's own hot breath. Twisted leafless branches and twigs reached out like greedy hands. The otherworldly trees were anchored upon a network of roots that undulated under the surface of the ground like hungry anaconda. Hannah dared not step behind one of these trees to relieve herself if she valued her continued well-being.

Crows flocked everywhere. Hundreds of them perched upon the limbs of the trees, their beady black eyes following Hannah's every step. Here and there, as though posed in a macabre form of art, were the bloodless bodies of what had once been humans. Their grisly remains were impaled upon long metal spikes as crows greedily feasted upon their eyes and entrails. Everything was shrouded in a thick foggy mist. At the centre of it all was *Castellum Regnum Mortuorum*, the Castle of the Dead.

Most castles were built from earth, timber, and stone, but the seat of the dark prince was built from the powdered bones of the vanquished and mortared in the blood of unrepentant sinners. It was a demonic military fortress, designed to keep enemies out and prisoners in. All who approach do so at their own risk.

The central keep was surrounded by six towers, three on each side. The towers were so high Hannah had to crane her neck to see the crenellated tops. The arrow slits appeared as evil eyes staring down on her, waiting for the right opportunity to destroy her.

The wind carried the sound of swords clashing, grunts, and shrieks of agony. Countless battles, demonic laughter, and screams of torture resounded like a huge bell clanging in her head. The den was so deafening, Hannah had to cover her ears. She spoke in a frightened voice just above a whisper, so fearful was she that she might inadvertently awaken yet another group of unseen monsters.

"Tell me what is this place, Micah?"

"This is the seat of the Son of Satan's own kingdom and the place of countless battles. Here is where the fallen gathered after their expulsion from the celestial choir. They were warring angels, every one of them. Their thirsts for power did not end after the fall. Many have tried and failed to unseat our mighty prince. Just as sure as we are born of a woman and have to die, those like you, Hannah, have to face the master. Come, I will take you to him."

They were at the end of the walkway. Rusty chains groaned as the castle drawbridge was lowered, sending a wordless invitation for them to enter. Hannah hurried across the drawbridge to escape the threat of snapping sea beasts coming from the moat below and the foul smell that seemed to envelope the area surrounding the castle. She took comfort in hearing Micah's steady footsteps behind her.

No sooner had Hannah entered into the gatehouse through the inner ward of the castle's scarred wooden door than a question came to mind. She turned to Micah, but instead of the tall, familiar figure who had stewarded her across miles and miles of fire and brimstone, she found herself staring into the accusing dark eyes of her grandmother Zahara.

Zahara's slit throat made for a second lipless mouth beneath her chin, similar to the manner Hannah had left her on that fateful rainy night in Zanzibar. The castle door slammed behind them. Hannah was trapped like a rat and would have to fight for her spirit life.

Zahara had a ceremonial dagger fisted in her hand which, had Hannah not turned when she did, would have been plunged to the hilt in her back. Instead, the knife's sharp blade grazed the tip of Hannah's shoulder, opening the skin and exposing bone in a painful three-inch gash.

Zahara's body had the look and smell of advanced decay. Her clothing carried dust from the grave with each step she took. Rotten flesh hung from her bones. Insects crawled in and out of every opening of her body, temporarily pausing their feast on her flesh.

This can't be happening, Hanna bemoaned. *My grandmother is dead. Hell, I killed her!*

Remembering that she too was dead, Hannah acknowledged the knife-wielding corpse in front of her was all too real. There was no time to wonder about the sheer absurdity of the situation she was in. Hannah knew she was in a fight for her life.

Zahara was unstoppable, advancing like something without feeling while wielding her vicious blade with alacrity. Zahara continued to slice at the defenceless Hannah's arms, chest, and face. Hannah was at a disadvantage with one bad eye and no weapon with which to defend herself. Already she bore deep defensive wounds in her palms and forearms, and she was near blind from the blood running into her one good eye.

There was bloodlust in Zahara's eyes as she moved in for the kill. A flash of bright blue light slashed through the darkness, temporarily illuminating the room before Zahara could deliver the blow to finish Hannah off. Hannah caught a quick glimpse of a man whom she somehow knew without being told was Rajab bin Mohammed bin Said el Murgebi—her grandfather.

He was dressed as men of old and had the same cruel twist to his lips as her father. The grandfather Hannah never met had died before she was born. He threw her a weapon.

Yes. Now the odds are even! I killed the old bitch once, and I'll do it again.

Hannah grasped the weapon in both hands and fearlessly countered the dead woman's attack with stabs, feigns, and thrusts of her own. Zahara appeared to feel none of the wounds Hannah inflicted upon her, but then Hannah saw an opening. She moved forward with authority, plunging the weapon into Zahara's heart. Her grandmother vanished in a puff of smoke along with her grandfather.

Covered in blood and heaving from exertion, Hannah spun around with the knife in her hand, waiting for the next attack. There was no one else to fight. She was utterly and completely alone. Fear returned to claim her when the walls around her started to breathe in excitement.

There was no handle on the inside of the castle's main door. Even if she could find a way to open the huge wooden door, Hannah didn't know if she had the courage to face what lay outside now that she was alone. She felt like she was on the deck of a ship as the floor upon which she stood started to move in concert with the walls. Heavy breathing filled the room. For obvious reasons, she could not remain where she was.

Guided by a scant bit of light from the moon coming through a small high window, Hannah felt along the writhing walls until she came upon a torch mounted in a sconce. She fumbled in her pocket for the flint she'd taken from the old man's pocket at the banks of the River Styxx, hoping against hope she had not lost it. She sighed with relief when her hand closed around the treasured item.

She lit the torch and made her way to a wooden door on the opposite side of the room. The door was black and scarred with grooves that looked suspiciously like scratch marks. Were it not for the torch, the door would have appeared as one with the wall.

The door dared Hannah to enter, mocking her with its ominous silence. Taking a deep breath, Hannah opened the door with shaky hands to what lay beyond. Its squeaky hinges reluctantly opened into a large foyer with yet another small window, a cold stone floor, and naught else but a huge tapestry that took up the entire left wall.

Hannah stood before the tapestry, transfixed. She had never seen anything so disturbing, yet at the same time so beautiful. Whoever designed the tapestry was a master of the art. The attention to detail was exquisite, making the tapestry all the more frightening.

It depicted a monstrous horned man with thick muscular thighs and black demon wings, sitting astride a huge black charger. The man was dressed in full black chainmail. Hannah couldn't miss his long, barbed tail hanging over the destrier's wide barrel or the menace that radiated from the piece. Man and horse appeared ready to leap from the wall at any moment.

It took a great deal of effort for Hannah to look away, but when she did she spied two more closed doors—one directly in front of her, the other to her right. She opened the door on her right. The flame from the torch she held cast an eerie shadow on the wall behind her and left a trail of swirling black smoke as she descended the stairs.

Hannah saw light in the distance. She wanted to pick up the pace, but her bare feet were slippery with sweat and the stone steps were slick with moisture. Plus, she had only one good eye. She had to tread carefully.

She heard the clanging of metal against metal and the hissing of steam or bellows.

"Could this way lead to the smith?" she wondered aloud. There was only one way to find out.

CHAPTER 30

SURELY THIS CASTLE *is a maze,* she thought when she left the last step behind her and saw what lay ahead. She was faced with three more doors. Never a patient person under the best of circumstances, it seemed to Hannah that the castle was playing a cruel, twisted game with her and she didn't like it one bit. The sounds she'd heard from the steps proved to be illusive, escaping to a place beyond reach as the castle drew Hannah deeper and deeper into its bowels.

This time Hannah didn't hesitate to open the door nearest her. She was most anxious to find out where the mysterious closed door would lead her. She moved her hand toward the knob and returned it to her side three times before she could summon the courage to grasp the knob, turn it, and pull the door open.

She was relieved to find there was only another flight of stairs leading her to a lower level in the castle. She hurried down the stairs to put as much space as possible between herself and the spectre of her long-dead grandmother.

The clashing of metal upon metal grew louder as each step drew her nearer. By the time she reached the bottom of the steps, she also heard voices. Hannah followed the voices down a narrow torch-lit hall which opened up to a huge room. She had unwittingly found the castle's torture chamber.

If the stairs leading down to the basement were the intestines of the castle, surely the room she'd been led to was its anus—dark, moist, and crammed with all kinds of wicked shit. The room was long and narrow with walls of blood-covered brick on stone. The smell of death, excrement, and fear crawled through her nostrils and travelled down her throat, threatening to turn her inside out.

Hopeless screams of the dying echoed off the walls. There was nowhere to look and nowhere to hide to escape the horrors.

Hannah had endured much before, during, and after her spirit had broken away from her body on Magnolia Hill, but nothing could prepare her for this. If the evil in the castle was trying to break her, it had succeeded. Hannah walked trancelike—an invisible intruder—around one torture device after the other.

A man was screaming for mercy as the soles of his feet were being slowly roasted over a bed of hot coals. The sickening odour of charred human flesh was nauseating. His plaintive cries were like nails being hammered into her eardrums. Hannah raised shaking hands to cover her ears.

The bellow Hannah heard earlier was being used to control the intensity of the heat. The man working the bellows didn't pause or acknowledge Hannah's presence as he brought his helpless victim to the brink of true death and then snatched him back from the precipice in time to prolong his suffering.

Yet another unfortunate soul screamed for mercy while a huge bald-headed man clad in only a leather facemask and breechcloth approached with a tongue tearer. All Hannah could see was the man's broad, sweaty back when he straddled the screaming victim. She heard a squeal of pain and then ominous silence after the victim's tongue was torn out with the large metal pliers.

A scantily dressed young girl was tied to a contraption called The Rack. She lay across a hard wooden board by her ankles and wrists. Her eyes were huge with fear. Hannah watched as another masked man turned rollers on either side of the board, pulling the girl's slender body in opposite directions. She screamed again and again as every joint in her body was dislocated.

A torture device called Iron Maiden stood in one corner. Hannah deduced it was occupied based upon the blood pooling around its base and the whimpering sounds from within. The device was aptly named because of its iron cabinet. The inside of the cabinet was lined with metal spikes, strategically placed to impale the average-sized victim in the eyes, chest, and back. There were no spikes placed where there were vital organs to ensure maximum suffering and protracted pain before death.

Yet another man was strapped by the neck and completely immobilised by a torture device called a Heretic's Fork, which resembled a large metal horseshoe. In the centre of the metal horseshoe was a horizontal metal bar with two sharp tines at each end. At one end of the device, the tines were partially embedded under the man's quivering chin; the lower tines were gradually pushing into his sternum, causing the hapless victim what appeared to be indescribable pain. One wrong move and he would be impaled chin and belly. Hannah couldn't take anymore.

If there is a way out of this hell-hole, I will find it, she thought with renewed determination.

Hannah was bound and determined to get out of the castle, even if it meant retracing the steps she'd already tread. It would be better to take her chances outside than to meet the fates of any of the people in this room. She was about to make good on her plan when the man in the Heretic's Fork called out to her.

"Please help me. I beg of you. Please help me."

Hannah debated whether she would go to him or not. Deciding he could do her little or no harm, she stepped closer.

"What do you expect I can do for you, old man?"

He turned his jaundiced eyes in the direction of several sharp objects lined up on the wall behind her. "Please. Take down one of those knives and cut the strap to this device. Set me free."

"And what will you do for me if I set you free?"

The old man looked at Hannah like she was out of her mind.

"I assume you want to get out of here. I can help you. I know the way out. I can get you to safety, but you must first help me get out of here."

Hannah was not easily misled.

"How do I know you will not do me harm once I set you free? I do not trust you or anyone I encounter in this terrible place."

Tears came to the old man's eyes, yet Hannah was unmoved.

"Pon my word," he said, "I will lead you out of here and you need never look back."

Hannah didn't have anything to lose. She chose a wicked-looking blade from the assortment of weapons and torture devices lining the wall and went to work sawing at the thick leather strap.

"Hurry! They can't see you, but they can see me!"

The "they" he was referring to were any one of the five massive, sweaty brutes performing acts of torture in the underground dungeon.

"Once you get me free, we will away down the hall to the right. There is a door which leads to a lower level where a small floor-level window leads outside. Please hurry!"

Hannah did the opposite. She slowed down. She needed to know if this old man really knew what he was talking about.

"How do you know about this window?"

"I know about the window because I have escaped through it, but these old legs ain't what they used to be and they caught me before I could get very far. That's how I earned a spot in this blasted place. This time we will make directly for the woods and hide ourselves until the danger passes. So hurry! Let us away from here!"

Finally, there was hope. There *was* a way to get out of the castle. Hannah placed her hands on both sides of the old man's head in an affectionate gesture. Her expression softened. The old man thought she was about to kiss him. Instead, she tightened her grip on his head and slammed his face into the sharp metal tines. Hot blood sprayed out of the wounds in his chin, covering the front of Hannah's gown. His eyes were wide open and his expression one of incredulity as Hannah walked away without a backward glance.

I'm getting the fuck out of here, and I'm getting out now. The last thing I need is a wounded old man slowing me down!

Hannah's eye was throbbing under the rag patch as she made her way down the hallway to the right of the dungeon door. The itch in her eye was so bothersome she would have gouged it out of its socket had she the courage to do so.

A sticky substance on the floor adhered to the soles of her bare feet, making a squishy sound with each footfall. The way was dark, the hallway narrow. Her wounds and limited vision made her fearful of what lay ahead. She was three quarters of the way down the hall when something overhead swooped down and grabbed her by her long hair, lifted her off her feet, and rendered her airborne.

CHAPTER 31

HANNAH WAS UNCEREMONIOUSLY dumped on a stone-flagged floor in what she surmised was the castle's great hall. She landed in a crouched position like a cat. Having accomplished the task at hand, the harpy who absconded her joined three others who were noisily flying overhead. Her scalp throbbed where the harpy's claws had pulled her hair out by the root. She appeared less than human—like a feral animal, chest heaving, and her big yellow teeth revealed in a snarl. She cast her head to the side like the animal she had become. She could hear a soft whisper inside her head. "You are in a monster's lair," it said. "Be wary."

She angrily pushed the dark veil of hair out of her face in response to the inner voice and raised her head to take in her surroundings as best she could with her one good eye.

Directly in front of her was a black iron throne so massive it could comfortably seat any one of the fabled giants of old. The imposing royal seat had an exaggerated high back with intricately soldered demonic symbols running along its borders and on its thick squat legs. The armrests were made of powdered bone and thousands of teeth that glowed like mother of pearl.

The seat and back of the throne, and several furnishings throughout the great hall, were upholstered with the flesh of countless enemies whom the prince had vanquished. He took apparent pleasure in placing his royal ass upon the flesh of his victims.

Hannah couldn't suppress a shudder as she took in the rest of the hall. To the left of the demon prince's throne was a whipping post. Hannah blinked the sweat out of her good eye several times. *Surely I am hallucinating.* Micah, whom Hannah now clearly recognised as Binta's son Hacim, was slumped against the splintered wooden post with ribbons of flesh dangling from his lifeless body.

An invisible fist forced the memory of Hacim's last day of life inside Hannah's head. Against her will, she now vividly recalled that hot afternoon when her father had ordered the innocent young slave boy beaten in the courtyard for all to witness and her role in his demise. Hannah did not recant her lie even after she was made aware the innocent youth was none other than her loyal nursemaid's only son.

She could clearly see the direction this visit to the great hall would take and she didn't like it one damn bit. Now she wasn't so sure she wanted to meet the infamous prince. But like it or not, before his "royalness" deigned to show up, it appeared she would have to take an unpleasant stroll down memory lane.

Her next unwelcomed visitor was Zahara. This time, however, she was not surprised when her late grandmother reappeared. Dressed in a burial shroud befitting African royalty, her grandmother's body was on display in a wooden funeral bier lying upon a stone altar surrounded by black candles. Zahara appeared to be sleeping as the light of the candles cast an eerie glow upon her smooth mahogany skin. There was no evidence of the wounds Hannah had inflicted during their previous battle.

The soft whisper inside Hannah's head became a scream. *You have to get out of here. You have to get out of here. You have to get out of here. Now!*

Hannah spun around, looking for a way out. Every exit was barred by a red-eyed demon. The harpies still flew in the rafters, waiting for her to make one false move so that they could pick her off. She had treated Hacim and Zahara unjustly.

Too damn bad. They are dead, she thought with no remorse. It appeared they wanted to exact their revenge, even if it need be from the grave.

But not if I have anything to do with it. When you can't flee, you must fight. Hannah was prepared to stand and deliver.

A gigantic chimney was set in the south wall between two small, high windows that were illuminated by the light of the blood-red moon. The walls were decorated with spears, banners, and mediaeval weapons the likes of which she'd never seen before.

The heat from two huge fireplaces with carved-over mantels outlined her sorry condition and contributed to the sheen of sweat that stuck her night-rail to her battered body. Her palms dripped with sweat.

Hannah ran in the direction of the weapons mounted above one of the fireplaces. In her haste to get her hands on one of the weapons, she knocked over a chair, causing a lantern to topple. She dragged one of the skin-covered stools over to the base of the fireplace. She would need it to gain the height necessary to reach a huge sabre she intended to use to defend herself.

She never did get her hands on that weapon because seemingly out of nowhere her father's dead wife Salme popped in front of her. Salme wore a bloody night-rail and clutched a dead baby tightly in her arms. Pretty little Salme's corpse showed the ravages of the grave. Part of her flesh had melted away with time or been eaten by grave-burrowing rodents. Her once glorious mane of coal black hair was thin, wispy, and bald in places. Her lips were blue from the poison Hannah had used to kill her and her unborn babe. Her eyes were accusatory, but nothing could disguise her intent.

No. No. No. No. No. This can't be happening, Hannah thought with despair.

Before she could fully process what she was seeing, her old nursemaid Binta quietly entered the great hall through a door behind the throne. Binta paid less attention to Hacim, Zahara, and Hannah than she would pay to a stranger on a busy street. She walked past her son's dead body, cradling a tiny kitten in her plump brown arms. The kitten had one blue eye and one green. It purred with contentment while Binta stroked its fluffy fur, cooing in that soft sing-song voice Hannah remembered so well.

"Sweet kitty kitty. That's my sweet little kitty."

Binta shuffled along like a human marionette, drawing closer and closer to the corner Hannah had backed into. Unaccountably frightened by this new, seemingly innocuous threat, Hannah backed even further away like a cornered animal. Binta drew ever nearer, with a look of madness in her eyes and the smell of the grave about her.

Something had freed Hacim from the whipping post. He inched toward Hannah, shambling step by painful step, leaving a trail of skin and blood behind him. A low keening sound rose from his throat and exited his mouth like a hot spring geyser.

Slowly, as if summoned by some unseen master, Zahara rose from the casket, hoisted her slight body out of its wooden confines, and slid over the side of the altar. Hannah picked up the smell of burning cloth as one of the sleeves of Zahara's burial shroud brushed against a candle and caught fire. Like the others, Zahara immediately focused her attention on Hannah. The hate radiating from her dark eyes was scorching. Zahara moved inexorably closer to Hannah as the flames greedily licked their way up her arm.

Hannah's lips trembled. They were all closing in on her: Binta, Hacim, Salme, and Zahara.

Her attention shot back to Binta.

"No one will ever hurt you again, little kitty," Binta said, before tossing the kitten in the air near Hannah. The tiny kitten transformed in mid-air into a swamp lynx with teeth bared and claws poised for attack. Hannah curled up in a ball to protect her face.

"Enough!"

That one word, spoken with unquestionable authority, undoubtedly saved Hannah's spirit life. Demons and the dead alike fell to their knees, and Hannah followed suit. Shaken, she slowly raised her head to look at her timely saviour. What she beheld caused her to piss on herself.

An eerie quiet came over the great hall. The quiet was so profound, the sound of the piss running down Hannah's legs resounded like the beat of a thousand drums.

The Dark Prince had arrived to hold court. He was evil incarnate, and yet so very beautiful in face and form that it hurt Hannah's eyes to look upon him. Instead, she focused her timid gaze upon his boot-shod feet. She was compelled to prostrate herself. Like the lowest snake in the Garden of Eden, she crawled on her belly to kiss the toes of his boots.

Though chains had bound her physically during her captivity, she had never claimed a master spiritually—that is, not until now. Her true master stood before her in all his splendid, wicked glory. She was enraptured.

He wore his shoulder-length hair pulled back from his face in a long slick braid as thick as sailor's hemp. His skin was a beautiful burnt copper and, except for his eyes, his features were almost feminine. His eyes held the secrets of every evil and every evildoer, and they were as dark as the deepest pit in the lowest level of the seven hells.

He strutted back and forth in front of Hannah, preening like a proud peacock before finally standing still to unabashedly strike a pose. Dressed in an ankle-length great coat over unrelieved black clothing that hugged his body like a second skin, he proffered an obscene display of his tight muscular thighs, taut buttocks, and bestial-sized genitals. He was a little under six feet tall and covered with muscles that rippled through his form-fitting clothing with every move he made.

After he gave Hannah adequate time to drink in every aspect of his magnificence, he swept his long coat out of the way to reveal a long-barbed tail. The Dark Prince regally strode to the front of the great hall to sit upon his throne, followed by an entourage of six hideous demons.

The Dark Prince looked down on the mess that was Hannah as if she was less than dung beneath his feet.

"I see you know your place," he said imperiously. "Rise. I will have a word with you."

Hannah rose on shaking feet.

"I suspect you are wondering why you are here and not left to the devices of my clever band of torturers as you so rightfully deserve, yes?"

His question was met with silence. "You may speak."

"Yes, Your…forgive me, but I do not know how I should address you," she stuttered in a shaking voice.

The Dark Prince was quick to respond. "You will address me in accordance with what I am—the Great Abaddon, the Angel of the Bottomless Pit, Ruler of Demons, the Roaring Lion, the Great Dragon, the Serpent of Old, the Son of Perdition or the Angel of Light. I am known by many names, but, for the time being, I will allow you to address me as Master."

"Master, I would like to know why I am here," she inquired respectfully.

Quicker than a bolt of lightning can strike a tree during a thunderstorm, the Dark Prince's long, barbed tail struck Hannah a glancing blow in the face, opening her cheek about a quarter inch below her bad eye to her chin. The pain was knee-buckling. Hannah flung her hand to her injured cheek to staunch the copious flow of blood.

"I did not give you further leave to speak, worm, nor did I give you permission to question me. But since I happen to be in a magnanimous mood, I will answer your impudent question."

"We are in the midst of a war, a war that has been raging since my father and his followers were unjustly expelled from the heavens by that lackey Michael and his band of pseudo warrior angels. I was but a defenceless babe when it happened and unable to prevent being brought into Michael's household. I was patient, however, and I waited, eventually convincing the fool that he had somehow changed my nature. All the while I was in the service of my father. I misled Michael and his master once, and I shall do it again," he stated proudly.

"The Watcher Angel, Azazel, lies trapped somewhere on earth, his powers bound by celestial chains. I need for him to be free. One day we will regain our rightful estate, and I will claim my true throne at the right hand of my father."

He began to pace.

"In the interim, there are several obstacles that need to be overcome before I can achieve my ultimate goal to claim total domination of the heavens, the earth, of the entire universe. Most of these obstacles exist on earth. That is where you come in, little worm.

"I am trapped, bound by the powers that be, and forced to reign in this dark kingdom for at least the next thousand years. I intend to significantly shorten the time of my banishment. You and your line will destroy every earthly impediment and tear down every boundary standing in my way. I have waited a long time for the Angel of Death to bring you to me, little worm. A very long time."

"May I speak, Master?" Hannah asked, taking extreme care to couch her question in a respectable tone. The demon nodded his ignoble head in assent.

"Why have you chosen me for this colossal task, Master?"

"Cain's punishment for slaying his brother Abel was to have the melanin stripped from his body and to bear the mark of white skin in a sea of blackness as he wandered in the Land of Nod. He didn't suffer his banishment alone, little worm. There were children born to Adam and Eve other than Cain, Abel, and Seth. Cain took with him several of his own sisters when he travelled into Nod, and he bore children with them.

"Cain's grandson, Lamech the Murderer, sired a daughter. That daughter, named Naamah, bore my child during the time when I was a member of the Order of Watcher Angels. I have chosen you because you are the last remaining descendant of the line of Cain with the correct temperament that is required for the task, little worm. Most of your ancestors are currently slow-roasting in Tartarus and are of no use to me for this purpose.

"You belong to me, little worm, mind, body, and soul. You and your seed will serve me in all things or you will die a thousand deaths, and I will revive you again and again so that you will continue to suffer until the end of time."

"Upon my honour, I will serve you faithfully, Master," Hannah vowed, fervently declaring fealty to the son of the Satan. The Dark Prince's responding laughter shook the walls of the great hall.

"You have no honour, little worm. That is one of the reasons why you are the perfect choice for the job I have set before you.

"It is a shame that you will not live long enough to enjoy the sweet taste of my victory. By the time my plan takes root, you will be a distant memory, and the worms will have eaten the flesh off the bones of your descendants, and the bones themselves will be naught but dust. But I will see that you get everything you deserve for your service to me, little worm. I promise you that."

The Dark Prince rose from his throne and strolled to stand directly in front of Hannah.

"First, I will send you back to the land of the living. It is not your time yet, little worm. You have much work to do. There is danger from the slave woman named Flossie and those of her line," he forewarned.

"Upon your return you must go to the wooded area abutting Magnolia Hill and retrieve King Solomon's *Grimoire* which you buried near the base of the red maple tree. I have supplemented it with dark majick. Take it and memorise its contents, for therein lies the key to defeat my earthly enemies."

Hannah couldn't help but wonder if the *Grimoire* she had penned mirrored the one she had stolen from Zahara and subsequently lost.

He placed his hand upon Hannah's forehead. The fire from his touch burned every cell in her body. She felt her spirit spiralling through a swirling void as he spoke.

"Serve me and you shall prosper in all things. I will give those of your blood power and wealth beyond your wildest imagination. You and yours shall prevail over your enemies. You have but to open the door for those who follow me and prepare the way for my coming, Mehwish Shumaila bin Said al-Murgebi."

Hannah closed her eyes in utter and complete bliss.

Ah, his voice is music to my ears. He called me by my true given name, Mehwish Shumaila. Beautiful as the moon.

CHAPTER 32

Magnolia Hill

ANNAH'S BURIAL TEAM consisted of Nina Mae, Merle, and Jessie—all field hands. They assisted Flossie in preparing Hannah's body and that of her babe for burial. All three women would sooner spit on Hannah than speak to her, but they were all professed Christians in their own fashion who believed even a she-devil like Hannah deserved a decent burial.

The women worked quietly and efficiently. The body of the stillborn baby girl had already been cleaned and lovingly swaddled in a pristine white towel taken from the Big House. She would be buried in the casket alongside her mother.

Flossie broke the silence, humming a familiar song old Cook used to sing, as she tilted Hannah's naked body to the side so that Nina Mae and Merle could wash the back of her body clean. Jessie solemnly stood holding the plain white shroud they would bury Hannah in.

Flossie had been able to force Hannah's mouth shut and lower the lids of her eyes to hide her final accusatory stare, but there was not much she could do to mask the obvious suffering she'd endured.

Even in death there was a menacing look about her. It showed itself in the blood pooling underneath the surface of her yellow skin and in the down-turned curve of her mouth. A crevice filled with a lifetime of spiteful ire had taken up residence between Hannah's close-set eyes. She had died blaspheming God's name and with a curse upon her lips. Flossie doubted there would be any forgiveness for a creature such as Hannah.

Flossie submerged a bloody washcloth in water heated by a low fire. She wrung out the cloth and, one by one, gently uncurled Hannah's clinched fingers so that she could wipe each one clean. Flossie was thorough, getting beneath the nails and around the cuticles where dried blood was embedded.

Gently, as if she were ministering to her own child, she washed the blood off Hannah's face and cracked lips. *The bible says 'Love thine enemy. Bless them that curse you.'*

Even now Flossie didn't want to touch her, but, as always, she did what was right. It was not for her to judge. Hannah would be judged by the Almighty and all the lesser Gods for each of her crimes and not by a lowly slave woman like herself.

Once Hannah's body was clean and wrapped in the white burial shroud, Flossie positioned the dead woman's hands across her chest. She then placed a metal plate on top of Hannah's hands to prevent her spirit from leaving the confines of the coffin. Hannah had been hell on wagon wheels when she was alive. Flossie didn't want to think about what kind of evil spirit would come out of the likes of someone like Hannah.

Best to keep the spirit of that bitch bound, she thought.

"She sure did have some pretty hair," Nina Mae commented as she brushed the dead woman's hair until it shone.

The texture of Hannah's thick curly hair had been a source of envy amongst the slave women.

Hannah stoked the fire of that envy every chance she got by flipping her long locks in the faces of the slave women whose short, nappy hair could not be coaxed into white folk's hair styles. Hannah's cruelty would not be missed.

Burials were attended to quickly and efficiently on Magnolia Hill. Due to the oppressive heat, decomposition advanced at an accelerated rate, feeding upon flesh and blood and rendering what was left of the deceased to nothing but bone and dust. The burial would take place that very evening after the day's chores were completed.

Generally speaking, burials were well-attended by resident slaves and slaves on neighbouring plantations. Hannah's burial would be the exception. Other than Saul, the grave digger, and his grandson Joseph, the carpenter, Flossie doubted there would be anyone to attend Hannah and her babe's burial. Flossie would follow the casket to the grave for no other reason than to make sure the evil woman was truly dead. Once Hannah and her babe were planted in the ground, life would go on as if they had never existed.

The burial team was completing the final details on Hannah's body. The rickety wheels of the carpenter's wagon could be heard pulling up outside Flossie's cabin. The coffin sat in the bed of the carpenter's wagon. Flossie turned to Jessie.

"Joseph will load the bodies into the coffin. Go to her cabin and see if you can find some personal items to place in the coffin with her."

Jessie scurried off to do Flossie's bidding. It was customary to place some personal items inside the coffin to appease the spirits. Hannah may have rejected her African blood and spurned her slave brothers and sisters, but Flossie intended to see to it that she and her infant would be buried in the same manner as all the other slaves on Magnolia Hill—east to west with her head facing east and her feet to the west toward their African homeland across the vast ocean. In that position, neither she nor her infant would have to turn around in their graves to face the mighty angel Gabriel when he blows his trumpet on Resurrection Day.

By the time Jessie returned with a piece of red ribbon and a crudely carved small wooden statue of a man with a ponderous belly, long thin arms and legs, and exaggerated facial features, Joseph had already carefully arranged Hannah and her babe's body in the coffin. Flossie placed the two items inside the casket before Joseph put the lid on the coffin and nailed it shut.

The mewling of a kitten and the listing of the wagon over the pits and ruts dotting the dirt road leading from the slave quarters to the burial grounds jostled Hannah awake as if from a deeply disturbing sleep. Her eyes sprang open. She was fearful the kitten in her dreams was the same monster cat that had attacked her while she was in Incarnadine's domain.

She opened her eyes to total darkness, stifling heat, and limited movement.

The smell of fresh pine wood surrounded her. Her hands were weighed down with a smooth metal object. She pushed the metal plate aside. When her fingers touched the face of the baby lying next to her, she was able to fully comprehend what was happening to her.

It wasn't a kitten that had awakened her from the dead. It was the plaintive cries of her baby. Reality slammed against her face like a careening carriage crashing into a solid brick wall. *I'll be damned; they've buried me alive!*

She panicked. The baby's cries echoed inside the wooden coffin. A scream burned the inside of Hannah's throat. It tore its way out of her mouth, only to bounce off the insides of her pine death trap.

She banged on the lid of the coffin, but the limited space prohibited her from extending her arms and striking the fresh wood with enough force to be heard from beneath the soil. The walls of the coffin were closing in on her and she was finding it hard to breathe. Out of her mind with fear, she clawed at the raw pine, ripping off her fingernails in a desperate attempt to fight her way out.

Suddenly she heard voices and felt movement. They had not put her in the grave yet. She must be in the carriage on the way to the slave graveyard. There was still a chance!

She frantically felt around in the dark coffin for the metal plate. It had slipped between her hip and the side of the coffin. When her bloody, fingers touched the plate, she grabbed hold of it like it was a lifeline. With both hands, she rammed the end of the metal plate against the lid of the coffin. When the wagon carrying her coffin stopped, she renewed her efforts until she heard instruments prying the nails sealing the coffin loose.

Hannah sucked in a deep breath of air when the lid of the coffin was lifted, allowing the light of the sun to shine upon her face. She heard Flossie exclaim, "My God. My God. The devil's handmaiden has arisen."

CHAPTER 33

RIGHT AFTER CLAUDE'S eldest son, Henri, was sent to Europe under a dark cloud of shame, Claude's youngest son, Julien, set a date to marry Justine Drayton, his fiancée of several years. After trying to get pregnant for five years and just as many miscarriages, Justine finally managed to push a living child out of her scarecrow-thin body. It was a boy. Every white person within a fifty-mile radius was coming to celebrate as if the baby was the return of the messiah instead of another monster with the last name Etienne.

Carriages were already lined up along the long circular drive leading up to the front door of Magnolia Hill. As soon as the sun rose, the ornate double wooden doors would be flung open in welcome to the remaining guests. A big "down-home" southern style cookout with all the fixins' was planned for Saturday following a fancy ball the night before.

From the look of things, and the pulsing ache inside of Flossie's bones, there wasn't going to be any fancy cookout, planned or not. Dark clouds were gathering overhead and the smell of rain was in the air. The Etiennes thought they were gods, but even they couldn't control the weather.

Claude Etienne and his wife Janine wanted a special meal prepared today. Justine's parents, William and Caroline Drayton of Drayton Hall, had arrived two days ago to assist in ironing out all of the final details for the celebration. Claude's wife, Janine, specifically requested fried green tomatoes with two kinds of shrimp for dinner—shrimp remoulade and sugarcane shrimp.

The Draytons were frequent visitors to Magnolia Hill. They were partial to Flossie's hot and spicy blackened drum fish fillets. Flossie would instruct

Perline on how to prepare the fish along with dirty rice and asparagus in cream sauce. Perline would complete the meal with some of her mother's renowned bread pudding for dessert.

Since most of the plantations were a fair distance from one another, guests frequently stayed the night. For breakfast on the morrow, Flossie intended to rouse herself enough to cook up some grits and grilliards, crawfish etoufee omelettes, and whipped cream biscuits with citrus compote.

As Flossie had predicted, her daughter Perline had earned her keep many times over. She was a seamstress extraordinaire and skilled in cooking and midwifery. Under Flossie's tutelage Perline was becoming a renowned herbalist as well.

Perline had been enlisted to sew Justine and Janine's ball gowns for the Etiennes' ball. She had a bright gold gown and another gown in a delicate shade of peach draped across her arm. Perline needed to put the final touches on the completed gowns. Flossie had also been summoned to the Big House. Janine wanted to go over the menu for the parties with her.

"We had better go, Mama."

Perline's sweet voice roused Flossie from a sound sleep. It was the middle of the night and still dark, yet Perline had already prepared breakfast for the occupants of the Big House and prepped the ingredients for lunch and dinner because her mother was too sick to do it.

It was becoming harder and harder for Flossie to get off her pallet every day. She hadn't been able to hide her declining health from her daughter. Perline took on Flossie's daily responsibilities and dosed her mother every day with herbs from their garden. Flossie didn't have the heart to tell Perline that God didn't make herbs for what ailed her. She'd been bleeding from her female place for nigh onto a month now and was wise enough in the ways of the body to recognise the familiar scent of rot that starts from the inside and eats its way through you until there is nothing left. She was dying.

Perline helped Flossie get dressed after she packed herself with clean white cloths to catch the blood. They slowly made their way up to the Big House. They had a busy day ahead of them.

Hannah stared Flossie and Perline down as they passed her on their way to the Big House. *Damned if that old crippled bitch ain't glaring right back at me as if she were whole. One day Flossie is going to let her guard down, and when she does I'll be right there to take advantage of the moment,* she thought viciously. For now, Hannah would content herself with rolling her eyes and looking Flossie up and down with a nasty expression on her face.

Time has not been kind to the old woman or her lame daughter, Hannah thought. *Both of them look like they have one foot in the grave. If I had my way, both of their twisted feet would be in a pine box facing due west.*

The enmity between Hannah and Flossie escalated on that unforgettable afternoon fifteen years ago when Hannah and her daughter Anna literally came back from the dead. Hannah nearly lost her mind when she returned to her secret hiding place in the woods a few days later to find her precious Grimoire gone. She now knew that the demonic tome had not been inspired by an exceptional memory as she once thought, but by the voices of long dead wizards and arch mages sent to her by the Satan's youngest son. She couldn't prove it, but she knew in her gut that old witch had it.

The fear Hannah felt when she thought she had been buried alive was nothing in comparison to the rush of indescribable terror that ran through her body at the mere thought of what Incarnadine would do to her if he discovered the Grimoire was no longer in her possession. She had to get that Grimoire back, and she needed to make sure that her master never found out she lost it. If he did, there would be hell to pay—literally.

For fifteen years she'd been searching for that book. For fifteen years she'd come up empty-handed. The only place she had not been able to search was the kitchen, where Flossie and her daughter laid their little nappy heads. Flossie had somehow warded the place. Hannah couldn't so much as put her foot on the front step without getting incredibly sick. To make matters worse, apparently whatever ward Flossie used also extended to anyone Hannah sought to send inside the kitchen in her stead.

Flossie offered no denial when Hannah confronted her with the theft. Hannah knew her time would come. When it did, she intended to crush

Flossie and anyone else foolish enough to stand in her way. Once Hannah got her hands on the book, she would see to it that Flossie suffered for that last bit of arrogance.

CHAPTER 34

"I DECLARE, JANINE, you really should let me buy Flossie. I swanny, Flossie is worth her weight in pure gold for this bread pudding alone. It's absolutely scrumptious," Caroline Drayton exclaimed, after she shovelled another spoonful of pudding into her mouth.

Janine and her daughter-in-law, Justine, were hosting Caroline Drayton, Emmaline Pele, and Angelique Themezy at a ladies' lunch. It was clear to anyone with eyes in their head that Flossie was terribly ill, yet Janine Etienne insisted she sit in a corner in case she needed her. Flossie sat in silence while Caroline Drayton batted her big poppy eyes in what she hoped was a coquettish manner when, in fact, she looked ridiculous. Emmaline stared down at her plate with longing after seeing Caroline's reaction to Flossie's pudding.

"Aren't you going to have some of the dessert, Em? I assure you it is as delicious as Caroline says," Janine urged.

Emmaline had a weakness for good food. She was attractive enough, with dreamy brown eyes and a head full of unruly copper curls, but she was also pleasingly and unfashionably plump.

"Oh, I really shouldn't," she said, staring at the dessert like it was her last meal. "If I put on any more weight, your guests will think that I am the one who had a baby and not Justine." She giggled.

"Go ahead and enjoy yourself, Em," Janine coaxed. "After all, you only live once."

That was all the prompting Emmaline needed. She dove into the dessert like a hungry dog who feared its food would be snatched away. She ended up having three servings of the rich dessert before her gluttony was finally appeased.

"Caroline, I cannot allow you to purchase Flossie because I intend to," Emmaline stated, pushing the empty plate away from her with a groan. She turned to Janine. "Whatever Caroline is offering, I will double it!" The ladies broke into peals of laughter when Angelique piped in.

"Emmaline and Caroline can fight over Flossie. She's old and won't last long. I'd like to make an offer on her daughter Perline. I have yet to meet anyone, white or slave, who is as good with a needle and thread as she is."

Janine beamed at the praise. After all, both Flossie and Perline were Magnolia Hill slaves; thus, they were a positive reflection of her husband Claude, their master. Be that as it may, Janine had absolutely no intentions of getting rid of Flossie or Perline. She hastened to tell the women that.

"My apologies, ladies, but I would not sell Flossie or Perline for all the tea in China," she said with a fake look of contrition on her face. Janine didn't add that she couldn't sell either of them if she wanted to. Janine was given absolutely no authority to make even the smallest decision on Magnolia Hill. In fact, her husband Claude acted as if she didn't even exist. For the next few days she would pretend that theirs was a happy home while it was anything but. The only advantage she'd been able to enjoy was the fact that her daughter-in-law Justine shared her misery. Janine waited for one of the slaves to refill her cup before continuing.

"Claude told me Perline had a twin sister who, unlike Perline, was as healthy as an ox when she was born. As you all know, we rent Perline's services out. I declare, every time I think of the money we could have made off of Perline's twin sister over the long term, I get positively sick to my stomach. Surely she must have inherited at least *some* of her mother's and sister's talent."

"Well, what became of her?" Angelique asked, as if the mother of the slave they were discussing was no more than a piece of furniture in the room. Janine let out an exaggerated sigh.

"Oh, you know how men are. In a fit of pique, Claude sold her to a wealthy French planter in Natchez."

"Oh shoot," Justine said childishly. In the short time she and Julien had been married, he had successfully managed to smother her personality and her self-confidence. The ladies, her mother included, were surprised to hear her speak since she so rarely opened her mouth. "I suspect that now her current master is enjoying her special talents," Justine added.

Well, I declare, Janine thought. *She does have a brain in her little head.*

Despite Janine lowering her voice to a whisper, Flossie heard every single word.

"I don't know how true it is, but I heard the planter she ended up with settled her on her own plantation after he put five pickaninnies in her."

"No! Surely you jest," Caroline said in an outraged voice. "It is against the law for slaves to own property in Louisiana!" Caroline's face was flushed red. She clinched the cloth dinner napkin in her hand so tightly her fingernails made half-moon imprints in her palm.

"I wish I was jesting," Janine said solemnly. "But not only did the Frenchman settle her on her own farm after he took himself a white bride, he freed her. She married one of those redskin savages from a nearby tribe and popped out four half-Indian/half-nigra babies for him. They made that farm so profitable she was able to buy the freedom of all five of the slaves she had with the Frenchman."

Flossie held on to the side of the chifferobe to keep from falling. Their conversation continued, but Flossie didn't hear any of it. The only sound that filtered through her mind was the echo of a distant voice, repeating over and over again.

She is alive. She is alive. All this time my daughter Minette has been alive in Natchez. And Lord have mercy on my soul—she free!

Flossie knew what she had to do.

CHAPTER 35

THE GUESTS AT Magnolia Hill were going through the bed linens as fast as Anna could wash them. She was hanging sheets on the line when she saw Marcel Benoit riding toward the stable on his chestnut brown horse. He rode every morning at the same time. Anna made it a point to be occupied doing any nature of task that would place her directly within his path.

She looked around to make sure no one was watching before grabbing the half-full clothes basket against her hip. She hurried in the direction Marcel was riding in, slowing down to a more casual walk as she drew nearer to the stable. As always, she'd timed their encounter perfectly.

Marcel could barely hold back the look of pleasure that blossomed on his handsome face. He wasn't fooled by Anna's antics. He easily saw through the pretty young house slave's contrived efforts to gain his attention. He took his morning rides for the sole purpose of seeing what outlandish lengths she would go to next.

Marcel Benoit III was a French artist, specializing in portraiture. He had a reputation for capturing his subjects on that slippery slope somewhere between honesty and flattery, thus making him popular among the colonial aristocracy. He also had the reputation of being a ladies' man.

Marcel's grandfather, Marcel Benoit "the first," and his father, "the second," had both also been artists. His grandfather, an artist of great renown, had been blackballed. He'd lost everything, ending up doing courtroom portraits of infamous criminals for a Parisian newspaper after he'd been caught dallying with the wife and young daughter of one of his wealthy patrons. The young daughter had been Marcel's own grandmother Genevieve.

He did the right thing by her and saw her properly wed, but she found herself disowned by her family and widowed in less than a year. Marcel's grandfather was murdered while trying to capture the likeness of an infamous murderer named Pierre Antoine Wolf on his way to the gallows. The murderer used Marcel's grandfather as a human shield to make his escape. Once he eluded his pursuers, Wolf cold-bloodedly slit Marcel's grandfather's throat and scalped him.

Claude Etienne hired Marcel to render the likeness of his daughter-in-law and grandson on canvas. That placed Marcel somewhere in the middle on the social acceptance scale—too good for the slaves, but not quite good enough to associate with Claude's high-brow elitist guests. Other than the fact that Marcel was invited to take his meals with the Etiennes, he was never allowed to forget that he was one step above poor white trash and little more than hired help.

Marcel slowed his horse down to a canter and then a clean stop a few feet from Anna. Anna balanced the clothes basket on her hip and raised one hand to shield her eyes from the early morning sun. Marcel looked like a handsome prince sitting on his mighty horse. Every time he looked at her he made her feel like the princess her mother had once been in a faraway place called Zanzibar.

"How you doing on this fine morning, Mr. Marcel?" she asked with a bright smile.

Marcel's breath caught in his throat. He noted that she had the signature Etienne grey eyes and light brown hair with blonde highlights. He wondered which of the Etiennes had fathered her. When she was looking up at him, as she was right now, with the sun catching her profile just so, for one brief moment she resembled an angel even though Marcel knew for a fact that she was anything but. She was too much the seductress to be anybody's angel. Marcel enjoyed Anna's flirtatious nature. A big smile split his face.

"Well, Annie, I'm doing mighty fine now that I've laid these eyes of mine on you. I declare you are a sight for sore eyes and a vision to behold, little dahling." Marcel dismounted, needing to get closer to her.

Anna purred like a well-fed kitten, preening in Marcel's extravagant praise. The two of them had been playing a dangerous game of flirtation since Marcel's arrival at Magnolia Hill. Anna was anxious and ready to take their mutual attraction to the next stage.

Mimicking the exaggerated mannerisms she'd frequently observed in her betters, she said, "Why, Mr. Marcel, that's awfully kind of you to say."

Marcel's response was quick and simple. "Well, Annie, it's easy to speak the truth."

They were out in the open, where just about anyone could see them. Thank goodness the hour was early and most of the occupants of the Big House were either still abed or breakfasting. Anna, whom everyone but her mother Hannah called "Annie," didn't care. She wanted Marcel Benoit, and from the look of hunger burning in his dark eyes, Marcel wanted her too.

Anna was no stranger to that look. She'd seen it on the faces of every man who looked at her. She was beautiful and she knew it. The only thing that marred her classic beauty was a small star-shaped birthmark on her right temple. She shared the same mark as her mother.

Now that the Big House was filled to overflow with guests and attentions diverted, she planned to take advantage of the wonderful opportunity she had to be alone with Marcel. The man she knew to be her father had been sniffing around her of late. Hmph. *If anybody is going to put a sucker in my belly, it's going to be this handsome Frenchman and not my fat drunkard daddy*, she vowed determinately.

"It's powerful hot out here, ain't it, Mr. Marcel?

She ran her finger down the opening in her collar, dragging it to the centre of her cleavage, nice and slow. She held Marcel's gaze with her big grey eyes. Next, she placed the tip of her finger in her mouth. Without once breaking contact with his hungry gaze, she swirled her tongue around the tip of her finger in a very suggestive manner. Marcel got the message—loud and clear.

Marcel groaned in agreement. It was hot alright, but the heat had absolutely nothing to do with the weather. All he could think at the moment was how much he would love to render Anna's form on canvas—that is *after* he'd bedded her.

"It's powerful hot indeed, Annie," he said in a husky voice. The timbre of his voice sent chills down Anna's spine.

Anna closed the distance between them until they were in what would be considered in polite society as indecently close. Anna's next words came out as a sweet, sultry whisper in a southern drawl.

"It's cool in the stable, Mr. Marcel. Might be a good idea to go in and cool off for a spell, especially after that hot ride you just had."

Her suggestion made Marcel's dick harden. Basket in hand, Anna sashayed to the stable door, mesmerising Marcel with the sensual swing of her shapely hips. Anna had one hand on the latch. She turned to give Marcel a sultry look over her shoulder. "You coming or not?"

Marcel let loose a vulgar curse. *Fuck yeah, I'm coming.*

Annie opened the stable door halfway and slid inside. Marcel followed. Once inside, Annie got rid of the basket and walked backward toward an empty stall, undoing her clothing with every step she took. Marcel quickly stabled his horse and joined her.

As soon as they found the security of an empty horse stall, Marcel took control. He pinned her against the back wall of the stall. Anna raised her knee around Marcel's waist. She couldn't get close enough to him. She wanted to press herself so hard against him that they blended together as one—blood, flesh, and bone. The horses in the adjacent stalls neighed when their bodies came together.

Marcel took her mouth in a hot scorching kiss. Anna was no longer a slave, and Marcel was no longer a travelling French artist with a line of debts to settle in France he could never repay. For the space of a short while, they were just a man and a woman finding pleasure in one another.

Anna's slender fingers got lost in his silky auburn hair. The calluses on the tips of her work-roughened digits scratched a non-existent itch on his scalp and provoked a brand new one in his crotch. They inhaled each other, swapping tongues, spit, and air while their hands roamed one another's body.

Marcel whispered nasty words in French and English in Anna's ear as she struggled to get her hands inside his shirt. She wanted to feel his hot flesh, to knead his powerful muscles in the palms of her hand. He'd long since discarded his riding jacket. As badly as he wanted to, he dared not totally disrobe.

Marcel had an artist's hands, elegant with long, blunt-tipped fingers. He ran his warm palm up the inside of Anna's raised thigh. She growled like something inhuman when Marcel shoved two fingers inside that weeping swollen place he ached to get in. Anna bore down on his hand, trying to get his fingers deeper.

"You like that, don't you, gal?"

It felt so good. All Anna could do was nod her head in response. She looked like a wild abandoned gypsy with her hair all over the place and her eyes wild with passion. Marcel was hypnotised.

He leaned back to watch his work, slipping his fingers in and out of her. She was squishy and wet inside. His fingers glistened with her juice. Marcel could feel her slick insides laying claim to his fingers. Her walls hungrily snatched at his digits, loath to let go.

Anna cried out in alarm when Marcel abruptly pulled his fingers out. Before she could make further complaint, Marcel gave her one more long blistering kiss, then he whispered, "I'm ready to fuck. Lay down and spread yourself for me."

Anna scooted down the stall wall to sit in the hay. She barely felt the rough wood on the stall scraping the skin on her back. Her grey eyes were locked on the impressive bulge between Marcel's legs. Panting, she kept her eyes locked on his hands while he unbuttoned his pants. He was nice and thick. Just the way she liked it.

Marcel dropped to his knees, holding his ruddy-tipped manhood in his hands. He stroked himself a few times, causing pre-ejaculate to weep from the tip. Now he was ready. He grabbed Anna by the back of her knees to pull her closer. Anna used her fingers to spread herself wide. Her actions reminded Marcel of a well-known *demi-monde* he'd once fucked in Provence.

When Anna spread her legs there was no hint of expensive French perfume or flowery bathwater—only the sweet musky smell of hot, natural woman and desire mixed in with the smell of horseflesh, hay, and dung. Marcel's nostrils flared.

He held his breath as he pressed himself into Anna's haven one inch at a time. Her hips rose to meet him. She let out a guttural grunt when he was finally seated to the hilt. Marcel bared his teeth and flattened his hands on the wall above Anna's head for leverage. She alternately squealed and grunted as he ploughed into her. The sounds Anna was making were driving Marcel wild.

They rocked into one another so hard the walls of the stall began to shake. Marcel felt hot blood building up, threatening to rise to the top of his head and explode. There was no kissing, no caressing—just heart-pounding, hot, sweaty sex. Marcel was so close to cumming, his teeth ached. He could tell Anna was close too. Her insides felt like tiny hands grabbing hold of his cock and refusing to let go.

Suddenly Marcel stiffened. He heard the stable door open and close. Realising Anna would soon climax, he smothered her abandoned cry of release with a brutal kiss. They were no longer alone.

Next, he clamped his hand over Anna's mouth and raised a finger to his lips signalling her to be quiet. She nodded in understanding. It would not turn out well for either of them if they were caught by Claude, Julien, or one of the many guests wandering the grounds.

Marcel's grandfather had a problem keeping his cock in his pants. That problem eventually got him killed. Marcel didn't plan to follow in his grandfather's footsteps. There were two voices—a man and a woman. Anna went stock still when she recognised one of the voices belonged to her mother.

CHAPTER 36

"WERE YOU ABLE to get the guns?" Hannah asked in an urgent tone. She'd taken a big gamble having Charles Deslondes meet her in the stable. She would have been missed had she tried to sneak off the plantation, so she sent out a signal for him to meet her here.

"Yes, but not nearly as many as we will need," Charles replied. Manuel Andre of Woodlawn keeps a large store of weapons on his plantation. Harry will try to get as many of them as possible. Those who don't have guns will have to use machetes, hoes, axes, and cane knives."

Charles Deslondes knew the risk he was taking in coming to Magnolia Hill in broad daylight. He was primed and ready to disappear back to the swamps and eventually make his way back to Deslondes Plantation where he served as a driver.

Hannah didn't miss the fervour in Charles' eyes. It started as an ember years ago, only to fan into a full-fledged flame for freedom as he reached adulthood. His was a perfect coattail to ride upon for her own selfish purposes.

"There should be a large enough supply of machetes and the like," she stated. There was a brief moment when Hannah and Deslondes shared a sinister laugh at their private joke.

Hannah's words were clipped and business like. "Drake locks the machetes up after the hands come back from the field each day. I know where he keeps the key. I'll make sure the shed is conveniently left unlocked on Friday night."

"Good," Deslondes said, nodding his head in approval. His voice was rich and deep. He spoke with the diction of an educated man, but the timbre in his voice gave proof to the fact that he was a son of Africa.

"By the time your army reaches Magnolia Hill the Maroons will have joined us. We will be at full force," Hanna added. "And Charles," she said, grasping his arm, "Do as you will with the whites on other plantations, but as for Magnolia Hill, I don't want to leave one of them alive—not a man, not a woman, or a child. And that includes any slave foolish enough to get in our way. Kill them all. Kill every last one of them. Oh, and make sure you slice up that baby first. You can leave the master and the mistress to me. I'll personally take care of them," she said with an evil look on her face.

The air in the stable had suddenly turned to ice around Anna and Marcel. Hannah was planning a rebellion.

Janine Etienne kept Perline up at the Big House late into the night. Flossie was passed out by the time her daughter returned to their cabin. Exhausted, Perline laid down to catch a few hours of sorely needed sleep. She woke the next morning to find her mother in a pool of blood. There would be no work for Flossie today. She was too sick to even lift her head.

Perline silently banked the cooking fire and hurried to the well to fetch water. Not one word passed between the two women as the daughter gently bathed her mother. It was as it should be, Flossie thought: "Once a woman, twice a child."

Flossie's huge feverish eyes were filled with so much love they fairly lit up their humble cabin. One good eye and one milky eye followed her daughter's every move. Perline had learned a long time ago to move with economy, limping from place to place to accomplish her tasks. Before long, the smell of breakfast foods danced with the sickly sweet scent coming from Flossie's diseased body.

Perline knelt to feed her mother before packing up the breakfast for the housemaids to deliver to the Big House. Sick or well, the white folk needed to be fed and tended to. She held her mother's hand until the food was picked up. Flossie opened her mouth to speak, only to break out in a paroxysm of coughing that threatened to sap the little strength she had left.

"Mama, please don't try to speak. Rest yourself," Perline said anxiously. She'd seen this kind of sickness before. Her heart was breaking because she knew it could only end one way.

When Perline made to get up and retrieve a cup of water to wet her mother's parched lips, Flossie grasped her wrist so tight Perline actually flinched.

"What, mama? What can I get for you to ease your discomfort?"

Flossie knew Perline had already steeped some poppy seed and laudanum to take away her pain, but the powerful potion would also befuddle her. There would be time enough for that later. Right now, she needed all her senses about her. She fought to bring forth every single word. When the words finally did come, they were in a voice that was hoarse and little above a whisper.

"Sit, chile." Flossie watched her daughter struggle to the ground. When she was finally seated next to her, Flossie began to talk. "Your daddy was a fine black angel by the name of Ajuma," she began. "You got angel blood running in your body, through and through, and don't you never ever forget it!"

Perline was stunned, but there was no time to absorb what her mother had disclosed to her about her parentage because Flossie was not quite done with her revelations. Perline sat spellbound while her mother's story continued to unfold.

"One day while I was tending the herb garden in the woods, I spied that nasty Hannah slipping something under a rock. The heifer never knew I saw her. I knew she had to be up to no good, and I was curious about what she felt was so important that she had a need to hide it. My spirit told me to wait and bide my time. So I did."

"My opportunity finally came on the day that yalla heifer Hannah was labouring to bring forth her demon seed. I made a detour past my herb garden to her hiding place while she was screaming her fool head off in this very cabin."

"I found what she was trying to hide. It was a book filled with all nature of wickedness. I know what was in it because your daddy taught me how to read and write. I tell you, chile, that book nearly burned a hole in my hand.

It had to have been written by the devil himself."

"When I returned to the cabin, I had that evil book hidden on the bottom of my herb basket, just as nice as you please. I'd covered it up with herbs I planned to steep to calm down my rheumatism."

"The first thing to come out of her mouth when she rose from the so-called dead was, "Where the fuck is my *Grimoire*, old lady?" Up until that moment, I had no idea what you call that kind of book other than just plain evil."

The gods can't stand a liar, and neither can the Lord. I went toe to toe with her, never once denying I had it. I never admitted it either. Over the past fifteen years, she's tried to do everything in her power to get her hands on that blasted book. At first I didn't know what to do with that kind of evil. As if I had asked out loud, the gods of our ancestors told me what to do with it. Now I'm going to tell you."

Flossie directed Perline to remove a loose floorboard under the kitchen table. Inside was the book of which her mother spoke and a balled-up dirty rag that had at one time been white. Perline hastened to bring the items to her mother's bedside.

"This here cloth contains the afterbirth I dug out of Hannah when her baby was born. That gal ain't the only one who knows how to cast a spell. This is what I used to bind her. As long as her innards were in this house, she couldn't come in and she couldn't send nobody else in either."

"As soon as Joseph is done digging my grave—"

Perline's big green eyes welled up. She started to cry. Flossie reached for her daughter's hand.

"Please don't cry. I'm so tired, baby. It's time for me to go, and I'm ready."

With the strength that could have only come from her parents, Perline dashed her tears. Her mother had something to say. She would not tax her flagging energy with interruptions. In fact, Flossie's words were now coming with great effort. Her voice was as weak as her body, but Flossie didn't intend to go anywhere until she had her say. Perline moved closer so as not to miss one word. Flossie began again.

"As soon as Joseph is done digging my grave, I want you to place this book and this rag at the bottom of it. Make sure you throw enough dirt over it so that nobody but you, the gods and the good Lord Jesus know what's there. Don't leave my body unattended for even a minute. Get Merle and Jessy to sit wake by my body while you tend to the grave. They'll know what to do if that gal tries anything.

"Then I want all three of you to sit wake by my body all night so that yalla heifer can't work no evil on my spirit. Come morning, Joseph will bury me deep enough to bind that bitch and that baby that came out of her with eyes like the Etiennes. We need to bind their evil powers forever." Perline could no longer keep silent.

"Mama, you can't expect me to place your body atop something so evil. We talking 'bout eternity, Mama!"

Flossie was losing her patience. She needed Perline to follow her instructions to the letter. That was the only way she could go to her reward and know her daughter would be alright.

"You think I don't know what we talking 'bout?" Flossie snapped. "Don't you worry 'bout me, angel girl," she said in a gentler voice. "Surely, after all I have been through, the Gods will expand my resting place and grant me the bliss of the grave and none of the torment."

Next Flossie told Perline what she knew about her sister. "Wait until you know the time is right, chile of my heart, then I want you to walk down River Road and don't look back. Go to your sister. Tell her who she is. Make sure she tells my grandchildren who they are. Every one of you carries the blood of an angel. You will be free!"

Flossie was dead before sunrise.

Deep in the Atchafalaya Swamp

Feo was nervous. He couldn't keep still. The traitorous imp swung from limb to limb like a monkey outside one of the many secret lairs the demon Emesis maintained in the swamps. The imp was anxious to get this clandestine meeting with the demon over and done with. Feo was taking a great risk in meeting the disgraced demon, but with great risk comes even greater reward.

Emesis promised Feo he could have the newborn Etienne baby in exchange for information Feo had relating to an upcoming demon surprise attack. If Zuet or any of his officers found out about his betrayal, Feo would be lucky if they merely killed him.

But then again absolutely nothing tastes sweeter than newborn baby—nothing at all. He would give Emesis the information he requested and more, for a tiny drop of that tasty little infant's blood. He swung from the limb and dropped to his feet when he smelled the demon's approach.

Emesis was a low-level demon, not even afforded the privileges enjoyed by demons on the fringe of the demonic hierarchy. The demon was nothing if not enterprising. And he was not without resources. His spy was skulking near the opening to his secret lair, anxiously waiting to see how Emesis would receive the information he had for sale. The life of the Etienne baby was a small price to pay for the information he sought. The demon didn't waste any time with niceties.

"Tell me everything you know about the attack. Leave nothing out."

"Yes, master," the imp said deferentially. "As you know, the humans are celebrating the birth of Justine Etienne's baby, the baby you will help me kidnap. They have invited families from as far away as Virginia. They will have a fancy ball tomorrow night and cook outside on Saturday during the day."

"There is a slave named Hannah on the plantation. This slave and her daughter Anna are direct descendants of the line of Cain. Both belong to The Satan, mind, body, and soul."

"Tomorrow, while the whites' guard is down and they are replete with food and drink, Hannah will lead a slave rebellion. It is her intention to kill every man, woman, and child on the plantation."

Emesis paced back and forth with his hands at his back, processing everything Feo disclosed. "How can this woman expect to prevail against the might of the whites?" he said. "Surely she and her cohorts will be cut down and their rebellion quelled."

"They will have help. For the past five years, a half-white slave named

Charles Deslondes and two Asante warriors named Kook and Quamana have been holding clandestine meetings in cane fields and taverns up and down the coast, hoping to emulate the successful slave revolt that took place in Haiti to abolish slavery. They have also enlisted the aid of the swamp-dwelling Maroons. The woman Hannah has aligned herself with this group. Little do they know that they harbour a snake in their midst."

Emesis silently absorbed Feo's information. "Okay, even should the slaves prevail, what does all this have to do with Zuet's surprise attack?"

"Zuet will use the slave uprising as a smoke screen to flood the area with demons. His goal is twofold. Wipe out the line of humans that serve as his personal thwart, and catch the Nephilim in every town and county unaware. He seeks to smoke Zion Shemyaza out and bring him to his knees."

CHAPTER 37

JANINE HELD HER body ramrod stiff in Claude's arms as they shared the obligatory first dance to commence the Etienne ball. They were halfway through the ordeal when Claude's valet, Stanley, approached for a private word with him. Whatever information the slave divulged put Claude in a tizzy. Janine could barely hide her relief when Claude stalked off with a thunderous frown on his face.

If Claude remained true to form, she would not get another opportunity to dance with or even speak to him until the conclusion of the ball. That suited her just fine.

She made her way through the crowd of dancers to the area where another matron was seated. It no longer mattered to Janine that her husband had no feelings for her. She was used to being left to her own devices. By the time Claude excused himself, the ball was in full swing.

Janine joined Estelle Bene of Destrehan Plantation, who was excitedly fanning herself while keeping an eye on one of her two daughters as they swirled on the dance floor in brightly coloured ball gowns. Estelle was a natural-born chatterbox and happy for the company.

"Is it hot, or is it me?" she asked before Janine could even take a seat.

Janine had to admit that it was unseasonably hot for January. She had enlisted several of the field hands to stand at strategic places throughout the ballroom to fan the guests. One of those slaves was even now stirring the hot air with a large palmetto leaf fan right next to Janine and Estelle. *Maybe if Estelle pushed away from the table more often she would not get so hot,* Janine thought uncharitably.

Instead of saying what she actually felt, Janine chose the diplomatic route. After all, the whole purpose of this weekend was to win the wives of the local planters over so that they would include her on their exclusive invitation list.

"I assure you, Estelle, there is nothing wrong with you. It is indeed warm. We are probably in for a storm," she added.

"A storm, you say?" Estelle acted as if she had never heard of a storm in Louisiana during the month of January. "It seems to me that your decision to host an outdoor soiree in January was an ill-fated decision on your part and not well thought-out, at best," she said snidely.

Janine judiciously bit her tongue. She was past the point of insult. She didn't know why she continued to curry the favour of these women. She promptly tuned Estelle's annoying voice out as the corpulent matron went on and on about how uncomfortable she was feeling and how she feared she would get caught out in the rain on the morrow. Janine couldn't make herself care one way or another about how Estelle was feeling.

The weather was the least of Janine's concerns. Every time she thought about how Flossie had had the audacity to up and die days before one of the biggest events of her life, Janine got mad all over again.

She could have at least waited until Monday! If that goddamn worthless slave wasn't already dead, I swear I would kill her myself. Now Janine had to figure out how to accommodate the culinary needs of her many quests tomorrow.

It made Janine even angrier that Perline requested time away from the Big House to bury her mother and to sit by her dead body all night. *Hell, it wasn't like the old crow was going anywhere. That body would keep.* But Janine didn't know whether her reputation would. She made a mental note to take a switch to Perline's little black ass upon her guests' departure for her lack of consideration.

Her invitation list included the "who's who" of New Orleans society; the Bienvilles, Kenners, Hendersons, Destrehans, La Branches, Picous, and Deslondes. Janine had even invited the Honourable James Brown and his wife Nancy, who is the sister of Lucretia Hart Clay, the wife of the esteemed Henry Clay. Because of Caroline Drayton's familial connection with her daughter-in-law, nearly all had accepted. She would make these people forget her tawdry past and accept her, even if it meant she had to bend down and kiss their aristocratic asses.

Justine wasn't faring any better than Janine. Her baby was little more than a fortnight old and she just recently out of the delivery bed. Julien had been drinking since early morning. You wouldn't know it by looking at him, but he was a nasty mean drunk. He'd threatened to come to Justine's room tonight. A shudder went down her spine. It was getting harder and harder for her to hide the many bruises he'd placed on her body.

Justine hadn't wanted this celebration. Nor did she relish the attention that came along with it. It was easy to convince her parents that she was happy through false words written on expensive perfumed stationery, but impossible to hide her misery from family and friends while face to face. The fancy ball and festivities scheduled for tomorrow had been her mother-in-law's idea— all engineered in a twisted bid to gain acceptance she would never receive.

No one who knew her would believe that Justine Elizabeth Drayton, the belle of five counties, would find herself stuck in a social setting she was no longer comfortable in and married to a man she no longer loved. There was no doubt about it, Justine no longer loved Julien Etienne; she despised him.

Wasting no time, Julien showed his true nature on their wedding night. His inadequacies as a man bubbled out of him like so much acid, burning everyone he touched. Fearful she would disclose his dreadful secret, he intimidated her with his size and utilised fear tactics. Now that he had gotten a son on her, she didn't know what awaited her. Justine schooled her face in an inscrutable expression as they danced across the shining ballroom floor. She couldn't allow anyone to know her inner fears, especially her parents.

Julien's cologne was a bit too strong and his grip far too tight as he masterfully negotiated his wife through the intricate dance steps. By this time Justine's head was spinning. Beads of sweat dotted her forehead. She kept swallowing to keep the excess saliva building in her mouth from opening the door to sickness. She silently prayed she wouldn't humiliate herself by losing her supper all over her husband's fancy suit. If she did, he'd make sure she regretted it.

Just when she thought she couldn't take it anymore, her father-in-law interrupted the dance with a tap on Julien's shoulder. He pulled his son aside to whisper what appeared to be an urgent message in his ear.

Just like that, Julien took his leave to go only God knows where to do only God knows what. Justine didn't care where he went off to as long as he took himself away from her.

Claude Etienne resembled a grand inquisitor as he hovered over Marcel with a face as angry as a storm cloud. Marcel feared Claude intended to "shoot the messenger," and that was the last thing he needed at the moment.

"Now tell me again. What *exactly* did you hear?" Claude demanded for the umpteenth time.

Marcel's hands were shaking. He was sweating bullets, and not from the heat. Marcel had never been a good liar, but sometimes a lie is better than the truth. In this case, Marcel hoped his cleverly weaved tale would save his life.

When Marcel requested to speak to Claude Etienne on an urgent matter, his manservant bade him wait in his master's study until he could fetch him. Marcel was now surrounded by not only Claude and his big brute of a son, Julien, but several other prominent gentlemen planters with plantations in St. John the Baptist Parish, all staring at him like he'd committed the worst sort of crime. The lies Marcel was about to tell felt like ash on his tongue. He thought it best to stay as close to the truth as possible.

"I was currying my horse in the stable when I heard the stable door open," he said for the third time. "Something told me not to let my presence be known when they started speaking in low voices. There were two of them. They were black slaves from what I could tell. One was named Charles. The name of the other slave was never mentioned, but the voice was that of a woman."

The gentlemen stood stone-faced while Marcel disclosed everything he and Anna heard in the stable the day before, omitting Anna's presence and what he had *really* been doing in the stable. He made it appear as if he'd just overheard the conversation.

Claude's grey eyes were trained upon Marcel. "Stanley!" he bellowed.

The trusty slave had been standing on the other side of the study door like a well-trained dog. He responded to his master's call at once.

"Tell Drake to saddle up. I need him to ride like the wind. He must warn the militia that there is going to be a slave uprising. Hurry!"

"Yessir, Masta, sir."

Stanley wasted no time carrying out his master's orders.

Claude turned to the men assembled with a grave look on his face. "I declare that Magnolia Hill will be ready when the insurgents come!"

When Sally Mae heard the tread of footsteps ascending the stairs, she feared they belonged to yet another guest wanting to pop her head in to "oooh" and "ahhh" over Claude and Justine's funny-looking little baby. She made herself appear to be busy refolding baby clothes and bedding.

White folk don't like it when you appear idle.

Sally Mae, a young mother herself, was Claude Junior's wet nurse and nursemaid. Justine had difficulty bringing her baby into the world, and she had no milk to feed him.

Sally Mae quickly responded, "Please come in," at the sound of the soft knock at the door. A huge grin split her face when she saw it was none other than her father's brother, Stanley, who served in the Big House as Masta Claude's valet and doubled as the butler.

Bless his sweet heart, Uncle Stanley hadn't come empty-handed. He pressed a fancy linen napkin into her hand filled with tasty tidbits he'd purloined from the party.

"Oh bless you, Uncle Stanley. I've been sitting up in this stuffy room all day long without one bite to eat. I was just about ready to go crazy. I sure do thank you," she repeated with sincerity. Now it was Stanley's turn to grin.

"You sure are welcome, Sally Mae. I'm happy I was able to do it for ya."

Sally Mae couldn't help but feel resentful. After all, here she was feeding somebody else's baby while her own baby was forced to suck on a rag soaked with sugar water and a little bit of breast milk. The least Mistress Justine could have done was seen she had something to eat. *Thank God for Uncle Stanley.*

"Now, I can't stay long, baby girl," Stanley said in a rushed tone. "That French fellow that come to paint Mistress Justine's picture had one of the house slaves come fetch me, all in a dither. Said it was powerful important he speak with Masta Claude right then and there. Said it was a matter of life and death.

"Well, I delivered the message to Masta right there on the dance floor, I did. Next thing I know, Masta, young Masta, and 'bout five other white mens is holed up in Masta Claude's study with the door closed. I tell you, Sally Mae, something don't smell right."

Stanley had now transferred his curiosity to his niece.

"What you think is 'bout to happen, Uncle Stanley?"

"I don't rightly know, Sally Mae, but when a white man says something is a matter of life and death, it usually turns out that one of *us* ends up dead," he said solemnly.

"Well, ain't that the truth," Sally Mae readily agreed. Stanley turned to leave.

"Well, I best to get myself back downstairs afore I'm missed. Enjoy them vittles, honey," he said with a smile.

Enjoy them she did. Sally Mae dove into the victuals with gusto. Before long there was nothing left but crumbs in the cloth napkin Stanley had wrapped the food in. After she ate, she checked on the baby to make sure he was dry, then she sat in the nearby rocking chair listening to the strains of soft music drifting from the party below.

Several guests were wandering through the intricate gardens in an attempt to escape the crush of heat inside the ballroom. High above their heads, the imp Feo hung upside down from a limb on the Magnolia tree outside the nursery. Feo was not alone.

Emesis' semi-transparent form hovered in front of the partially open nursery window. Slowly, his barely visible body took on the form of a mist. Like smoke from a smouldering fire, the demon became a dark cloud, snaking through the open window on a gust of humid air to coalesce behind the rocking chair on which the unsuspecting Sally Mae sat. Emesis engulfed the slave in his essence, swirling around her like early morning fog.

When Sally Mae's eyes grew heavy and closed like the shutters before a storm, the demon fully materialised in all his hideous glory. He waited patiently until her head bowed forward and her chin rested upon her chest. He canted his hideous head to the side to listen for any approach. He heard none.

Feo's breaths were coming fast and loud with excitement. He leapt from the tree limb to hang by his three-fingered hands from the outside window ledge. He itched to get his hand on the sleeping baby and wanted to know what was taking the demon so long.

When Emesis looked up, the impudent imp's ugly head was fully inside the open window as he peered inside the nursery. Emesis growled deep in his throat, threatening dire consequences if the imp did not back off, but Feo was too far gone to heed the demon's warning.

Seconds later, Emesis' long black tongue shot out of his mouth to wrap around the imp's neck like a whip. Emesis had Feo's attention now. The imp dangled from the window ledge by one hand, his wide-set eyes bulging out of his head as the demon tightened his deadly grip.

Just when Feo thought the demon would snap his head off with his lethal black tongue, Emesis snapped his tongue back into his mouth, ripping out a chunk of imp meat from the side of Feo's face. Emesis returned his attention to the crib.

The baby's eyes were wide open when the demon snatched him.

CHAPTER 38

MARCEL RACED FROM Claude's study and out of the back entrance of the house like a runaway slave with a pack of bloodhounds on his trail. He couldn't remember what excuse he'd given to get out of the presence of the accusatory eyes of the planters or whether it had even made sense. There was death in the air, and he couldn't put the sight of Magnolia Hill and all it represented behind him fast enough.

Fearful that Claude or his son would call him back or send someone else to fetch him for more questioning, Marcel did a fast walk-run away from the house, stumbling a couple of times as he looked over his shoulder. His explanation for what he'd purportedly heard in the stable had been paper thin, becoming thinner still with each new telling. He would not be able to stand up to another round of interrogation. He headed for the stables. Every stall was occupied. A slave was brushing a brown mare which Marcel assumed belonged to one of the guests at the ball.

"Boy, I need you to stop what you are doing and saddle that horse," he commanded, pointing to the horse he generally rode in the mornings. "And be quick about it. I'm in a hurry."

In under five minutes, the horse was saddled and Marcel was flying through the wind toward the plantation northern acreage. He didn't slow down until he saw the plain buck wagon he'd partially hidden between the trees. Anna stepped out of her hiding place behind the wagon.

"I thought you would never get here!" Anna said anxiously. "Did you speak to Claude?"

It didn't escape Marcel's notice that Anna had conveniently dropped the title "Masta" from her vocabulary. It was as it should be because soon she would be his wife. She would be free.

"Yes. Not only did I speak to Claude, but I was also extensively questioned by his son, Julien, and every single planter in attendance at the party. For a while there I wondered why I even bothered to warn them. I should have let the savages tear them apart," he said bitterly.

Anna planted a hasty kiss on Marcel's mouth before climbing under some blankets he'd placed in the back of the wagon. She would conceal herself until they were away from the environs of Magnolia Hill, and then she would ride beside her man like the white woman she always wanted to be.

"But, Perline, what if they catch you?"

Jessie's big grey eyes followed Perline around the kitchen and cabin while Perline packed her meagre belongings in an old white tablecloth taken from the Big House.

There wasn't much Perline wanted to take with her. She'd already packed every one of her mother's ceremonial items inside the cloth and enough dried fruit and herbs to last her for the four days it would take her to walk to Natchez. She would find water in brooks and creeks along the way.

God willing, I'm gon' see what I would have looked like if the devil named Claude Etienne hadn't entered my mother and father's life.

Perline continued with her packing. "If they catch me," she said without emotion, "I guess I'll be dead. I'm damn near there already. My heart just don't know it yet."

When her mother's spirit departed her body, something resembling it jumped inside Perline. She was the daughter of the conjure woman, Flossie, and a black angel named Ajuma. She was no longer afraid.

Perline paused a second to look around the kitchen where she and her mother had toiled and suffered. The place had never been their home.

So many memories, few of them good, she thought.

If it was up to the Etiennes, she would live, work, and die here, just like her mama. That's not what Perline wanted. She had a sister named Minette. Her sister and her sister's children needed to know how special they were.

Perline's eyes were warm when they landed on Jessie. "This ain't no life, Jessie. Wasn't no life while my mama was this side of living, and it's gon' be even less of a life without her. I plan on leaving here or I'm gon' die trying. Either way, I be free."

Perline reminded Jessie of a delicate bird with its wings broken. The idea of little fragile Perline going off on her own into the dark, uncertain world frightened Jessie to the core.

"But where you gon' go, Perline? How you gon' live?" she asked with eyes that implored Perline to reconsider her decision to leave.

Perline's body may have been twisted, but her spirit was like tempered steel. She'd been bent, but not broken. Jessie couldn't recognise the quiet resolve and strength that flowed through Perline's spirit. She was too blinded by her own fear to see the strength in someone else. Perline sat down. She took the hand of the woman who had been in her life for what seemed like forever and had been such a true friend to her mother.

"I'm going in the direction of Natchez," she said in a firm voice. "And I'm gon' live by the will and grace of the gods. I don't want you to worry about me, Ms. Jessie. Before she died, Mama told me who my daddy was. He was a black angel who went by the name of Ajuma. My mama met him in the woods one night while she was making a sacrifice to the gods. Now they together again in heaven so I know they are looking down on me. They will protect me," she said with assurance.

A frown wrinkled Jessie's forehead. A fleeting memory of a mist-shrouded night when she was returning from the arms of a lover long dead tickled the surface of Jessie's brain. A beautiful black male wept at two fresh graves. One belonged to an old slave whose name Jessie no longer recalled; the other belonged to Flossie's son. Two more beautiful black men with huge wings that could not have been anything but angels touched down on the sacred grounds of the old slave graveyard to take the grieving man away. Jessie now realised the weeping man had probably been Flossie's Ajuma.

Mistaking Jessie's expression as continued disquiet, Perline pressed her case.

"I promised my mama that I'd leave this place behind me the first chance I got. My spirit tells me the time to do it is now, Ms. Jessie, or I ain't never gon' go.

"Ms. Jessie, I sure am gonna miss you," she said with tears in her clear green eyes. "You was a good friend to my mama and like a second mama to me. I won't never forget you."

Jessie knew she would never forget Perline either.

CHAPTER 39

Woodlawn Plantation, LaPlace, Louisiana

FIFTEEN SLAVES WALKED away from Woodlawn Plantation in LaPlace, leaving years of brutality behind them and the main house and several ancillary buildings in flames. There was a brief scuffle when a group of rebel slaves sought to get their hands on Col. Manuel Andre's small cache of stored arms, leaving the colonel gravely wounded and his son Gilbert dead with an axe embedded in the centre of his face.

The rebel leader, a labourer named Harry, didn't plan on there being any bloodshed. He'd already seen enough violence to last two lifetimes, but something in him snapped when Manuel Andre declared in a cruel voice, "Boy, you best put that axe down if you know what's good for you."

Even unarmed, Manuel thought he could exert his special brand of superiority over Harry—as if Harry was too stupid to realise that he had the advantage since he was the one with the weapon in hand. Before Harry realised what he was about, he'd raised the back of his axe and struck the man he had once called Master a vicious blow to the head.

"Father!"

Manuel Andre's son Gilbert's cry of anguish hung in the air like a bad odour. Thinking his father was dead, Gilbert charged Harry with a whip in hand and hate in his eye. The expression on Gilbert's face when Harry's axe cleaved his forehead made Harry catch his breath to keep from getting sick. The die was cast. The blood of white men had been spilled. There would be no turning back now.

There were eleven plantations involved. Each had their own separate leader with Charles Deslondes and Asante Warriors Kook and Quamana presiding over all. Woodlawn was the first plantation. They were scheduled to move on to Deslondes Plantations next to pick up their leader. The Maroons would join them once they reached the end of the line at Magnolia Hill, where they would meet Hannah, the only female rebel. There was no time to spare.

Deslondes Plantation, St. John
the Baptist Parish, Louisiana

Even though both mistresses of Deslondes Plantation had packed two days ago to attend a party at Magnolia Hill, Charles took the precaution of having his men sneak off the plantation one by one to hide in the dense brush along River Road.

You can never be too careful.

Deslondes was the mastermind of the uprising. The revolt was fashioned on what he saw first-hand when the white Deslondes brothers were forced to flee in fear during the slave revolt in the French colony of Saint-Domingue. Deslondes was one of the valued slaves they clamped in chains to take with them. That uprising culminated in the end of slavery in Saint Dominque, Charles Deslondes' birth place, and the founding of the Haitian Republic. He was determined to set up a similar republic in New Orleans.

One of the late Deslondes brothers—Charles did not know which—had been his father. Both of them used his mother and ran her into an early grave. Since both Deslondes' deaths from fever three years ago, Charles worked himself into a position of trust as a driver and overseer on Deslondes Plantation. Charles spat on the Deslondes brothers' graves every chance he got.

He thought he saw light up ahead. He left his companions where they had secreted themselves to investigate. He had no way of determining if the light bearer was friend or foe. If the light belonged to a white man, it would mean the brothers on Woodlawn Plantation had been apprehended and their rebellion was over before it started.

As the light drew nearer Charles was able to make out several black men on foot, all familiar faces of slaves from Woodlawn Plantation. In front of the line of orderly slaves was Harry. Charles sent up a silent prayer.

Thank God they made it.

After years of clandestine meetings and dangerous planning sessions with enslaved men living on plantations miles apart, the time had finally arrived to take their freedom.

Charles embraced Harry like a long-lost friend, thankful his band of fifteen rebels had made it safely to their rendezvous point. Deslondes Plantation, owned by the widows of Jacques and Georges Deslondes, was right next door to Woodlawn Plantation. To Harry and the slaves he'd convinced to follow Deslondes, every single step on that dark, wood-banked stretch of road that ran the length of St. John the Baptist Parish seemed like ten miles.

"I am so happy to see you, brother. I could kiss you!" Charles said enthusiastically. "Were you able to make your escape smoothly?"

The smile disappeared from Harry's face.

"One of the house slaves betrayed us while we were trying to get our hands on the guns. Manuel Andre confronted us before we could make a clean escape. He demanded I drop my weapon if I knew what was good for me. I struck him, and when his son Gilbert came to his aid I was forced to kill him. My only regret is that I did not finish Manuel off."

Charles' face held a look of concern when he patted Harry on the back in commiseration. Harry was not a killer. None of them were. The ratio of blacks to whites in St. John the Baptist Parish was three to one. If they were killers, the whites would have been dead a long time ago. Leaving Col. Andre alive had been a big mistake. Charles hoped it would not come back to haunt them.

Harry glanced at the frightened faces of the eight men standing with Charles.

"Are these the only men who will join us from Deslondes?"

Both men had anticipated a greater number. At least twenty had attended their meetings.

"The men on Deslondes are afraid. Can you blame them?" Charles asked, a note of disappointment in his voice. "Many slaves talk about freedom, but are unwilling to risk their lives to get it. Some think it is better to be miserable with the familiar than risk everything for the unknown."

Charles was afraid too—so afraid that even now there was a ball of lead sitting in the centre of his belly. But he was more afraid of living as a slave than he was of dying like a man.

"We will have to make do with what we have, Harry."

Harry and his men fell in line with Charles and the five who joined him from Deslondes Plantation. As they proceeded down River Road, their ranks grew as small groups of slaves joined them at every plantation they passed. They marched in an organised fashion—a ragtag army of slaves, from the states, Africa and Haiti, many of whom spoke different languages. Their weapons were pikes, hoes, axes, and a few firearms. As they picked up momentum, their feet sounded like the beat of their native African drums.

James Brown Plantation

It was not in the Ashanti psyche to capitulate, no matter the odds. Before he was captured, Kook was a commander of an elite troop of Ashanti infantrymen, skilled in the use of the spear, the bow, and the musket. Before his capture, Quamana served under him. It was in Kook and Quamana's very natures to offer up fierce resistance until the end, even if it meant their deaths.

Ashanti commanders carried Afena swords. They would behead their enemies with these curve-edged swords and place effigies of the severed heads upon the Golden Stool, a sacred symbol of their people.

Kook had neither spear nor bow nor musket as he prepared to go into this important battle. Contrary to what Charles Deslondes might believe, Kook knew for a certainty that their freedom would not be won without bloodshed.

Kook hefted the heavy axe that he had rendered to razor sharpness. *This axe will serve as my Afena.* He lifted a nearby hoe with the other powerful arm. *And this, will serve as my spear.* Kook stood in front of the plantation of James

Brown where he and his men would join the insurrection. It had only been five years since he was taken from his native Africa, and Kook still had the taste of freedom surging through his veins.

Quamana and Kook stood strong, with twenty-eight slaves and a large contingency of Maroons hidden in the dark recesses of the barn. Quamana and the men were waiting for his whistle signal to join him.

Kook's heart rate accelerated with excitement. He could see a light in the distance, and he could clearly hear the sound of drums and marching feet. He brought two fingers to his lips and whistled. The rebellion had officially begun.

Brown and his wife were at a party at Magnolia Hill. The overseer was drunk in his cabin with one of the slave girls, enabling Kook, Quamana, and the other men to merely walk off the plantation unimpeded.

CHAPTER 40

LaBranche Plantation

WITH EACH PLANTATION they passed, their army grew along with Charles' confidence. He felt their quest was ordained by God. As such, the road on which they trod would remain as secure for his army as did the waters that God allowed Moses to part for the Israelites. Their Red Sea was the mighty Mississippi.

When they came upon LaBranche Plantation, all Charles' confidence vanished in a puff of smoke. The master of the manse, Francois Trepagnier, stood at the end of the drive with blazoning eyes and a rifle at the ready. His overseer and two white men, also armed, flanked him.

Before the whites could get a shot off, Kook sent his makeshift spear soaring. It pierced Trepagnier's chest cavity with a loud thump, toppling the man off his horse. The rider-less horse galloped down River Road at breakneck speed. Realising the odds were against them, the other white men took off on their horses in the opposite direction. Kook took control. He pulled his spear out of Trepagnier's chest.

"Come! That evil doctor's house is less than a mile down the road!" he shouted.

This was the same doctor that had allowed his woman to die a year before. He was determined the doctor would pay with his life, but when they arrived at the doctor's house, no one was there.

"Burn the house to the ground!" Kook screamed.

Meuillion Plantation

The slaves on Meuillion Plantation heard the drumbeat and the marching feet of the rebels long before they arrived. The rebels' approach was heralded by choking, billowing black smoke surging above the flames from plantations that had been reduced to little more than kindling. They were at Meuillion, the only home the plantation blacksmith, Brazile, had ever known. It was clear the rebels had every intention of burning Meuillion to the ground as well. Old Tom, the Big House butler, was determined to see that didn't happen.

"Old man, you either with us or you against us. Which is it gon' be?" one of the rebels demanded.

Brazile had to give it to him. Old Tom had a set of big balls—way bigger than his. Right now, the old man was the only thing standing between the rebels and the Big House. Old Tom wouldn't be able to look to any of the Meuillion slaves for assistance. Many of them had joined the ranks of the rebels or were hiding out like Brazile.

Brazile couldn't hear what Old Tom's response to the rebel leader's question had been, but he did hear the report of the gunshot that came less than a minute later. He heard it loud and clear.

I guess the rebel didn't like Old Tom's answer.

Poor Old Uncle Tom. "I told him to hie himself to the woods to hide until the human locusts passed us by. He thought surely they would not harm an old man and wouldn't listen. Now the man that I have known all of my life as Uncle Tom is probably dead, Brazile thought sadly.

Whispers of an insurrection had been tossed in the wind for years, but Brazile had never put any credence in them. Anyone with any sense had to know that the slaves could never withstand the might of the whites. Hell, even he knew that. But now it all made sense—all the suspicious looks and unfinished sentences whenever Brazile came upon a group of three slaves or more and the unfamiliar faces that would crop up on the plantation from time to time. They must have been fearful that Brazile would disclose dates and locations of their secret meetings and the names of the participants and the particulars to the master—and rightfully so.

The sound of looting and destruction surrounded Brazile as he burrowed his head in the fecund earth of the wooded area behind the slave cabins. Fearful of his fate should he suffer the misfortune of discovery, he tried to blend in with his surroundings—to become invisible. Information supplied by him to the master had resulted in many a slave's back getting stripped to ribbons. He knew there would be no love lost were the rebels to get him in their clutches.

Brazile waited long after the sounds of retreat could be heard before running from his hiding place in the direction of the crackling sound of hungry fire licking up the side of the Big House. His only thought was to save his master's house.

Woodlawn Plantation, LaPlace, Louisiana

"I tell you, Charles, when I opened my eyes, I didn't know whether I was alive or if I'd died and gone straight to hell," Manuel Andre said with fierce emotion. "Those black bastards murdered my son and left me for dead!"

Clearly shaken, Andre clutched Charles Perret's arm in desperation. "They killed my boy, Charles. My son Gilbert laid dead not far from me with an axe embedded in his face. I swear, everywhere I turned I saw nothing but blood and fire."

Charles Perret, a nearby planter and personal friend of Manuel's turned his head away out of respect while the old grey-haired war horse took a moment to break down and cry. Perret couldn't blame him. The man had lost his only son to a band of savages.

Perret's face grew red with dismay and anger as Manuel Andre quickly disclosed how, though grievously wounded and weak from loss of blood, he'd somehow managed to secure a mount and make his way to Perret's plantation which was several miles upriver from Woodlawn.

"I say we go after those brigands and cut them down," Perret said in a voice filled with rage and hate. "Manuel, are you strong enough to ride?" he asked.

Manuel seemed to grow ten inches taller.

"Not only can I ride, Charles, I feel the strength of righteousness infusing these old bones. Those nigras must be stopped!" he said with fervour.

That was all the incentive Perret needed. He walked to the open door of his study and shouted, "Joshua! Get Cricket to saddle up two fresh horses. And have Mamie bring me some bandages to bind up the colonel's head wound. We're going to fetch the militia!"

CHAPTER 41

New Orleans, Louisiana

B Y THE TIME Andre and Perret made it to the residence of Judge Saint Martin on the other side of the river to assemble an eighty-man militia, Drake, the overseer at Magnolia Hill, was pounding on the front door of Governor William C.C. Claiborne's residence in New Orleans as if his very life depended upon admittance.

Finally, a dignified black butler answered the door. He turned his nose up after one good look at Drake's unkempt appearance. Drake had ridden fast and hard all the way to New Orleans, and his sweaty clothing and wild countenance showed it.

"I need to speak with the governor at once!"

It was obvious the butler took exception to Drake's appearance and his rude tone. He was about to close the door in Drake's face when Drake stuck his foot in the door to impede the impudent black's actions.

Drake bunched the butler's collar in his fist, snarling in the butler's startled face with teeth that were as big and yellow as a hungry wolf. "Listen, you stupid black nigger," he spat. "You've got exactly ten seconds to either let me in this house to talk to the governor or tell me where the fuck I can find him. Or I swear before all that is holy, I will rip your black hide from limb to limb with my bare hands and piss down your throat!"

The butler stumbled back in alarm, wiping Drake's spittle from his face. Something in Drake's voice let the butler know he meant business.

"The governor is in attendance at a soiree at the residence of the

Honourable General Wade Hampton the First," he said in a shaky voice.

Drake didn't even bother to ask the visibly petrified servant where the general resided. Like most natives of New Orleans, he already knew.

General Wade Hampton was regaling the governor, Commodoure John Shaw, and several dinner guests with an exaggerated tale when Drake forced his way past his doorman to barge in on his dinner party.

"Here, here…I say, what is the meaning of this untoward intrusion?" Hampton sputtered in umbrage.

There was no time for niceties. Drake got right to the point.

"General Hampton, sir, my name is Drake. I am the overseer at Magnolia Hill Plantation. Claude Etienne bade me ride like the wind to get to Governor Claiborne at any cost. We are in the midst of a slave uprising. Several plantations have already been put to the torch, and I believe there has been loss of life. The rebels are making their way down River Road toward Magnolia Hill as we speak.

"The Etiennes are hosting a huge party there tonight. Planters from nearly every plantation in the parish are in attendance, including the esteemed Henry Clay and his wife. I fear if the Governor doesn't call up the militia, there will be a massacre!"

Hampton, Shaw, and Claiborne wasted no time marshalling two companies of volunteer militia, thirty regular troops, and a detachment of forty seamen to quell the rebellion. Less than an hour later, Perret and Andre's men joined forces with the governor's militia to converge upon the rebels.

The rebels had reached high ground at the Destrehan-Bernoudy Plantation when the militia rained down on them like a horde of angry locusts, boxing them in on all sides. It was the beginning of the end.

Colonel Manual Andre led the vanguard while the militia whooped and hollered, charging upon their horses and picking off rebels one by one like they were at a country turkey shoot. Those that were not shot point blank were hacked to death with bayonets.

Kook and Quamana took cover behind an old wagon that was tipped on its side. The Ashanti warriors fought side by side, each firing one of the few precious firearms from the ground until there were no bullets left for them to shoot. Both men knew they were going to die. Better to die than be returned to their owners in chains.

It was on the tip of Kook's tongue to tell Quamana that he would meet him on the other side when a bullet pinged through the opening between the spokes of the wagon wheel, striking Quamana in the chest. Quamana flew backward with a grunt, his dark muscular arms spread like wings and his eyes wide open in shock.

"I got one of 'em!" someone shouted in excitement.

Kook knew he had to abandon his friend. The sound of horse's hooves indicated the shooter was coming in his direction. Other than his hands, and a spirit filled with hatred, he had nothing with which to defend himself. He frantically looked around for someplace he might find temporary cover.

There, he thought. He saw two double doors on the far side of the house leading to what he assumed was some kind of root cellar. *If I can just slip inside…*

Kook kept low, crab-walking in the direction of the cellar. To his dismay, the doors wouldn't budge. They were locked from the inside. Without a second thought, he sprinted toward the nearby outhouse and slipped inside. He could see through the cracks and bullet holes in the warped wood of the outhouse. He grit his teeth in anger as two militia men dismounted from their horses to stand over Quamana's prone figure. Every muscle in his body was tensed as he waited for the white men to finish Quamana off. Instead of killing the warrior, they dragged him away to a location that was outside Kook's range of vision.

Screams of horror, smoke, blood, death, and pandemonium reigned at every turn. The few guns the Rebels possessed and their axes and hoes were no match against the mounted militia men who had guns and bayonets. Realising the odds were against them, many of the rebels took flight, disappearing into the nearby woods and swamps. Kook didn't blame them. It was far better to live among their Maroon brothers in the swamp to fight another day than to be massacred by white devils intent upon their decimation.

It was with that thought in mind that Kook darted from the outhouse to join his comrades in the swamps. He didn't get far before a bullet found one of his knees. He tried to make the cover of the nearby wooded area, dragging his injured leg behind him, but Manuel Andre rode him down, took aim, and lobbed yet another bullet in him. This one was aimed in the back of his good knee, dropping him like a rock.

The engagement was over in less than twenty minutes. Within that short span of time, more than fifty slaves were murdered. Many more than that, however, had managed to escape into the nearby woods.

The whites rounded up the eleven rebel leaders. Each of them was now on his back. They were tied up side by side like Africans on a slave ship. The only thing that was missing was the rock of a ship, fear of the unknown, and chains. Kook would leave in the same manner that he had come to this wretched place. He could see that Quamana, whose body was lying right next to his, was already dead. He silently wished his Asante brother's spirit a safe journey to the ancestors.

Even in the face of certain death, Kook was fearless. He turned his cold black stare to the men guarding them. He wanted them to remember his face. He wanted his face to come to them when they lay down to sleep at night, to rob them of rest and sanity.

He didn't know why the gods had placed this burden upon him and his brothers and sisters, but there was nothing for any of them to be ashamed of. They had fought for their freedom, even though it would cost them their lives. He would leave this world with the knowledge that he had sent at least one of these pale-skinned monsters to their maker.

When they dragged Charles Deslondes into the centre of the clearing, there was no fear, no crying, and no begging for mercy—just a sense of profound sorrow and resignation that their young lives would have to end as slaves on somebody's goddamned plantation.

Kook didn't flinch or turn away when Manuel Andre ordered one of his men to chop off both of Charles' hands. Then they shot him in both thighs until they were broken. Next, they proceeded to shoot him in several places in his body, making sure the bullets missed vital organs so as to prolong his suffering. Before he expired, they tossed Charles Deslondes' broken body in a bundle of straw and roasted him alive.

And they call us savages, Kook thought.

Kook's heart pounded like a bass drum when the colonel turned his mean blue-eyed stare upon him. It was his turn.

CHAPTER 42

Magnolia Hill Plantation

IF A DEMON wasn't smart, it could easily get trapped inside a host body during the human transition between life and death. Tyranny was an old hat at host-hopping, having been at it for millennia. He would never allow something so stupid to happen to him.

Tyranny had been forced to vacate Magnolia Hill on the same gust of foul air that exited Clidamont Etienne, a/k/a Pierre Wolf's, mouth during his last breath. The evil spirit found himself rudderless and without a physical home or domicile as he floated above the plantation he had called home for so many years. He'd had a mighty good ride inside that Wolf fellow and an even better ride after he'd re-invented himself to become Clidamont Etienne.

The slave woman named Hannah did Tyranny and Wolf a huge favour when she shoved those hankies down the old goat's throat. Tyranny had been chomping at the bit near the end when the old guy's body started to rot. Unfortunately, all bad things must come to an end.

Tyranny interrupted his musings to inhale deeply. *If I am not mistaken, I do believe there is death in the air at Magnolia Hill.*

He could smell it drifting upon the wind like the sweetest perfume. By golly it did his wicked heart proud to know that it would be served up on a silver platter by his father's chosen vessel. Shit didn't get any better than that.

Not every demon could claim Tyranny's special expertise. It was for that reason that weeks ago every demon on Magnolia Hill chose to exit the bodies of their hosts like rats on a sinking ship and hightail it back to their respective levels of hell. Without a doubt, in less than an hour's time there would be some serious dying going on. The last thing any respectable demon wanted was to be trapped like a rat without means of escape inside the body of a dying human.

No worry. Their departures would only be temporary. Once the Wizard Moultrie opened up the gateway in the swamps, legions upon legions of demons would make their triumphant returns, flooding not only Magnolia Hill but the city, the state, and beyond. Tyranny and his brothers, sans his youngest brother Incarnadine, would lead the charge.

The demons were not without purpose. If all went according to plan— and Tyranny saw no reason to believe that it wouldn't—the Nephilim would have their eyes on the conflict brewing between the slaves and the whites while the demons snuck in unawares to flood the swamp through the gateway Moultrie would open for them.

Once we decimate those pesky Nephilim, there will be nothing standing in our way. Soon—very soon, in fact—I will have my pick of human garments to slip on, and I can't wait! This time, I think I'll go for something more youthful and virile.

Thinking there was no need to draw undue attention to herself, Hannah walked toward the stables at a fast clip, even though she really wanted to run. She slowed down a bit to mull over the plan in her head for what must have been the hundredth time. It was simple. The rebel forces would stop at every plantation on River Road, starting at Woodlawn Plantation, picking up additional rebels along the way. It was expected that a large contingency would join forces with Deslondes from the Meuillion and Kenner-Henderson Plantations.

Midway between Magnolia Hill and New Orleans, half of the Maroons would come out from under their rocks in the swamps to add to the ranks of the rebels coming from Woodlawn, Deslondes, LaBranche, Destrehan-Bernoudy, and all the smaller plantations in between.

When Hannah gave the signal, at least forty Maroons were going to crawl out of the wooded area bordering Magnolia Hill on their bellies. They would start fires in every field on the plantation. While the whites were fighting to put out the widespread fires, a second contingent would set fire to the barn, stable, and, lastly, if all went according to plan, the Big House itself.

This was where Hannah's plan would drastically diverge from Deslondes'. Once Magnolia Hill was destroyed, Hannah was instructed by Deslondes to lead the Maroons and any Magnolia Hill slaves who wished to join her down River Road to Destrehan-Bernoudy where they would bivouac with the other rebels. From there, they would march upon New Orleans as a unified force. Charles' ultimate goal was to conquer New Orleans and establish a black republic on the shores of the Mississippi. Lofty goals indeed.

Hannah's objective was to use Deslondes' well-planned revolt as a smoke screen to burn Magnolia Hill to the ground and kill every single white inside the Big House, including the overseer, Drake. *We don't want to leave him out, now do we?*

She couldn't care less if the slaves remained in bondage for the next thousand years, just as long as she wasn't one of them. Her cohorts would have to fend for themselves. And since Hannah hadn't seen her daughter Anna for the past two days, the little slut would have to fend for herself as well. Hannah didn't care what became of her.

She slipped inside the dark, cool confines of the stable to choose a horse for her getaway. The Maroons would torch the stable and the rest of the horses to thwart any means of escape for the occupants of the Big House. Once she and her army of Maroons put the house and surrounding buildings to the torch, she planned to make her escape—alone. She had the money and jewellery she'd stolen from old man Etienne and several items of clothing that happened to "go missing" from Janine and Justine's extensive wardrobes. When she rode away from Magnolia Hill for the last time, she would do so as a white woman.

Hannah giggled to herself. While Jacques Fortier of Kenner-Henderson Plantation, James Brown, and a host of others were stuffing their faces with food grown and prepared by slave hands and dancing upon floors Hannah had personally scrubbed on her hands and knees, Hannah was leading one of

Claude Etienne's fastest stallions a safe distance from the fields the Maroons would soon set afire. It was show time.

So as not to alarm the women folk, the planters unanimously agreed upon keeping the disturbing information they received from Benoit to themselves until the militia arrived, at which time they would be better able to determine the veracity of Benoit's information and assure the women of their continued safety and well-being. The last thing Claude or any of the other planters needed or wanted was full-scale panic. After all, nothing puts the kibosh on a good old-fashioned southern plantation party quicker than the possibility of a slave uprising.

As a precaution, Claude posted several of his most trusted slaves around the periphery of the plantation in what he considered to be vulnerable positions. He doubted there would be any threat within the boundaries of Magnolia Hill, but he needed to make sure no outside troublemakers slipped in to rouse his people up. He would be alerted at once should anything untoward occur.

So far, their plan seemed to be working. All was quiet, and none of the women seemed to have picked up on the strained expressions each of their menfolk was now wearing. Claude was determined to keep it that way.

He had just excused himself from an animated conversation with Messrs. Kenner and Hendersen on the merits of the hot box for recalcitrant slaves as opposed to the good old-fashioned whip when his keen grey gaze landed upon his wife. He couldn't help but note that she was pretty well in her cups. There was no disguising it. Janine's countenance bore the telltale signs of a confirmed drunkard.

Her eyes were glassy and red. Her face was shiny with the sweat that comes when an excess of alcohol is fighting to escape the body. Wisps of hair had come undone from her carefully dressed coiffure, blowing around her flushed face to the rhythm of the palmetto fan the slave was using in an effort to keep her cool.

Claude was disgusted. He could drink until he passed out in the middle of a dirt road—and frequently did—but no man wanted a drunkard for a wife, especially at a social event. He narrowed his grey eyes to slits. The thought crossed his mind that it may well be time to plant another wife up on the hill.

Janine rose unsteadily, staggering in the direction of the punch bowl for yet another cup of the fruity concoction that had been spiked with Magnolia Hill's special blend of rum. The crème de la crème of New Orleans society was enjoying her hospitality at no small expense while not one of the matrons had missed an opportunity to snub or insult her at some point during the night. *Fuck all of them.* Janine thought, intent upon getting drunk.

Claude had seen enough. He changed his original course, silently vowing to take Janine in hand before she managed to make a complete fool out of the both of them.

He'd nearly reached Janine, who was pouring another liberal cup of the potent punch, when Samuel ran into the ballroom with a harried expression on his face.

"Masta Claude! The cane fields is on fire!"

The Maroons had outdone themselves. Not one, but three cane fields were already ablaze. The air was still, enabling the hungry flames to make short work of the fields, eating up territory, and rendering everything the fire wrapped its blazing arms around to ash.

There was immediate pandemonium in the Big House. In a panic at the mere thought of losing his precious crops and all the profit they would generate, Claude enlisted the aid of the other planters to assist in putting out the fires, leaving the women locked inside the Big House unprotected. Every one of the house slaves disappeared right after Samuel's announcement. If Claude wanted to put those fires out, he and his planter buddies were going to have to do it themselves.

Claude fared no better once he got outside. Not one slave was available to help put out the fires. With manpower spread thin due to the scarcity of helping hands and the distance between each of the fires, Claude and the planters were fighting a losing battle.

CHAPTER 43

T HE WOMEN PANICKED upon hearing gunshots and shouts outside the Big House. Janine stumbled to a nearby window. She screamed and covered her mouth after one look.

"Nigras!" she said. "There's Nigras everywhere, and they aren't from Magnolia Hill!"

Janine realised that could mean only one thing: an uprising. Suddenly she was stone-cold sober. Janine turned and bumped into Nancy Brown, who had been right on her heels.

"This is all your fault, you low-class whore," Nancy said. "You think we don't know about how you used to lay with the darkies and push their babies out? Disgraceful, that's what you are. Disgraceful."

The dislike Nancy was barely able to conceal while in Janine's presence was now coming to the surface and bubbling over. From the looks on the faces of the other matrons and young ladies in attendance, they were of one accord: this was all Janine's fault. In fact, since Nancy had said so, everyone else was jumping on the "insult Janine" band wagon. They were afraid, and their fear manifested in anger.

"I told my husband we shouldn't have come to this den of iniquity. The pair of you—both you and your husband—are lower than the dirt beneath my feet," Nancy declared.

Nancy was two inches from Janine, spitting in her face with every one of her spiteful words. When Janine hauled back and slapped her in the face hard enough to bring tears to the mean-spirited woman's eyes, she gasped in surprise.

"I don't give a shit if any of you like me or not," Janine stated.

That statement got their attention alright.

"From this moment forward you don't have to worry about me ever trying to gain your acceptance. You may not be able to get it through your feeble little minds, but it appears this plantation is being overrun with rebels, yet here you are casting aspersions on my rumoured sex life.

"There is no time for this. Despite your low opinion of me, *I* for one want to live. Either shut your pseudo-aristocratic mouths and find something to defend yourselves with, or you can stand here hurling insults at me until that wild band of nigras come in to get you. Your choice, ladies," Janine said in a voice dripping with sarcasm.

Janine's words sank in because the ladies scurried like field mice to find something to defend themselves with and a place in which to hide.

"Oh my God, *Claude Junior!*" Justine exclaimed, leaving the flustered women to their own devices to check on her infant. She tripped over the hem of her ball gown in her haste to get up the stairs to the nursery. Her single thought was to get her precious baby somewhere safe. By the time she reached the top floor landing, she was out of breath.

She flung the nursery door wide open to find a whole lot of nothing—no baby and no nursemaid. Fear like she'd never known before spiked through her body. Frantic, she ran from room to room, flinging each door open and calling out Sally Mae's name. Her answer was silence. She hoped and prayed Sally Mae had taken her son to safety.

Hannah waited until Claude and the other planters were out at the far fields, working at what she knew would be a vain attempt to put out the fires before giving the signal to attack. Twenty Maroons swooped down on the Big House like vultures on fresh kill. Hannah stood back while one of the Maroons battered down the front door, and then they charged into the house.

Hannah's face was devoid of emotion as she watched the Maroons destroy everything in their path. Feet covered with mud and dust stained the floors as the Maroons rushed through the entryway like whirling dervishes, smashing furniture, china, and crystal in their wake.

One by one, the Maroons routed each of the planter's wives from their hiding places, dragging the terrified women out into the open to dispatch them. When a Maroon snatched one woman out from under the long table in the dining room, she had the nerve to scream, "Please! Please don't rape me!"

With his lips curled in distaste, he said, "The only thing I wish to stick inside your pale body is this!"

He shoved his blade into the woman's belly with a grunt of satisfaction. Their eyes were locked when he jerked the blade downward, slashing her open from abdomen to groyne. He held the woman upright in a macabre embrace until the light went out of her eyes. He then lowered her to the floor, bent to wipe his bloody blade on the skirt of her ball gown, and kicked her out of the way to move on to his next victim.

The Maroons reminded Hannah of slaves chopping sugar cane. They sliced away at every one of the women they could find, beheading some, scalping others, and hacking a few to pieces. The rage inside of each of them blinded them to their savagery.

Hannah didn't so much as blink an eye at the utter brutality taking place all around her. Bits and pieces of brightly coloured ball gowns in satin, lace, and precious silk adhered to body parts held together with the sticky glue of their blood. Many of the Etiennes' fancy guests lay scattered like a rainbow of broken toys.

Hannah canted her head to the side in response to a muffled sound. Soon her feet were carrying her to the butler's pantry. She flung the door open, and there was little chubby Emmaline Pele, huddled in a corner in a ball like a big fat roll of pastel-covered dough.

"Please don't hurt me," Emmaline whispered. Her bow-shaped lips and her double chin quivered as she stared up at Hannah with big imploring eyes.

Hannah's lips tightened into a cruel straight line as she raised the machete. Emmaline squealed like a mouse and looked away, shutting her eyes tight like a child trying to block out a particularly bad nightmare. By the time Hannah was standing directly over her, she'd raised her hands before her face in a defensive motion. Hannah swung the machete—hard.

Hannah let loose a grunt of pure satisfaction when one of Emmaline's hands and three fingers from the other hand landed on the floor with a solid "thump." Hannah swung again. This time the top of the machete cut through Emmaline's collar bone. She toppled over. The little piglet should have known better than to appeal to Hannah for mercy.

Hannah's chest was heaving in excitement from her first kill of the night. It felt good. She stepped out of the butler's pantry like a female Viking, with a murderous look in her eyes and blood spatter on her clothing.

Hannah didn't even bother to engage in pursuit when she heard the backdoor open and slam shut. She cared not that some of the women were able to escape sure death in the house. She knew they would be picked off by the Maroons camped at strategic places outside. It was just a matter of time before their pitiful lives would come to an end.

The women Hannah sought were not among the dead—at least not yet. She directed one of the Maroons to barricade the back door so that no one else could escape, then she determinedly made her way upstairs.

Justine nearly jumped out of her skin, whimpering like a lost child when she heard a loud crash below. The crash was followed by gunshots, thumps, and a cacophony of hair-raising screams. Then there was silence.

The silence was even more ominous then the screams had been because it was followed by the sound of a heavy tread, walking up the stairs in an unhurried fashion. Justine slammed and locked the bedroom door behind her with shaking hands.

Her eyes frantically searched the room she was in to find something to defend herself with, but there was nothing. Frightened out of her wits, she pressed herself up against the far wall, holding her breath as the steps grew nearer and nearer. Someone was walking down the hall, finally stopping right in front of the room she was in.

Justine's breath hitched in her throat when, seconds later, wood splintered and the sharp bite of cordite filled the room as the lock was shot out. A loud crash reverberated throughout the house as the door was kicked in. The slave woman Hannah stood in the doorway with eyes filled with loathing, a bloody machete in one hand and a gun in the other.

The fear Hannah saw in Justine's eyes felt better than a lover's kiss. She could only imagine what was going through Julien's demure young wife's mind at that very moment. It's not every day one has a slave with blood-spattered clothing standing over them with murder in their eyes. An occurrence like this fits into the "once in a lifetime" category.

"Where is the baby?" Hannah asked in a voice that didn't betray her excitement. She couldn't wait to chop the little Etienne "messiah" up in front of his doting parents.

For a split second, Hannah saw a bit of hope flash across Justine's face. She knew exactly what the frightened young woman was thinking: *'Surely Hannah would not have inquired about my son if she meant him or his mother harm. Would she?'*

Hannah wasted no time in disabusing Justine of that foolish notion with a quick crack in the mouth with the butt of the smoking pistol. Pointing with the tip of the gun, she directed the horrified woman to sit in a nearby straight-backed chair. She could feel Justine's body shaking as she tied the woman up with several belts she found in one of the dresser bureaus. She faced Justine again once she had her securely trussed up like a Thanksgiving turkey.

"Now, bitch, I'm going to ask you one more time. Where. Is. The. Baby! And this time I want an answer."

Justine struggled to speak through her ruined mouth.

"I don't know where my baby is—I swear. He was with Sally Mae in the nursery. When I came upstairs to get him, both the baby and Sally Mae were gone." She silently prayed Sally Mae had gotten her baby to safety.

"I don't..." She broke down in a paroxysm of tears. "I don't know where my son is."

Hannah believed her. No one, not even a white, could put on an act like that. She moved forward to slip Justine's dainty ball slippers off her feet. The women's body shook like she was afflicted with palsy. Hannah bent to pull the slippers onto her dirty bare feet and stood.

Okay. Change of plans.

Hannah looked around the bedroom for a means to dispatch the blubbering woman. A wicked smile captured her face when her eyes lit upon a taper. Hannah lit the taper in the fireplace and stood before Justine with glee in her eyes. Justine's eyes were now wide with dawning horror.

"No. Oh God no. Please don't do this! Please! Noooooooooooooo!"

Hannah lit the hem of Justine's pretty ball gown and watched it and her wiggle and dance in that straight-backed chair as both went up in flames. The burning woman's shrieks scratched the surface of Hannah bone marrow, causing her to grit her teeth. Justine's body would serve as the accelerant to burn the Big House from the top down.

CHAPTER 44

TYRANNY KNEW HIS place was with his brothers in hell, but he couldn't tear himself away from the marvellous scene that was unfolding before him. The sense of death, despair, and destruction had a hold on him more securely than a tight fist on a horny man's cock. And he was just as excited. He was about to do something that was inadvisable, but he would do it all the same.

Tyranny had not had occasion to use a vessel's body as his host since Hannah dispatched Clidamont Etienne. This opportunity was too damned good to pass up. Tyranny licked his forked demon tongue and stroked himself to the rhythm of the tortured screams coming from inside the Big House. He paused mid-stroke when he saw one of the females run out of the back door in a state of hysteria.

Tyranny recognised the distraught woman as Claude Etienne's wife, Janine. The woman was a fright with her dress stained and torn in places and her hair in total disarray. She spun around in a circle, probably trying to determine the best place to hide. She finally ended up heading in the direction of the rickety row of old wooden shacks the slaves resided in.

Now this is an interesting development, the demon thought.

Less than ten minutes later, the same door Janine Etienne had exited banged shut behind Hannah who, unlike Claude's wife, had a look of clear determination and intent upon her face.

My word, is that a bloody machete she has in her hand?

The demon couldn't help himself. Before he had time to talk himself out of it, he swooped down from his lofty height to perch upon the roof of the Big House. He briefly felt scorching heat on the soles of his cloven feet before he shot through the air to burrow inside the crown of Hannah's skull like a fiery arrow shot from a demonic bow. Hannah's body jerked as if struck by lightning.

Jessie, Merle, and another slave woman named Gloria were too old to run and too afraid to fight. The frightened women were huddled together on the floor of Merle's dark cabin. They'd barricaded the door with pieces of furniture at the first sign of conflict.

They listened to the mistress going down the row of cabins on Slave Row, first pleading then demanding entrance, hoping against hope to find shelter and protection. The slaves had a different idea. Those who had not banded with the rebels or run for the hills barred their doors against her.

Merle's was next to the last cabin. The wood threatened to buckle under the force of Janine's fist pounding upon Merle's cabin door. Her voice was near unrecognisable. She was frantic.

"Please let me in," Janine begged between pounds on the wooden door. "If you let me in, I'll have your master free you."

The women were too afraid to acknowledge Janine's improbable offer. To let the mistress in meant they would also be letting in whoever was chasing her, and they had no intentions of doing that.

There was a brief moment of silence. Merle thought Janine might have given up and was making her way back to the Big House. She let out a deep breath of relief, then heard scratching at the tarp Merle had draped over the inside of the makeshift window. Merle sprang into action without thinking.

"I'll be damned if I let that woman in this here cabin," she muttered. She clutched a metal cooking pot in her hand and slammed it with all her might against the impression Janine's hand made through the tarp. Her hostile action resulted in a series of curses from Janine.

"You niggers had better let me in that goddamned cabin if you know what's good for you! Once your master hears how I've been treated I will personally see that every single one of you is strung up for the crows to feed upon. Let me in," she hissed, only to be met with silence.

Finally, Janine cut her losses and ran to the last cabin at the end of Slave Row—a cabin that had once been inhabited by Flossie and her dead son Jake, but which now stood empty due to reports of ghosts. Jessie sent up a silent prayer of thanks that, after becoming the plantation cook, Flossie and Perline moved into the slightly larger cabin which housed the kitchen.

By the time Hannah departed the Big House, flames were already engulfing the roof and licking their way down its stately white columns. The Maroons were fleeing the house like wild animals one step before a forest fire. They knew to join their brothers that were already hiding in strategic locations on the plantation.

Everything is working according to plan, Hannah commented to herself. She heard a woman's scream. The scream was quickly muffled, but not before Hannah zeroed in on the general direction it came from—Slave Row. Hannah caught a glimpse of the familiar gold material she'd seen Perline carrying up to the Big House earlier that week.

Tyranny was looking through Hannah's eyes as she turned in the direction of Slave Row to stalk the fleeing woman in the bright gold ball gown.

Oh this is going to be so much fun!

The gold material of Janine's dress stood out like a bright beacon against the night. Hannah took her time following the woman, swinging her trusty machete along the way to get her wrist loose and limber for the task at hand.

Hannah walked the familiar tree-lined dirt road, taking in each shack she passed with her thin lips turned down in disdain. She needed to savour every step, every moment of her last night on Magnolia Hill. In many ways the plantation symbolised everything that had occurred in her life from the day Martin Singleton betrayed her to the day she'd died, gone to hell, and been reborn. She'd finally come full circle.

She looked down at the toes of her pretty peach evening slippers. They may have been incongruous to the dusty dirt road she tread and inappropriate for the task she intended, but in Hannah's mind the slippers were somehow befitting as she made her last walk down the length of shacks belonging to the slaves who should have been serving her. She wondered how many of them were cowering behind their flimsy cabin doors, watching her every step. She would allow them to live, so that they could tell their children about this night, so that they would never forget.

A wicked smile captured Hannah's lips. Other than the wooded area banking the side of Flossie's old cabin, there was no place else for Janine to run. Hannah picked up her pace when she heard Janine close the door to the last cabin on Slave Row.

When the coast was clear and she knew Janine had moved on, Merle scrambled to the window. She raised the corner of the tarp to peer in the direction of Flossie's old cabin. She slapped her hand over her mouth to trap the sound of terror when she saw Janine run into the haunted cabin, only to be followed shortly thereafter by Hannah.

Sweet Lord have mercy Jesus! Hannah has a machete in her hand!

Merle watched Hannah's arm rise and fall again and again. She was sickened by what she saw, but she couldn't look away. The other two women squeezed their eyes shut at the steady thump, thump, thump of Hannah's machete as she hacked Janine Nelson Etienne to pieces.

The clouds that promised rain all week long finally made good on their threat. Claude and Julien Etienne stood side by side with their shoulders slumped in defeat. The rain soaked their smoke-stained evening wear as they stood in the midst of the steam rising from acre upon acre of destroyed cane field. The pounding rain managed to beat the fire into submission where the collective efforts of the planters could not. It was too late to save Magnolia Hill's torched fields. They'd lost it all.

The stench of burning cane rode upon clouds of billowing black smoke, surrounding the plantation like the worst kind of rot. The smoke choked the weary planters and brought tears to Claude's and Julien's matching set of gunmetal grey eyes.

"There is nothing else we can do here, Father," Julien said wearily. "I suggest we return to the Big House and see to our women."

Claude didn't answer. He couldn't speak. He couldn't move. It appeared to his son that he was in some kind of trance. In actuality, he struggled to take in the extent of the sheer destruction surrounding him and needed a moment.

"Did you hear what I said, Father? We need to gather up the planters and get back to the women."

Julien could see his father was in shock. He had to force the old man to deal with the reality that these fires had been purposely set. With the rumour of a slave rebellion fresh on his mind, Julien was anxious to get back to the house so that they could properly arm themselves.

The rain stopped as quickly as it began, creating a muddy morass surrounded by a soupy curtain of oppressive humidity. The clip clop of horses made skittish from tense riders and the recent fires heralded the return of the exhausted planters to the Big House. Other than an occasional whinny from one of the horses or a grunt or snort from the hogs in the nearby pen, it was as quiet as a ghost town. In fact, as far as Claude was concerned, it was too damn quiet.

Claude was the first of the planters to notice something was off. He reined his horse in and slowly cantered up the drive leading to the Big House with the other planters close behind.

They stopped cold, all staring in shock and dismay at the half burned-out smoking ruin that had once been the Magnolia Hill mansion. They were still staring in horror and disbelief when Hannah's army of Maroons ambushed them.

Julien's horse reared, nearly unseating him when a single gunshot was fired. Seconds later, Earlson Bene went down like a ton of bricks as a Maroon bullet struck him in the side of the neck. The shooter flew out of nowhere to jump into Bene's empty saddle, swinging his machete like a dessert Bedouin. Bene's left foot was still caught in the stirrup, and the Maroon dragged the dying man's body around with him, stripping the clothes and skin off Bene's back as he galloped.

The same Maroon engaged and quickly brought down yet another planter with a vicious swing of his blade before Claude was able to take aim and shoot him out of the saddle. There was no time to worry about the women now. The men were fighting for their lives.

To the whites, it felt like the Maroons were everywhere at once—like there were 4,000 instead of forty. New fires sprang up in the barn, the stable, and several ancillary buildings used to process the sugar cane. Screams of horses roasting alive in the stable, mixed with the insane cacophony of shouts of jubilation, screams of fear, and moans of despair.

The Maroons were a fearsome sight, striking trepidation in the hearts of whites and slaves alike, with tribal war paint on their faces, machetes in their hands, and assorted articles of Claude and Julien's tailor-made clothing on their backs. Some even had rifles stolen from previous raids which they didn't hesitate to use with precision.

One of the Maroons set a lit torch to one of the slave cabins. Slaves ran around in circles along with their children, scrambling to figure out what to do and where to hide. One by one the cabins went up like dry kindling. Some even thought it was the end of the world as the fire leapt upon the limbs of the nearby Magnolia trees to rain down on their heads. In many respects, they were right. It was the end of the world—as they knew it.

Somewhere between fear and disillusionment were tears of resignation from those pathetic black creatures who decided to sit on the ground and watch the only home they'd ever known go up in smoke, hoping and praying things would be better in the afterlife.

In the midst of all the excitement Hannah decided it was time to slip away to the kitchen which served as Flossie and Perline's living quarters after the attack that disfigured Flossie and killed her son. She hoped that with the old woman dead and in her grave, the powerful ward Flossie placed around her dwelling had died as well. The Maroons were torching all the buildings on the plantation. Hannah was fearful the kitchen would go up in smoke before she had an opportunity to retrieve the *Grimoire*. She would not allow that to happen.

She spun uphill, in the opposite direction of the fighting, hoping against hope that little crippled bitch Perline would be cowering behind that flimsy wooden kitchen door praying for protection.

Your mama ain't around to protect ya now.

CHAPTER 45

HANNAH'S WICKED SMILE grew wider with each step she took. She knew exactly what she would do with Perline when she finally got her hands on her. First, she would brand her as a traitor, and then she intended to toss Flossie's innocent little crippled daughter to the wolves for their pleasure. The Maroons were near crazed with bloodlust. If Perline somehow managed to survive their brutal use, she would personally wring her scrawny black neck.

Flossie may have escaped my wrath by dying, she thought, *but her daughter is still around. She will serve just fine in Flossie's stead.*

Not sure exactly what might greet her on the other side, Hannah pushed the door to the kitchen open with caution only to find it empty. Everything was neat, clean, and in its proper place.

Although the kitchen was empty, Hannah could still feel the dead woman's powerful presence. Shaking off the eerie feeling of being watched, Hannah commenced her search.

For the next twenty minutes Hannah blocked out everything that was going on around her to search every inch of the space, using a torch to light her way. She found nothing. With each passing moment her frustration and anger rose. In a white-hot rage, she broke dishes, tossed pots and pans, and ripped any and everything to shreds she got her hands on. Realising that Flossie had somehow bested her from the grave, Hannah derived some small measure of pleasure in destroying the dead woman's belongings. It was time to go. She tossed the lit torch onto one of the pallets on the floor and closed the door behind her.

Hannah's mean, dark eyes followed Claude Etienne from the vantage point of Flossie's old cabin. He fought like a mad man, using his gun and his massive horse's hooves as weapons. His horse stomped upon any hapless Maroon who was unfortunate enough to fall and on any innocent slave to block his path. He fought with a ferocity that always accompanies a desperate desire to stay alive.

Hannah's attention was temporarily drawn back to the house when James Brown broke away from the pack, screaming out his wife Nancy's name in anguish. La Branche and Destrehan, two other planters, followed him. Brown took a bullet in the shoulder as he galloped toward the smouldering heap. That didn't stop him. He kept on riding. His determination paid off when seconds later his wife and three other women rose like Lazarus out of the double root cellar doors on the basement level of the house with soot-covered faces and singed hair.

Hannah laughed when the planters pulled the women in front of them on their horses and rode off without looking back, leaving the Etiennes and the others to fend for themselves. In her opinion, each of them deserved to have their lives spared for that simple act alone.

It was at that moment when one of the Maroons slammed the butt of his rifle into the back of Claude's head, bringing him to his knees. When he delivered a second blow, a black curtain descended before Claude's eyes. This time Claude went down and didn't get up. The remaining planters were easily subdued.

It was Hannah's turn to exact her revenge.

Claude was abruptly jolted back to the here and now when someone tossed a bucket of brackish water in his face. He came to, sputtering and choking, and found himself trussed hand and foot tighter than a Thanksgiving turkey. He couldn't find one place on his body that wasn't screaming in agony and begging for relief.

Kenner, Henderson, Meuillion, and his son were similarly confined. The whole lot of them was surrounded by a nightmarish group of bloodthirsty blacks bent on exacting their special form of revenge. The table had turned. Claude recognised one of the Maroons as a slave that had escaped from Magnolia Hill years ago. He knew for a fact that, if he didn't think fast, things were not going to go well for them.

"I should have known you were involved in this," Claude hissed when the crowd of Maroons separated to allow Hannah to step forward. It was clear she was their leader. His grey eyes were like chips of ice-covered slate when they landed on Hannah. Even tied up and facing the possibility of imminent demise, he unknowingly exuded an air of superiority and remained defiant.

Of course I am the leader, you fucking fool, Hannah thought, not even bothering to respond to Claude's observation. *Who else could accomplish all this?*

She was still basking in the exhilaration of having the object of her hatred at a distinct disadvantage. Her hands were no longer tied, and she could finally do something about that acidic loathing that was nearly eating her alive.

"You niggas won't get away with this!" Julien spat with blood and teeth flying out of his bloody, busted lips. "The militia is on its way even as we speak. If they don't get here first, you better believe that Brown, La Branche, and Destrehan are rounding up a contingency to deal with you and your ragtag army. Brown will probably lead the charge, and when they get here, they're gonna rip the skin off each one of your hides and feed what's left of you to the vultures!"

Hannah looked at Julien once he concluded his impassioned speech as if he was little more than a pesky fly. The look on Claude's face was different. He looked at his son with pride in his eyes. *My son is a real man*, he thought. *He's nothing like his effeminate, weak, elder brother Henri.*

It angered Claude that the weak son was safe in a monastery in France while his favoured son was in peril. If he could just keep the stupid nigga talking, maybe—just maybe—he would be able to buy enough time so that he and Julien could get out of this bucket of shit situation they were in.

Claude assumed Janine and Justine were dead. *Good*, he thought. *That will save our having to get rid of them later. We will rebuild Magnolia Hill. Not only will it be bigger and better, but next time I'll make sure we have a firmer hand on our niggas so that nothing like this ever happens again.*

"You always did have a mouth that was way too big and a cock that is way too small, Julien," Hannah said spitefully.

Julien's face flushed red with anger and shame. There was a spattering of laughter at Hannah's comments and the obvious affect her words had on Julien.

"I'll tell you what," she said judiciously. "Since you have so kindly alerted us to the pending arrival of the militia, and since we are obviously running out of time, why don't we speed these proceedings up a bit—shall we?"

Both Claude's and Julien's eyes nearly popped out of their heads from her tone and her diction. During all the years they'd known Hannah, she'd always spoken what the whites referred to as "nigga-speak."

"Surprised I've mastered the king's English, Claude?" she said, as if she could read their minds. "I guess you would be. It was far easier to act ignorant to keep from getting whipped or worse. I became a master pretender, especially when I was forced to endure your pitiful sexual efforts. Everything about you makes me sick. You repulse me, and you smell like a mangy, filthy wet dog."

This was Hannah's moment in the sun. She intended to end the lives of both senior and junior Etiennes, but not before she humiliated them and made them feel like they were less than human.

"My name is *Mehwish Shumaila bin Said al-Murgebi.* Say it," Hannah commanded.

She whispered something to one of the Maroons when her request was met with stubborn tight-lipped silence. The Maroon raised a long sharp blade and hacked off one of Julien's fingers.

The veins in Julien's thick neck bulged.

"Shit!" he bellowed at the top of his lungs.

Claude screamed as if it was he who had been cut and not Julien.

"Now," Hannah said in a patient tone one would use with a rather slow-witted child. "I'm going to tell you one more time, Claude. Say. My. Motherfuckin. Name! Repeat after me, *Mehwish Shumaila bin Said al-Murgebi.*"

"Father, just say it," Julien begged as blood poured out of the place his severed digit had once been. "It doesn't really mean anything, Father. Just say it, please."

Claude's voice was trembling with rage when he repeated Hannah's given name.

"Your name is not Hannah. It is *Mehwish Shumaila bin Said al-Murgebi*." The hatred pouring out of Claude's eyes was as solid as a brick wall and, under the circumstances, just as impotent.

"Now was that so hard?" Hannah asked with a satisfied smile on her face. She didn't expect an answer, and she didn't get one. She returned her attention to Julien.

"I see you think your father's capitulation has no significance, Julien. I told you your mouth was bigger than your cock, didn't I?"

She whispered yet another order in the ear of that brooding Maroon who had chopped off Julien's finger.

Julien struggled in vain when the maroon reached his large hand inside the opening of Julien's trousers. There was a loud ringing in his ear along with the sound of his father begging, "No. Please! God no. Not that. Pleeeeeeaaaase!"

Julien couldn't see what the Maroon intended to do from the position he was in. However, Claude could. His father kept screaming "God. Oh God, please help us!"

But God wasn't present on Magnolia Hill. It seemed like *He* fled right along with the demons.

Julien felt a horrible burning sensation between his thighs. He wasn't aware of exactly what had been done to him until the grinning Maroon raised his bloody trophy between his thumb and forefinger for all to see. Julien's mouth slacked wide open in a silent scream as the Maroon shoved his thimble-sized manhood down his throat.

The pain was horrific. He wanted to die. Julien's body twitched from head to toe while the red stain at the apex of his pants grew larger and larger. Claude wept like a disconsolate child when God answered Julien's prayer. Claude's screams soon turned to whimpers.

"Claude, I suggest you not waste your tears on Julien," Hannah said succinctly. Her voice was cold and impersonal. "As you can see, he's already dead. Under the circumstances I think you should be more concerned about your own well-being."

"I have been setting things in motion for this moment for quite some time, Claude. I knew from when I worked at Maison Plaisir that your son Henri took it up the ass, and I knew who was giving it to him. So-o-o, I set big boy over there on his own brother, knowing full well what would happen. My only disappointment is that Julien didn't kill Henri along with his black lover. However, I must admit that your daddy's illness on that same night was an unexpected bonus. I killed your damned daddy. Yup, it was me," she boasted. "I made sure he suffered before I did it too. I wish I could bring that cocksucker back to life, so that I can kill him all over again. It felt *that* good."

She drew close to Claude so that she could whisper in his ear. "I sliced Janine up into bite-sized pieces this evening, and I tied your daughter-in-law to a chair and burned that bitch alive. So, you see Claude, I am singularly responsible for decimating your entire family. At long last, Claude, it's your turn."

She turned to the Maroon with the bloody knife. In a voice that was all business she said, "Feed him to the hogs," and walked away.

CHAPTER 46

NEVER ALLOWING HIMSELF to forget that he was dealing with a duplicitous, conniving, lowlife demon is what had kept the Wizard Moultrie alive and out of the clutches of Zuet and the Nephilim he had betrayed. He didn't doubt for a minute that, given the right incentive, the imp would serve him up to his enemies.

"Who do you serve?" the Wizard asked Feo the Imp in a voice that was wet and slimy, like mould on a window.

"It is you that I serve, Master. Only you," the imp replied in deference.

Moultrie moved closer to the imp, sucking up his personal space and making him decidedly uncomfortable. Feo knew what he was dealing with. The Arch Mage Wizard was as dangerous as a snake who had escaped its cage after a lifetime of teasing. No one ever knew when it would strike. Feo feigned interest in an object in the room to create an excuse to take a step back, but Moultrie wasn't fooled. It pleased him that the imp feared him. Fear was good.

"Do you have what I asked for?" the Wizard asked.

"Yes, Master, I have it."

Feo handed over a sack. It held a baby that had stopped crying hours ago.

Moultrie took the package from the imp with care, placing it on a table made of oily black wood.

"Tell me it is still alive," he said eagerly.

"Yes, Master. Of course, it's alive."

Feo didn't know if the Etienne baby was alive or not. The last thing the imp wanted to do was displease the Wizard. The Wizard reminded Feo of Satan himself when he was displeased.

He held his breath when Moultrie lifted the baby out of the sack and expelled an audible sigh of relief. Even though its skin was blue, there was still some life left in it.

"This will do just fine," Moultrie said. "Come. I will need your assistance in preparing the chamber."

Except for the light from three lit candles on a table in the formation of a triangle, the room was dark. In the centre of the candles was a round bowl filled to the top with rain water from the recent storm. Moultrie sat facing the centre candle. He placed two drops of conjurer's oil in the bowl.

An overpowering scent of burning incense filled the room. Before the imp's arrival, Moultrie consumed fly agaric mushroom, a mild hallucinogenic, to heighten his senses. He breathed deeply of the incense, then he raised an ornate chalice to his lips which was filled with the blood of a wizard more powerful than he—a wizard who died at Moultrie's hands. He drank deeply of the dead wizard's blood, thus transferring the dead man's vast store of power and knowledge onto himself. He drained the contents of the chalice.

Blood has powerful energy—a life force. It is for that reason that demons are drawn to it. The Wizard then used a ceremonial knife to slice a deep runnel in the palm of his hand. This would serve as his personal blood offering.

On the floor was a diagram of a pentagram, the Triangle of Solomon. In the centre of the pentagram was a stone dais whereupon the Etienne baby lay. He too had been given a bit of the mushroom.

Moultrie's head was shaved clean. He was garbed in a coarse black monk's robe. He began chanting in Dimoori Sheol, the universal language of demons, while alternately walking the outline of the pentagram, first clockwise and then counterclockwise in what is referred to by practitioners of majick as "wickersham."

"Spirits bound by the great Solomon, I summon thee!" he began in a deep rumbling voice. "Let your presence be made manifest. You will serve me as you served Solomon!"

The Wizard repeated this phrase over and over again while blood from the deep gash in his palm rained down upon the floor with his every step.

On the sixth revolution he pulled back his cowl and allowed the robe to slide down his body to his feet. He was naked beneath the robe. He was Nephilim and perfectly formed. His burnished skin, upon which he'd massaged precious oil, shone like burnt copper.

He was now ready to sacrifice the "goat without horns," a black magic euphemism for an innocent child. It mattered not that the Etienne infant did not fit into that category. Moultrie would still murder, dismember, and eat the flesh of the Etienne child, thereby opening the gateway that would allow Zuet's demons to flood the human realm.

Grato Quies, Baton Rouge

The Widow Solonge ghosted into King Zion's bedroom earlier that evening unannounced. She grasped the silver gargoyle carved into the handle of her cane firmly, with twisted fingers that looked like they had been broken more than once. Her free hand shook as she stood before her king, dressed in black from head-to-toe.

You wouldn't know it by the look of her, but Solonge of the House of Shemyaza had once been a breathtaking beauty, married to a valiant Gibborim warrior, and the mother of two lovely children. That, however, was several lifetimes ago.

Solonge's husband Tremaine, of the House of Shemyaza, served as a double-agent who infiltrated demonic hordes to supply the Brothers of the Dark Veil with invaluable information. Tremaine's role as a spy was discovered during his last mission. He barely escaped the fifth level of the hells with his life. A high-placed demon, who was demoted for not filtering out the mole, kidnapped his wife Solonge and their two children in retaliation.

Seven nights later Solonge was unceremoniously dumped in front of King Zion's Baton Rouge residence, horribly disfigured and barely clinging to life. The demons had tortured her, murdered the children, and starved her of the blood all Nephilim require to sustain life and heal. Her wounds became permanent.

When Tremaine learned of his precious children's death and saw what was left of his once beautiful wife, he fell to his knees beside her torn body, keening like a wounded animal. He blamed himself for his family's fate. The next morning, Tremaine walked outside and let the sun take him.

Widow Solonge had suffered much for the sake of the Nephilim Nation. When she spoke, the king listened.

"I've had yet another vision," she proclaimed, without preamble. "The news I will impart could not wait until the morrow."

Zion braced himself for the news. Since her abduction Solonge experienced visions of the future. The visions were never good.

"There will be a demonic uprising in the Atchafalaya Swamps."

This would not be the first time Zion acted on her counsel nor would it be the last.

Zion personally saw the Widow Solonge safely back to her cottage. He was well aware that no one in his right mind this side of the Dark Veil was courageous or foolish enough to accost her. His action was merely a courtesy.

Clearly, Solonge was mad. Zion would not dispute that, but inside that maelstrom of madness was the truth. It was because of that knowledge that Zion didn't discount her warning or demand that she reveal her source. His keen sense of smell allowed him to pick up a hint of demon surrounding her. He had a good idea from whence her information was derived.

Zion sniffed the air. The atmosphere was ripe for Zuet's intended invasion. Zuet and his youngest son, the Dark Prince, were bound by the Ancient of Days to remain trapped within the confines of the seven levels of the hells, however, Zuet's demons were not bound by that same restriction. Since they were hideous in their natural appearance, the demons preferred to operate under the guise of invisibility until they could slip inside the body of an unsuspecting human.

If the demons are allowed through the gateway, each demon will have a small window of time within which to find a suitable human host. The host would have to be a purveyor of evil deeds and meet the added criteria of godlessness.

The recent slave rebellion had been quelled in a manner so lacking in humanity that it bordered on demonic. All nature of evil deeds had been perpetrated by the whites against the slaves and vice versa, leaving chinks in their souls as wide as a canyon and chasms of godlessness deep enough for demons to step right on it and work their evil. It all made sense.

Zion's long-legged stride ate up the distance between Solonge's lonely little cottage on the outskirts of his vast property and his home. He chose to walk rather than ghost because he needed time to think.

Zuet's proposed act of aggression would have to be met with an equal show of force on Zion's part. He turned his handsome face toward the heavens, contemplating what course of action he would take. The shine in his vibrant gold eyes rivalled the brightest star overhead. There was much to be considered. In order to crush Zuet's demons Zion would need his full honour guard and a large contingent of each of their Gibborim, including Ajuma and the soldiers who served under his command. It pained him to admit that his dear friend, Ajuma, hadn't been quite right in the head since the death of his human. The last thing he needed was an unstable brother in the field with him.

But damn. This is Ajuma, he thought.

It seemed like yesterday that Zion and Nicodemus had rescued the broken male Ajuma had become from that old slave cemetery at Magnolia Hill. Thereafter Ajuma had refused to eat, drink, or feed. He would not speak or acknowledge anyone's presence. They thought surely they would lose him when he attempted to walk into the sun while in his weakened state. That failed attempt began a pattern of additional attempts which made it necessary for Zion to order Ajuma be taken to his castle in Germany where he was chained hand and foot and locked inside a dungeon cell. There he was force fed until he regained a fraction of his senses.

Ajuma's body eventually healed, but not his mind. When Zion looked into Ajuma's eyes he knew that the Ajuma he had once known and loved was no longer there. His familiar green eyes were empty. Zion missed the male Ajuma had once been. He sorely missed his good friend. Zion didn't know what a return to the swamp area that was so close to Magnolia Hill and his human's grave would do to Ajuma's already fractured mental state. It might send him off the deep end.

Zion reached the house, but he didn't go inside right away. He watched the Anakin servants through one of the many windows calmly going about their duties. He was surrounded by Nephilim on every inch of his property. Yet the presence of others failed to dispel the feeling of being alone.

Ajuma was not Zion's only concern. The demons were powerless on their own. In order to facilitate a gateway to accommodate that number of demons, someone had to conduct a particularly vile ritual—a ritual that would require the blood sacrifice of an innocent.

Zion would not only have to stop the demons at the gate, but he would have to ascertain the identity of the individual who was in collusion with Zuet. He had a good idea how he would accomplish the first task, and he would ask the Ancient of Ages to reveal to him what he needed to know as to the second. It was time for him to round up his males.

Zion's mental message calling up every member of the Brothers of the Dark Veil had been answered by everyone but Rephidim.

"Where is Rephidim?" he asked.

"I believe he returned from his residence in Mississippi more than a fortnight ago, though, admittedly, I have not seen him since then," Gideon offered by way of explanation for Rephidim's absence.

"Well, I guess someone will have to fetch him here immediately," Zion responded. His penetrating gaze landed on Nicodemus.

"It is not like Rephidim to fail to respond to a summons. Go to his townhouse in the city. Make sure all is well with the brother, and then bring him here," Zion ordered. "We have a lot of work to do."

Without a word Nicodemus ghosted out of the room.

CHAPTER 47

NICODEMUS POUNDED ON Rephidim's door. *Where are the Anakin servants?* he wondered. Frustrated after his repeated attempts to gain entry to Rephidim's New Orleans townhouse went unanswered, Nicodemus took the liberty of ghosting into the brother's house to see if anything was wrong. He stepped into Rephidim's master bedroom suite with a dumbfounded expression on his face.

Nicodemus quickly took in the scene. Rephidim was camped out in an uncomfortable looking chair at a sick woman's bedside. Nicodemus could see Rephidim was clearly concerned for the human's well-being. Other than the woman's shallow breathing, it was as quiet as the grave in Reph's house. It took Nicodemus all of ten seconds to recognise who the human was.

"Aw shit, Reph. Please tell me that is *not* who the fuck I think it is!"

A ghostly pale Monique Dubonnet was lying under a mountain of blankets in the centre of Rephidim's big brass bed looking damn near dead. Nico dibbled and dabbled in human meat on occasion, but this was definitely *not* Rephidim's style.

Nicodemus wiped the sweat that appeared on his face the minute he entered the room. A hill of logs was burning in the fireplace. It was stiflingly hot in the room. Nicodemus knew something was wrong when the ever-polite brother didn't bother to stand upon his arrival. *That* wasn't Rephidim's style either.

"What in the fuck is going on here, Rephidim?" Nicodemus asked, as he looked at the obviously ailing human with worry on his face. It was plain to see that something other than a casual acquaintance had developed between Rephidim and the human.

"You look like shit on a stick," Nico added. He tore his eyes away from Monique to focus his attention on Rephidim.

"I'm not even going to ask what's wrong with her or why she's in your bed, but I damned sure hope you will enlighten me anyway."

Rephidim was too damned weary to take offence at Nicodemus' tone or the invasion of his privacy. For the past fortnight he had been sitting vigil at Monique's bedside, watching her chest rise and fall, and praying to the Ancient of Days that each laboured breath she took would not be her last. She had come to mean a great deal to him. He'd dismissed the Anakin to care for her himself, virtually cutting himself off from the outside world, and he couldn't recall when he had last fed.

Nicodemus moved closer to the bed to get a better look at the human. His innocent action caused Rephidim to go on the defensive. His deep brown eyes went totally black and a warning growl rolled out of Rephidim's throat. Nicodemus took a step back. He raised both hands toward Rephidim, palms up.

"Whoa, stand down, brother. I'm not going to touch her, I swear. Look, Reph, I apologise for barging in on you like this, but when you didn't respond to Zion's mental message, he sent me here to personally fetch you."

Three shades of black faded from Rephidim's face. He'd been so preoccupied with Monique's care that he'd done the unthinkable. He had missed a summons from the king. Zion rarely called them on short notice, but when he did you best believe it was important. Rephidim felt like he would be sick to his stomach.

Nicodemus could clearly see how upset Rephidim was. Rephidim was a reliable brother. It was not like him to blow off a summons from their king, yet there was no time to delve further into what was going on with the brother now. That was a conversation that would have to wait until later. They had a surprise party to throw for a bunch of demons, and Nico didn't intend to be late. Nicodemus filled the ensuing silence with an explanation for the summons.

"We have a situation. Zion has it on good authority that a powerful arch mage wizard in league with Zuet will open a gateway for a horde of demons in the swamp tonight. Zuet intends to flood the swamp with the demons and take us by surprise.

"To add insult to injury, all hell broke loose in St. John the Baptist Parish. The slaves up and down River Road staged a rebellion."

"I didn't know anything about a slave uprising."

"I can't believe you didn't know anything about it," Nico said incredulously. "There are severed heads mounted on poles the entire length of River Road. You can smell the stench of rotting flesh ten miles away. Shit, man, the rebels killed ten people, and from what I heard the ten they took out deserved killing.

In retaliation, the whites severed the heads of all the rebel leaders and chopped up several of the participants like stew meat. I don't know how true it is, but I heard they roasted the rebel leader alive."

Rephidim bent his head and rested his elbows on his knees in a posture of defeat. He couldn't even look at the Nicodemus. He'd missed so much, and he was so weary. He had been at Monique's side the entire time. Nicodemus's next words got his attention.

"We are about to battle, Reph. We need you."

Each of the Brothers of the Dark Veil have a special supernatural talent. Some had more than one. They were at their strongest when they fought as a unit.

"Let's ghost, brutha."

"I can't leave her, Nico." Rephidim said, looking Nicodemus square in the eyes for the first time that night.

Nico's response was quick. "Sure you can, man. Get one of the Anakin to sit with her."

He got it that Rephidim had feelings for the human, but business was business. They had some demons to kill.

"I sent the servants to the house in Mississippi. I didn't want any of them to know," Rephidim said cryptically.

"Didn't want any of them to know what, man?"

Nicodemus's earlier frustration was now turning into uneasiness. His question was met with silence, so he asked again.

"Reph, what didn't you want the servant to know?"

Nico was starting to get nervous. Rephidim was so slow to answer, he was fearful that Rephidim would not answer at all. Nico drew closer to the bed, not caring if his close proximity to the human riled Rephidim or not.

"What the hell did you do, Reph?" Nico asked in a voice just above a whisper.

When Rephidim finally did speak, Nicodemus thought he hadn't heard him correctly. "Say that again, man."

Rephidim took a deep breath and spit it out. "I dismissed the Anakin. I didn't want them to know that I gave Monique Dubonnet the dark kiss," he said. "She won't wake up, Nico. It's been nearly two decades, and she won't wake up."

Stunned, Nico merely stared at him. For the first time in his centuries-old life, Nicodemus Urakabarameel was completely and utterly at a loss for words.

Rephidim's secret was out. Now that Nicodemus knew he had granted Monique Dubonnet the dark kiss, Nico would surely tell Zion. Tired of all the deceptions and half-truths that had piled up from the size of a mole hill to a mountain, Rephidim told Nicodemus everything.

"Two weeks ago, Monique came down with a fever. I almost lost her. The worst part is over, but as you can see, she still isn't out of the woods."

"I have been fearful for her well-being for years and worried about how long I will be able to keep this secret from Zion and the rest of you Brothers of the Dark Veil. Now, here you appear, Nico, like magic.

"The weight of my lies by omission is weighing heavily on my soul. In my mind, your untimely appearance could only mean one thing. It is the will of the Ancient of Days that I finally unburden this weight with the truth. So here goes.

Monique has been in a coma ever since I gave her the dark kiss nearly two decades ago. She didn't ask for this, Nico. I am worried that she will remain trapped inside that grey world of a shade—not dead and not quite alive, for eternity. The guilt of what I have done to her weighs heavily on my shoulders.

Maybe that is why I feel that I have to care for her myself—that I owe her. Anakin have a tendency to gossip. Out of all the Anakins I employ in my Mississippi residence and here in New Orleans, I could only trust a couple of my servants to care for her. I rely upon them when I am not around to care for her myself."

Rephidim was still unable to verbalise the fact that every single breath the Ancient of Days allowed Monique Dubonnet to take was for him a precious one. This unexplainable devotion he felt for a stranger, and a human at that, was taking its toll. It had been days since he'd fed or taken his rest.

"Listen, Reph, I don't know what to say other than you can trust me with this confidence. Upon my honour, I will not go to Zion with this. It's your story to tell if and when you feel comfortable."

Rephidim let out an audible sigh of relief. It was no secret that their king had a decided dislike for humans. If Monique ever did wake up, Rephidim would have to bring her into one of the Nephilim communities. Zion didn't trust humans. The last thing he would want is to have one live among them.

"This is what we are going to do," Nicodemus said, taking command of the situation. "I will summon an Anakin from my residence in the city to sit with your human. I trust her implicitly. Now, when is the last time you fed?" he asked.

Rephidim ran his big hand over his face before answering.

"It has been far too long, Nico," he responded.

"That is as I suspected," Nicodemus replied. He raised his wrist to his mouth. There was a flash of fang as he opened a vein in his wrist and offered it to Rephidim.

"Drink, brother. We've got some demons to kill."

Once Rephidim had his fill, they ghosted to Zion's residence. Nicodemus and Rephidim arrived in time.

Every eye was on Zion. "Now that everyone is finally present and accounted for," Zion stated, looking directly at Rephidim and Nicodemus, "let us proceed with our war council. I have given the current situation a great deal of thought and have decided how we shall proceed. This is the plan."

CHAPTER 48

The Atchafalaya Swamps

THE STARLESS NAVY blue sky served as a backdrop to shimmering gold dust as one by one, Nicodemus, Gilead, Simeon, Boaz, Antioch, Rephidim, Ajuma, and 500 Gibborim warriors ghosted into the middle of the swamp. To ensure Zion's safety, it was the custom of the Brothers of the Dark Veil to always precede their king into battle. Tonight would be no different.

They were frightening to behold—tall, brawny males with supernatural senses, paranormal powers, preternatural gifts, and no-nonsense, harsh expressions on their otherworldly handsome faces. Their eyes missed nothing. They scanned their surroundings with enhanced vision and listened for even the slightest movement with their superhuman hearing. When the area was secure and all was deemed clear, a blinding blast of light heralded the arrival of their king. It was eerily quiet as they waited for Zion to speak.

"We have come full circle," Zion began, as his eyes swept over the Nephilim warriors. "I know that all of you is remembering our fruitless search for Ephraim so many years ago in this very same swamp. I am also grappling with those memories, and I shall never forget that a link in the mighty chain of the Nephilim Nation has been broken nor shall I forget who and what was responsible for breaking it." His gold eyes burned with emotion as they swept the assemblage.

"Those cocksucking demons were involved in young Ephraim's disappearance. You know it. I know it. We will dedicate tonight's battle to the memory of Ephraim of the House of Armers and may the Ancient of Days bless and find favour with his young soul."

"To Ephraim!" the warriors shouted collectively before they moved out.

The sprawling million-plus acres of the Atchafalaya River Basin were hauntingly beautiful, with moss-draped bald cypress trees that thrived in its fertile soil and fecund wetlands, bayous, and marshes that served as home to 300 species of birds, ninety species of fish, and fifty-four species of reptiles and amphibians. All of them flourished in the murky waters of the swamp. Zion knew this because he made it a point to know even the most minute details when the safety and well-being of his subjects was concerned.

He cast his stately profile in a curious fashion, blocking out everything to allow his senses to become one with his surroundings, then he closed his eyes to allow his spirit to truly hear.

The silence in the air was ominous, made even more so since there was no sign of birds, fish, reptiles or four-legged creatures of any kind. Even the mighty gators had run to ground on this night. Animals were always quick to flee in the face of danger. Their absence leant Zion to know that not only was the information given him by the Widow Solonge accurate, but that he was in the right place at the right time.

The king took a moment to absorb the power pulsing out of each of the Brothers of the Dark Veil. He knew that they would gladly lay down their life, not only for him, but for the good of the Nephilim Nation. Each looked to him for direction. He said a silent prayer that the Ancient of Days would strengthen him and let him not grow weary. The Satan was always busy, and there was much work to be done.

He directed his attention to the Gibborim. They were 500 strong. Many of them were on their first mission and had not yet seen a demon, never mind killed one. Their faces revealed myriad emotions—excitement, anxiety, and, in some instances, fear. All of those emotions were normal before a battle. Only a fool would be unafraid to face Zuet's demons. Zion wondered how many of them would die tonight. He would not allow the neophytes to go into battle without at least a few words from their king.

"The demons we will fight tonight believe they are taking us by surprise. They will not be expecting us. We will initially have the advantage of surprise, but make no mistake about it, all of you will be fighting for your lives and the lives of the Nephilim Nation we are sworn to protect."

He paused to let his words sink in.

"There are rules of engagement set down by the Ancient of Days that preternatural beings are commanded to adhere to. According to those rules, we are preempted from killing any of the Fallen. Scripture states that their time and place of death will be determined by the will of the Ancient of Days."

Zion savoured the moment, knowing he had every one of the Gibborim's attention.

"I say fuck the rules of engagement, and fuck the scripture. Feel free to kill every single demon that crosses your path, and make sure that you do it with extreme prejudice. Oh, and remember this. Since theirs is a demonic nature, the Fallen don't believe in playing by the rules either. So, watch your backs."

Nicodemus broke the oppressive silence that followed Zion's words to speak the obvious. "Okay, now that the pep talk is over, how do we determine where the gateway will open, Zion? This swamp consists of millions of acres. There is no way we can comb it before daybreak."

"I'm glad you asked that question," Zion replied. "We will simply follow the smell of shit, my brother. I suspect that at this very moment those pesky demons are pressed against the other side of that gateway, anxious as all hell to get out. With that much demon power packed together, they will smell like one thousand backed-up outhouses."

No sooner were the words out of Zion's mouth when a strong gust of wind blew past them, carrying with it the familiar smell of roasted excrement. Without a word, the brothers allowed their supernatural sense of smell to take over as they moved in that direction.

It wasn't long before they found it—a nasty sink hole not far from a dried-up bog and a huge leafless tree. The tree was distinctive. It had a gnarled black trunk and twisted limbs that appeared to reach out angrily in all directions. The smell coming from the sink hole alone was powerful enough to bring tears to their eyes.

"Damn, that shit stinks," Boaz stated, bringing his hand up to cover his nose.

Antioch was quick to choke out an agreement.

"Who the fuck you telling, brother?"

The other brothers remained quiet, fearful the demon stink would travel into their mouths and burrow down their throats.

Ajuma stood at a distance. He was deemed unstable after Flossie's and Jacob's deaths. When he finally did come to his senses, Zion posted him as far away from Louisiana as possible. For years, he and his men battled evil in Asia. Asia might seem like a world away from Louisiana, but it was not far enough to out-distance Ajuma's memories. He wasn't the same male he had been before Flossie and Jake died. To make matters even more uncomfortable, he had not seen his brothers in decades. After what he had been through, he no longer knew how to relate to them. All he knew how to do was kill, and he was anxious to be about it.

A band of 100 Gibborim formed a circle around Zion and the Brothers of the Dark Veil in a solid wall of muscle and protection. The brothers quickly went into action, pulling sticks of dynamite out of their pockets and from the lining inside their flowing ankle-length coats. They shoved the sticks of dynamite in strategic places around the circumference of the sink hole, burying several sticks under the accumulated deposit of dead plant material inside the bog. They performed their tasks with silent efficiency, communicating anything that needed to be said telepathically. Once everything was in place, the Brothers of the Dark Veil looked to Zion for direction. With a nod of his noble head, they cloaked their figures in invisibility and prepared to wait the demons out.

Minutes later, the earth beneath their feet began to rumble. Like a huge yawning mouth, the sink hole gaped wide open, belching forth a menagerie of at least thirty or more monstrous demons.

But who the hell was counting? Zion thought.

The Nephilim were hard-pressed to maintain their invisibility as the demons knocked one another down to be the first to clear the gateway. The Nephilim watched the demons cavort at their successful entry into the human realm, waiting for the right moment to attack. The more demons they could take down during the initial strike, the better.

Clearly the demons hadn't expected any interference in their dastardly plans since they hadn't even bothered to present themselves in their customary illusion of comely looking males or females. They were in their true form. The Ancient of Days stripped all of the Fallen of their angelic countenances when he cast them out of the heavens. Since that time they have been forced to cast an illusion of their former beauty while among humans. Zion knew them to be lower than the scum Zuet scraped off the fucked-up walls in the lowest level of the hells. It was almost time to strike. Zion sent a telepathic message to Ajuma.

"Aim for the centre of the bog. Make sure the peat in the centre of the quagmire catches. I will concentrate on the circumference of the sink hole. Let's do it now!"

Zion and Ajuma became visible to all, momentarily shocking the demons into utter and complete stupefaction. Before the demons could register what was actually happening, the remaining Brothers of the Dark Veil became visible and the Gibborim Warriors, most of whom were still in a circle of menacing muscle around the battle site. Zion and Ajuma faced the demons fearlessly in a wide legged stance, their feet firmly planted in the moist swamp soil.

The demons recognised Zion as the infamous King of the Nephilim and Ajuma as the green-eyed Nephilim who fought more like a demon than one of his own. They could feel the aggression coming off of them in waves.

Zion focused his blindingly bright golden gaze on the area surrounding the sink hole while Ajuma focused his green eyes in the centre of the nearby bog. Soon, a ring of fire surrounded the sink hole and the moss and peat-covered bog, creeping toward the concealed sticks of dynamite.

Zion and Ajuma's massive chests swelled as they took a deep inhale. When they exhaled, a joint plume of white-hot fire shot out of their mouths, torching the stunned demons and lighting up the night sky in a manner more fearsome than the mythical dragons of old. Soon the demons were engulfed in a huge ball of flame.

Inhuman screams rent the silence as some of the demons ran in circles, trying to distance themselves from the fire that clung to them like a second skin. Others writhed on the ground in an attempt to beat out the flames. Fifty Gibborim warriors broke rank at Zion's command to fly overhead to ensure none of the demons could escape via air. The demons were boxed in.

The plume of fire ignited the sticks of dynamite, catching the second wave of demons and causing a conflagration fueled by demon flesh. It blew the next hundred or so demons foolish enough to come through the open gateway to smithereens. Chunks of fiery demon flesh flew through the air to rain down in charred bloody pieces on the heads of the Nephilim. The pieces that hit the ground crackled and popped like a greased pig on a spit.

Loud, successive explosions shook the foundation of the swamp, finishing off the demons that hadn't already been blown to bits. The Gibborim hooted and hollered at the slow-motion dance of some of the demons while the fire ate away at their flesh.

Zion looked on dispassionately at what he had wrought. He knew the fire alone wouldn't end the demons' existence. The only way to kill a fallen angel-turned-demon was to take their heads and their hearts. He was gratified when several of the Gibborim rushed forward with swords in hand to perform the thankless task.

Despite the wall of fire, the demons kept crawling through the gateway. Antioch, Nicodemus, and Ajuma flanked Zion as he cut a bloody swath through the demons. The demons trembled in his wake, attempting to flee only to be trapped inside the circle of Gibborim warriors surrounding the battle zone.

Some of the demons even tried to return through the sink hole only to be cut down by the Gibborim surrounding it. Zion noted that the gateway was now partially closed. Apparently, there was only a short window of time for the demons to come through, and that window had almost elapsed. Once the gateway was sealed, the only way the demons would be able to return to the hells would be the hard way. Zion and his men would have to send them there.

The Brothers of the Dark Veil quickly dispatched every one of them. If

Zion didn't know any better, he would have sworn the Satan was chasing them. He laughed to himself, thinking that Zuet probably stood at the end of a dark tunnel on the other side of the gateway with a pitchfork in his hand, poking and prodding the demons through the gateway to their certain death. Zion was more than happy to accommodate him.

Finally, there was a brief lull in the fighting, but Zion knew the shit wasn't going to last. He shook his head in complete disgust when a funnel of black smoke rose from the sink hole and none other than Buer and Harbourym, both well-known presidents in the hells, grabbed hold of the sides of the sink hole to pull themselves up and out. Zion frowned at the look of exultation on their ugly faces. His frown deepened when an army of nearly 1,000 demons crawled out behind them.

Damn. We should have saved some of that dynamite, he thought.

Zion snorted in disgust when Belphegor, a particularly vicious demonic duke with the head of a goat and the body of a man, followed close behind them, leading his trusty hell hound Cercebus by a thick black chain.

The triple-headed hell hound had a long dragon's neck and tail. Serpent heads ran along the length of its back. It struggled against the confines of the chains, snarling and frothing blood-speckled foam from its mouth. The demons' look of excitement quickly turned into rage when they stepped over what was left of their army. Their collective gaze settled on the Nephilim, and all hell broke loose. What ensued was a melee of unparalleled proportions.

CHAPTER 49

BELPHEGOR ASSESSED THE situation in an instant. Somehow the details of their plan had been revealed.

"*ATTACK!!!*" he screamed through cruel lips twisted in a hateful rectus. His scream echoed through the swamps as if it had been shouted from a deep canyon seconds before he released the hell hound.

Cercebus bounded forward like a rabid beast with razor-sharp, blood-flecked teeth bared and three sets of yellow demon eyes pointed in one direction. Boaz was directly in the hound's path. He would have taken the full brunt of the hell hound's powerful charge had he not used his power of telekinesis to bend a large twisted tree and block the vicious hound's path with the thick black trunk.

The hell hound's triple set of nostrils flared from the delightful smell of blood. He was eager to sink his teeth into the Nephilim general—to tear him apart—but his charge had too much power behind it for the beast to stop or to jump over the makeshift tree trunk Boaz had magically erected as a fence.

Cercebus yelped like a beaten bitch when his canine-like body slid like a carriage careening out of control, only to slam full force into the side of the tree trunk. One of the sharp tree branches impaled one of the beast's eye sockets.

Boaz was on it in a second, straddling the stunned hound, his mighty fist rising and falling as he repeatedly stabbed Cercebus in all three of his heads. He eventually sawed the hound's centre head off, and tossed it at its master's feet with a look that clearly said, "*Come and get me if you dare, motherfucker.*"

"Cercebus!!"

Belphegor bellowed the hell hound's name in anguish. He turned his bloodshot rage-filled eyes toward Boaz, slashing and stabbing everything in his path in his haste to get to the Nephilim general. Belphegor's sole focus at this moment was to wipe that arrogant smile off the face of the son of a bitch Nephilim who had murdered his hound.

Belphegor never reached Boaz. A gust of freezing cold air from Gilead's mouth swirled around him like a spider's web, freezing him as solid as a block of ice in the middle of the Antarctic.

"I got this one, Bo!" Gilead shouted in Boaz's direction.

Gilead took his time, striding through the battling demons and Nephilim toward the frozen demon like a powerful avenging angel. He stood before the demon to examine his handiwork. Belphegor was completely and utterly helpless. Gilead smiled when he heard the strangled sounds coming from the demon's throat.

Gilead raised his mighty sword to swing. A loud "ping" sounded as he hacked off one of the demon's arms and then the other. Next, he severed the demon's legs. Gilead took his time breaking up the ice that had once been the demon's torso, saving the head for last.

He held the demon's frozen head in his hand, savouring the fear locked in its eyes. He tore his gaze away from the demon long enough to search for a nearby brother. He spied Antioch, who was returning to the fray after dragging one of the wounded Gibborim to safety. He motioned Antioch over.

"You got any bullets left?" he asked with a sinister smile on his face. Antioch pulled out his gun.

"Sure do," Antioch replied, raising his gun. "What can I do for you brother?"

"You in the mood for a little target practise?" Gilead asked.

Antioch didn't answer. He merely smiled, stepped back, and pulled out his gun. Antioch's bullet made short work of the target when Gilead tossed Belphegor's frozen head into the air.

Nicodemus had dispatched a particularly nasty demon when he turned to see Ajuma pull his fist out of a demon's chest, firmly gripping its heart. Ajuma took a bite out of the heart before tossing the still beating organ on the ground, then shot forward to single-handedly engage three more demons.

"Ajuma, no!" Nicodemus shouted.

It was not the number of demons that concerned Nicodemus. He was sure Ajuma would be able to handle them. What bothered Nicodemus was the fact that Ajuma had yet to pull out any of his weapons.

Either Ajuma hadn't heard Nicodemus, or he didn't care to acknowledge his warning. Without a care or concern for his own well-being, Ajuma slaughtered the demons with his bare hands. If Nicodemus didn't know any better, he would think the brother was on a suicide mission.

Nicodemus still had a worried look on his face when yet another demon engaged him in battle. There was no time to think anymore—just fight.

Once the dead bodies of the latest set of demons were lying at his feet, Ajuma's lethal green gaze landed on the back of a demon he knew very well.

Buer, the tenth of the seventy-two spirits of Solomon, was a president in the hells where he governed more than fifty legions of demons. The demon was a colossal ball of muscle, covered in coarse black hair, with a long-barbed tail and five donkey legs that protruded from the circumference of his body. He walked upon two legs. Two more legs stuck out of his sides. And the last donkey leg stuck out of the back of his neck, giving him the appearance of a hoary wheel. In the centre of it all was the face of a grinning lion.

It was from Buer's lair that Ajuma extracted young Jihad's nearly dead body so many years ago. Now it was time for the demon to pay. Ajuma drew a wicked blade out of his coat lining and strode with an evil grin and purposeful intent toward the unsuspecting demon.

Angry at the turn of events, Buer ripped out the heart of a young Gibborim whose only crime was that of being within reach. The heart was still pulsing when he mimicked Ajuma's action and took a bite out of it.

Because the Nephilim king had somehow learned of their plan, their well-orchestrated plan had gone to shit. Zuet would not take this defeat lightly. Buer would rather die facing the Nephilim than return to the hells with his head hung in defeat and his tail tucked between his legs. Buer realised he had nothing to lose, so he fought like a madman, his lethal donkey hooves stunning his enemies before he struck out with his murderous serpent tail.

I will have to kill as many Nephilim as I can and find someplace to hide until the dust settles, he thought before he felt a white-hot pain in the centre of his back. He looked down to see the point of a blade protruding out of his chest.

Ajuma pulled his blade out of Buer's back. He was prepared to plunge it in a second time when the demon spun around to wrap his long serpentine tail around Ajuma's neck.

Buer had a comical grin on his face as he felt the muscles in Ajuma's neck bulge and saw his face turn dark red. The demon continued to squeeze, cutting off Ajuma's air supply, and threatening to crush the bones in his throat from the unrelenting pressure.

Ajuma's eyes blazed an otherworldly green that was terrifying to behold as the blood capillaries exploded in both eyes. He grit his teeth in pain while the demon tried to choke the life out of him. Ajuma didn't even try to break Buer's lethal grip on his throat. Instead, he wrapped his big fist around the closest portion of the demon's tail that wasn't encircling his throat to pull the demon closer to him. When the demon's face was close enough to kiss, Ajuma's sabre-length fangs burst through his gums, and he clamped down on the demon's thick throat like a bloodthirsty animal.

Buer relinquished his grip on Ajuma's throat at once, fighting for his life in a desperate attempt to dislodge his neck. He pounded his hooves into Ajuma's back, opening his flesh to the bone, but Ajuma was like a hungry dog on a bone. He wouldn't let go. Instead, he growled and snarled, swinging his head back and forth while pulling huge chunks of flesh and muscle from the demon's throat, finally bringing the demon to his knees. Still he wouldn't let go.

General Simeon of the House of Ramuel was engaged in hand-to-hand combat with a naked demon named Harborym. The demon had the body of a man, a huge python penis, horns protruding from its head, a large pointed nose, donkey ears, and a long, pointy barbed-tipped tail. The head of a cat protruded from one side of the demon's shoulder blades, and the head of a poisonous asp sat squarely upon its other shoulder. Blood flew in the air as Simeon grappled the demon to the ground, pummelling its ugly face.

Demons liked to fight dirty. True to form, Harborym fisted a handful of dirt. Simeon jerked his head back when the demon tossed the dirt in his face, temporarily blinding him. In the seconds it took to clear his vision, the demon pulled out a lethal blade. Harborym let the blade fly, expecting to catch Simeon right between the eyes, then shook his head in confusion. Not only had he missed the mark, but now there were three Nephilim who looked identical to the one he'd just tried to kill. Simeon had the gift of replication. It was up to the demon to determine which image was an illusion and which was the Nephilim. Simeon gutted him before he could resolve the quandary.

The demon Balam, a former member of the angelic order of Dominions, was cloaked in invisibility, seething as he watched Zion Shemyaza and his men cut down the army of demons like they were little more than human children. He looked at what was left of Buer, Belphegor, and Harborym with disgust.

Zuet should have known better than to send boys to do a man's job, he thought angrily.

Balam was a powerful demon in his own right, holding the title of king in the hells, with forty legions of demons under his command. *Had Zuet authorised me and my demons to lead this mission, the outcome would have been different*, he thought spitefully. The gateway would close soon, he thought with disgust. It was too late to summon his demons now.

If you want something done right, you have to do it yourself.

Balam dropped his cloak of invisibility to ride into the thick of the fighting on the back of an angry bear. He was naked and held a goshawk on his right fist. The bear stomped forward on ponderous fat feet the size of elephant hooves while Balam swung his free arm, knocking the ineffectual demons out of the way with his huge fists until, finally, he was face to face with Zion.

Zion saw the demon coming. He turned his head in Rephidim's direction with a questioning look on his face as if the demon was of little or no threat to him.

"Correct me if I'm wrong," he said, "but didn't we chop off that motherfucker's head, what, about two decades ago?"

Rephidim took a moment to ponder the question.

"If my recollection serves me correctly, I believe we disembowelled him and burned him to a crisp," he replied succinctly.

"Ahhh," Zion said, shaking his head, as if that explained the demon's unwelcome reappearance.

Balam was the fifty-first of the seventy-two spirits of Solomon and monstrously ugly. The tripled-headed demon stared at Zion out of the head of a bull, a man, and a ram. He had a serpent tail and eyes of flaming fire. His blazing, deep-set eyes took in Zion's appearance from head to toe.

Zion stared right back at him with clear golden eyes that could make a woman's pantaloons melt and a face so perfect it bordered on beautiful. Balam wanted nothing more than to crush that perfect face and tear that comely body limb from limb. When Balam finally did speak, his voice came out rough and gravelly, like someone swinging a sack of wet rocks.

"You have the look of your mother about you. I will be sure to give her your regards when my men and I fuck her tonight," he said disrespectfully.

Zion recoiled when the demon's flatulent breath hit him full in the face. He waved his hand in front of his nose.

"Now see, why'd you have to go and bring my mother into this? That's plain wrong on so many levels."

Balam didn't know what hit him when Zion opened his mouth and exhaled a burst of flames that incinerated him and his damned bear.

The battle zone was littered with dead and dying demons that Zion and his men had personally granted a one-way ticket back to the hells. With no new influx of demons, Zion determined it was time to stop toying with the wounded and end it all. He sent out a mass mental message for all of the Gibborim to ghost. When he was sure that every Gibborim had exited the swamp, he expanded his mighty chest on an inhale. When he released his breath, he let loose a plume of fire the size of a building, burning the remaining demons to a crisp before he too ghosted out of the swamp. All in all, for Zion it had been a good night's work.

Rephidim, who had the power of controlling the elements, closed his eyes and spread his muscular arms wide. It began to rain, dousing the fires.

The Brothers of the Dark Veil lingered to perform the luckless task of cleaning the site. Once that task was complete, all but Ajuma ghosted back to Zion's residence in Baton Rouge.

Ajuma didn't know he would ghost to Magnolia Hill until he had actually done it. Once he was there, he didn't know if it was the Satan himself or The Ancient of Days that had whispered the compulsion in his ear to return to the source of his greatest pain.

Magnolia Hill was a smouldering ruin, as ruined and dead as his wife, son, and every soft emotion he had ever possessed or ever would. In a way its destruction symbolised all he had lost. His beloved lived and died here.

He pressed a hand to that place in his chest that housed his heart. The pain from loss was physical, almost more than he could bear. He closed his eyes to let the pain take him. It washed over him like a mighty wave, taking what was left of his spirit with it.

He didn't know when next he would come this way or if he ever would. But right now it was the only link he had left to Flossie and Jake. So, he stayed. And he cried. And he hurt.

CHAPTER 50

The Port of New Orleans

MARCEL KEPT ANNA holed up in a small but respectable boarding house in the city for three days while he arranged for their passage on a ship headed east. Anna thought she would lose her mind during those long stretches of time when he was gone. Every time he walked out the door, she was fearful he wouldn't return.

The rebellion had been quelled nearly a week ago, yet there remained a palpable air of unrest in the city. Scores of New Orleans natives departed the city for safer locales, fearful there would be more violence. It was therefore a stroke of sheer good luck that Marcel was able to secure a small berth for them on La Duchesse de Noailles, a ship out of France destined for New York.

Anna was sitting in the enclosed carriage Marcel hired for their transport to the docks, wearing the white lady finery Marcel purchased for her out of his earnings from the paintings commissioned by the planters. Finally, she would be able to put memories of Magnolia Hill and Louisiana behind her.

Anna nervously fanned herself, peeking out the carriage window while Marcel confirmed their accommodations with the ship's first mate. He instructed Anna to remain in the carriage until he returned for her. She was so close to freedom she could taste it. She hoped nothing went awry.

A week had passed since the Deslondes slave rebellion and Perline's courageous departure from Magnolia Hill. Since then a tribunal was held at

Destrehan Plantation. Forty-five rebels were either sentenced to death or sent on to New Orleans for what could only be described as sham trials. The leaders of the rebellion had been swiftly and brutally dealt with. Many were cut into little pieces and their body parts displayed as a deterrent to any other slave foolish enough to contemplate freedom.

Deslondes, the mastermind of the rebellion had been roasted alive, while Kook, and the other leaders were executed before a firing squad, beheaded, and their heads mounted upon poles and placed at intervals along the river levee from New Orleans to LaPlace Plantation. It was even rumoured that one of the rebel leaders had been a woman from Magnolia Hill, and that her head rested on a pole alongside that of Deslondes.

Perline didn't know if there was any truth to the rumours, but she did know one thing for a certainty. The city was a tinder box, primed like a row of war cannons, and ready to blow. She couldn't get out of New Orleans quick enough.

Thanks to the kindness of a family of Quakers who spied Perline alongside the road while they were fleeing the turmoil on River Road, she was able to safely make it as far as New Orleans. They took pity on her and offered her a ride.

The gods were with her. The Quakers were abolitionists. Before they parted ways, they dropped Perline off at Saint Louis Cathedral where she met Father John Denis, who hid her inside the cathedral in an empty room the size of a prison cell. The good father gave his solemn word to Perline that he would see her safely delivered to her sister in Natchez. This promise was made at great risk to himself.

It was no secret that the Catholic Church was one of the largest slave holders in Louisiana, if not the country. In helping Perline, Father Denis was going against the church where he was domiciled and the current interpretation of biblical doctrine.

Perline would not be the first runaway slave Father Denis shepherded to freedom. To allay her fears on that first night, the Father assured her that there had been many before her. He need not have proffered any assurances. Perline was not afraid. The gods were with her.

Anxiously awaited church supplies were shipped in from the Holy See in France four times a year. It was Father Denis' responsibility to watch for the arrival of the ship and see that half of the supplies were delivered to their sister church in Natchez. Since the ship with the supplies had docked last night, Perline would soon put New Orleans behind her.

Father Denis maneuvered his wagon through the hustle and bustle at the busy seaport, his heavy wagon laden with church supplies. Perline quietly sat beside the priest, playing a role she was intimately familiar with—that of a slave. She doubted anyone would recognise her without her signature limp. Her face and form were totally unremarkable, but she couldn't say the same about her unusual coloured eyes so she kept her head down.

Suddenly the wind shifted and the nappy hairs on the back of Perline's neck stood on end. A sickening sense of disquiet took control of her body, alerting her that she was in close proximity to evil.

In spite of her previous resolve, Perline raised her eyes in the direction of the danger to find herself staring directly into Anna's threatening gaze. The two women locked eyes. Neither of them was in any position to call attention to the other, and in the few seconds it took for Father Denis' carriage to come adjacent to and pass the carriage Anna was in, a silent message passed between them.

This was far from over.

ABOUT THE AUTHOR

Carolyn learned at a very young age that words would give her the power to soar through time, space, and alternate dimensions; words were pure magic! As a child, she would hold a flashlight beneath her bed covers so that her parents would not know she was up reading long after her bedtime. Little has changed. Carolyn still reads and writes late into the night.

The progression from avid reader to author was not without a few bumps in the road. She did not set out to write a series that would scare the fancy dress socks right off her beloved father's feet. And it certainly was not her intention to write novels replete with erotic scenes so graphic they would make her sweet mother blush to the roots of her steel gray hair. Carolyn intended to write something altogether different. The spirits, however, had other plans for her.

The world of "spirit" is real. It is evidenced in every whispered warning that saves us from calamity and in every dream that gives us clarity. Once Carolyn stopped fighting her destiny and allowed her beloved Ancestors and Spirit Guides to have their way, the words began to flow effortlessly, gifting her with a saga featuring sensual, alpha, *Nephilim*, and the powerful melanated queens they desired above all others.

Carolyn was born in New Brunswick, NJ, and raised in nearby Plainfield. She is interested in anything relating to the spirit world, classic eroticism, and the day-to-day trials and triumphs of melanated people. Her enthrallment with literature began while studying for her B.A. in Philosophy at West Virginia State University. Her fascination with the "spirit world" stems from her southern and Caribbean roots and a host of "intuitive" family members who are gifted with the ability to see, hear, or dream about things before they occur. As to her affinity for erotica? What do you expect? She's a Scorpio!

Carolyn is employed at a prestigious international corporate law firm by day and writes thought-provoking, erotic, spirit-infused literature at night. She has a weakness for wide-brimmed hats, stilettos, rare books, music, interesting people, and a good bottle of cabernet. She currently resides in Hillsborough, New Jersey, along with her spirit guides and her cast of other-worldly fictional characters.

Are you interested in connecting with Carolyn? Here's how you can do it.

BODV@carolynhollandbooks.com
Facebook: https://www.facebook.com/carolyn.holland.39
Instagram: https://www.instagram.com/behindthedarkveilllc/
LinkedIn: https://www.linkedin.com/in/carolyn-holland-b33446106/
Twitter: https://twitter.com/Holland459
www.carolynhollandbooks.com